THE THIEF WHO WASN'T THERE

Amra Thetys: Book 4

by

Michael McClung

Copyright 2015 Michael McClung

THE THIEF WHO WASN'T THERE

Dedication

For my crazy chickens.

Michael McClung

~~Abanon wields the Blade that Whispers Hate~~
Moranos holds the Dagger of Desire
Ninkashi grips the trembling Blade of Rage
with which she pierced the heart of her mad sire

Heletia grips the Knife called Winter's Tooth
Visini wields the Blade that Binds and Blinds
Husth fights with the Kris that Strikes Elsewhere
and woe betide the soul it finally finds

~~Kalara hones the Knife that Parts the Night~~
Grim Xith commands the Dirk that Harrows Souls
Eight Blades the Goddess has, and one
from eight will ren-

PART I: BELLARIUS

Michael McClung

ONE

"**T**here's a bunch of soldiers downstairs," the boy, Keel, announced.

I ignored him. Insinuating my own intangible, extemporaneously fashioned command key into the Telemarch's wards was a finicky, delicate business. It was not unlike picking an imaginary lock with an imaginary set of picks, except the consequences of failure wouldn't be imaginary in the least.

It would have been impossible were the Telemarch still alive. It required intense concentration, and it wasn't the safest magic I'd ever attempted. But if I could co-opt the deadly cobweb of defenses the Telemarch had laced into the stones of the Citadel, I wouldn't have to worry about anybody interfering with or interrupting my true work.

The mesh of magic woven about and through the tower was so dense and multi-hued, it was difficult to see through it to the physical world when using my magesight. Thank the dead gods I didn't need two eyes to see in three dimensions while working with the Art. Gently, gently, I pushed with my will against the node I was virtually certain commanded the wards, and perhaps much more. If I was right, well and good. If I was wrong—well. Being wrong about it would not be healthy. The wards were deadly the way water is wet, with enough power hardened into them to last a generation. Enough power to punish a failure on my part in a spectacularly conclusive manner. Rarely had I ever seen anything like them in our magic-poor age.

I could have left them alone and set up my own wards, nearly as puissant as the Telemarch's, given time, though not so durable. I did not have time. Every day, every *hour* that passed might mean Amra's death. But the time for haste had passed, and all my hurrying over the past week hadn't brought her back.

"Uh, Magister Holgren?"

"Just call me Holgren," I told the boy, not for the first time. "And magister is a little old-fashioned and formal in any case. What do they want?"

"They wanted to see the Telemarch. I told them he'd karked it. Then they said they wanted to see whoever was living here now."

"How do they know anybody is living here now?" I said, not really paying attention. I'd almost got my key to be accepted by the Telemarch's wards. If it wasn't simply luring me into committing myself to doing something I'd regret. The Telemarch, from what I'd seen of his applications of the Art, had a nasty turn of mind. But the node I was trying to infiltrate was definitely the heart of the wards. If I could subvert it, it would give me mastery of the Citadel's defenses. How much more it would afford me access to, I didn't yet know. There were strands that ran deep into the mount, and there were other strands that spread out across the city itself. All of them were intriguing.

I realized Keel had been talking, and that I had no idea what he'd said.

"Say again?"

"I said all the weird lights and stuff probably gave them a clue that the Citadel isn't empty."

Some of the spells I'd tried to locate Amra with had been rather flashy. Others had been incredibly loud. None of them had given me what I wanted.

"Magus? They said if you don't come down, they're going to come up."

With a mental and mostly imaginary *click*, the key finally punctured the disturbingly elastic membrane of the node and slotted perfectly, as far as I could sense, into the mesh of the Telemarch's commands. It was enough for now. Later I could explore just what I did and did not have access to, beyond the outer wards. For now, I had to deal with the locals.

They probably wanted their Citadel back. They weren't going to get it until I was finished. Messengers had come over the last few days, petitioning the Telemarch to take sides in the civil war that was burning sullenly through the city's streets. I'd given Keel instructions to ignore them. Soldiers, however, were a different matter.

I stood up, stretched, then with a swipe of my hand broke the circle of dust and blood I'd laid down for the work I'd just completed. Such things weren't strictly necessary, but I found they helped me to concentrate. I followed the boy downstairs to talk to the soldiers.

"What faction?" I asked him as we descended.

"Council. Steyner's men." Two of the Council of Three had survived the chaos, madness, magic and rioting that had engulfed Bellarius since the night of Amra's disappearance. Both of them believed they should be the next Syndic. The third faction, the Just Men, wanted to set up a democracy, Nine Cities-style. Or maybe something completely different. Keel's accounts varied, and my attention was less than complete. Apparently their leadership, and goals, were somewhat fluid at this point.

While I was rooting for the rebels in an abstract sort of way, I didn't have time for politics. The city of Bellarius and all the rest of Bellaria could have any style of government it wanted, or none at all, as far as I was concerned. Just so long as the various factions stayed out of my way and left me to my work.

"Uh, magus?" Keel said as we approached the main door.

"What is it, Keel?"

"Did you maybe want to put on your eye patch?"

"Ah. Yes. Thanks." I'd taken it off when I'd started work that morning. It was still new, and distracting. I hadn't wanted to be distracted. Well, no more distracted than losing an eye the week before made me. I pulled the thing out of my pocket and slipped it on.

"Maybe a little more to the right, magus," Keel commented. I gave him a glare. And adjusted it.

He nodded in satisfaction and opened the door. Gray, cheerless light dribbled in out of a gray, cheerless sky. Outside were twenty halberdiers in Steyner's maroon and yellow, their breaths pluming in the chill air. They were led by a captain in half-plate.

"You are the mage who has taken up residence here?" the captain asked, after looking me over.

"I am."

"You are required to vacate the Citadel immediately, by order of Syndic-elect Gabul Steyner."

"That's not going to happen," I said.

"Then we will be forced to remove you."

"You'll be forced to try. I warn you, captain, it won't go well for you or your men." With a mental whisper I activated the Citadel's base wards, the primary layer of protections the Telemarch had built into the tower using the Art. The ones meant to repel physical threats.

The captain stepped to the side and ordered his men to enter and evict me. I stood inside the threshold and watched, arms folded. I was curious as to what the Telemarch had wrought. I knew this layer of wards' purpose, but not how it would be made manifest. I hadn't had the time to study the wards in detail, and no opportunity to experiment.

The first pair of halberdiers tried to enter, and were rebuffed, as if they had encountered an invisible wall. They tried again, with the same results.

"Hack at it," their captain told them.

"Oh, yes, do," I said. One of the halberdiers glared at me. The other wore an expression that suggested he wasn't getting paid enough. He stepped back to give his compatriot room to swing.

The first hauled back with his overgrown axe and brought it down with not-inconsiderable force on the doorway's invisible ward. The halberd was immediately ripped out of his hands. It flew, spinning and with impressive speed, out and away from the Citadel, the haft cracking the halberdier in the face along the way. The man fell down in a moaning, bleeding heap. The halberd fell somewhere in the Girdle. I hoped that it hadn't split somebody's head open. In any case, it would likely end up in the hands of the rebels, so all in all I was not unsatisfied with the outcome.

"Right then," I said to the captain. "If you're done wasting my time, I have work to do."

"The Citadel is the rightful possession of the ruler of Bellaria!" he said in a tone that verged on whining.

"Yes, well. When he or she shows up, perhaps I'll be more accommodating," I replied. "Meanwhile, if you bother me again, I'll turn you into a pink mist."

I closed the door in his flushed face.

TWO

I'd given up on any quick solution to the puzzle of Amra's disappearance after exhausting every reasonable approach to the problem that Greytooth and I could come up with. That wasted a week, but I had, at least, confirmed three things: that Amra wasn't dead, that the Telemarch definitely was, and that Amra was almost certainly nowhere in the world.

That left everything outside the world. Which was a very large area to search. Technically, it was an infinity. Multiple infinities. But at least I had her point of departure. And so too, in a sense, it had me. I was tied to the Citadel, or at least keeping the Citadel from anyone else, because of that room where Amra had disappeared.

There was a very real chance that I would need that room to bring her back. I didn't know how big a chance; I had no way to calculate the odds. But as I wasn't willing to gamble her life on needing it and not having access to it, the Citadel had to remain in my control.

It was unfortunate that the Citadel stood at the top of Mount Tarvus. There is something, I have noticed, in those interested in power over their fellow men and women. Something that will not allow them to abide another looking down on them, figuratively or literally. Kings and priests sit and stand elevated above the masses to be seen, true, but just as importantly to separate themselves, to put themselves *above*. It is an unsubtle statement of relative worth. Lesser beings are made to bow and kneel for the same reason. It is more than show.

In Bellarius, the ruling class had taken it to an extreme with their useless tower building. The correlation of power to elevation was dyed into the fabric of Bellarian society as deeply as that of family and duty and revenge in the Low Countries. Why else was Hardside, the only appreciable stretch of level ground in the city, left for the desperate and destitute to inhabit?

It wasn't because of the occasional albeit serious flooding. That was a simple engineering problem that Gol-Shen had been dealing with handily for centuries, and at far less expense and inconvenience than it must have cost Bellarians to build vertically up the side of a mountain. No, in Bellarius the low ground was for lesser beings, and Hardside, being the lowest ground, was for the lowest of the low.

Which meant that the Citadel, squatting atop the mount's peak, was for the highest of the high. The various factions couldn't help themselves seeing my occupation of it as a challenge to their own notional authority.

If that were all there was to it, I wouldn't have much cared. If I knew for a certainty I would only need the Citadel for a certain, specific amount of time, I could have just ignored their belligerence. Weathered out whatever mischief they mustered up. But I didn't know how long I would need the Citadel for, and I couldn't just sit behind its warded walls. There were things out in the city that I needed, not the least of which was food.

So. In addition to setting my plan for finding Amra into motion, I was also going to have to play the part of a prospective ruler of Bellaria. To a degree, at least, and for a time. And all because of an empty room.

I climbed the stairs to the top floor, to look for the hundredth time at the Telemarch's inner sanctum. Or rather, the space that had contained his inner sanctum.

There wasn't a precise line where the room ended. Take the ugly, skull-shaped door, for example. The exterior of the door was as solid, and tasteless, as it had ever been. The interior of the door, however, no longer existed. Or at least the interior surface was as gone as gone gets.

It did not cease to exist at a precise point. The interior surface of the door, and the entire room, just *faded*. The nearest analogy I could manage was that of someone dipping a brush in ink and dragging it across a sheet of parchment. At first the line would be a solid black, but as the ink was used up, the line would become fainter, patchier, until it disappeared entirely.

In this case, the ink was reality itself. What the brush had been, and whose hand had guided it, I could only speculate. In all probability I had the metaphor reversed, and reality had been erased rather than applied. It made no difference, really, since all I had at this point was speculation.

I entered the room, wishing for at least the fiftieth time that I'd known what it had looked like before it had gone missing.

Keel had been following me. I hadn't really noticed until he failed to follow me into the room. He didn't like the room. Said it gave him the mimis, whatever those were.

"Hurvus will be around this afternoon to check your eye, Magus," he said to my back.

"What's to check? It's not there anymore." I'd burned it myself. Mages couldn't afford to leave body parts lying around. Too many nasty things could be done with them.

"You know what I mean," Keel said, discomfort plain in his voice.

I sighed, and nodded. "I do."

"We've nearly finished off the Telemarch's larder. Down to dried beans and ham bones. I have a little coin, enough for a few days' groceries, but I don't know what's available now."

"Why?"

"Because of the riots and the barricades."

I turned around. "No, Keel, I mean why are you still here? This last week I have not been the pleasantest person to be around. Why are you still here, telling me about appointments and provisions?"

His face got a little pale, and a little angry. "Did you want me to leave?"

"No. I just want to know why you're here instead of out there. You told me you were one of the Just Man's followers, before."

He nodded. "I was. But Ansen's dead. He doesn't need any help. And I don't much like the direction the Just Men have taken these past few days, if I'm being honest."

"What do you mean?"

He looked down at the floor and frowned. "They've brought back impalement. For captured gentry, and for Blacksleeves. For people labeled informants and collaborators. There's a lot of people sitting on spikes, down on the wharves." He shook his head. "Even the Syndic didn't do that."

"That's barbaric. I understand your reluctance to be associated with

THE THIEF WHO WASN'T THERE

it."

He shrugged. "Anyway, they don't need me. And Amra's alive, somewhere. I owe her."

"I'm doing everything I can to get her back, Keel."

"I know, magus. And I know I can't really help with that. But I *can* remind you your wound needs checked, and I can make sure there's food ready when you remember to eat." He shrugged again, clearly uncomfortable being forthcoming and mature. He was still young.

"I want to do what I can," he continued, "even if it isn't much." His narrow face broke into a grin. "Plus, I'm supposed to be gone from Bellarius. Since I'm still here, I'd rather be holed up in a fortress with a magus than out on the street where Moc Mien's crew can get hold of me."

I smiled. It hurt. "Ah. Amra's friend. I'd forgotten about him. All right. If you're going to be my representative in the city below, I can't have you dodging his crew all the time. Best to deal with him now rather than later." I left the inner sanctum, dug into a pocket and came up with a few marks. I passed them to Keel. "After you buy us something in the way of provender, I want you to invite Moc Mien up for dinner tonight. I want to talk to him."

"Uh, magus—"

"Don't tell me you don't know where to find him."

"It's not that. If he sees me again he's going to do very bad things to me. *Permanent* things."

"He won't." I dug out another mark, pulled a whisper of power from my well, and scribed the Hardic rune for 'parley' just above it. The rune floated and turned slow circles, as buttery gold as the gold mark it drew its reality from. I gave it enough power to last the day, and hardened it so that it wouldn't fade once I turned my attention away from it.

I flicked the coin to Keel. "Give him that. You'll be fine. He'll respect the parley."

"Not so sure about that," Keel said.

"Would *you* disrespect a mage's offer of parley? Trust me."

"All right," he said, both morosely and dubiously. "Anything else?"

I was going to need much more hard currency than I'd brought along with me on my voyage from Lucernis. If bad turned to worse, I'd need it in immediately spendable form. And I could not count on being able to pop down to the bank to make a withdrawal. Or that if I did, the bank wouldn't be razed to the ground. By all the dead gods, I disliked being stuck in the middle of a civil war.

"Do you know where the banking house of Vulkin and Bint is?" I asked him.

"All the banks are on the same street, so yes."

"I'll need you to carry a letter there for me. I'll write it out in a moment."

"They're not going to let me in the door. Especially not since the rioting."

"You don't have to go in. Just deliver the letter to the doorman. And on your way back invite Greytooth to dinner."

"So we're having a dinner party."

"It would appear so. Better buy some decent wine."

"Magus?"

"Keel, if you don't start calling me Holgren I'm going to write it on a stick and beat you with it until you remember."

He smiled. "That sounds like something she would say." No need to explain who 'she' was.

"Where do you think I got it from?"

"All right, Holgren. One more question?"

"Yes?"

"Why the change? For the last week you've barely spoken, or slept, or eaten. Everything has been about the magic. Now you're making plans like you're going to be here a while."

It was a good question. The boy was perceptive, if annoyingly young. "The change is because I've exhausted all my quick, relatively sane options for finding her."

"So? What now?"

"From this point forward, haste is a liability. She lives, that much I know, not hope. While that remains true, I must walk a knife edge regarding what I can and should attempt, to find her and get her back. I have to *walk* that edge. No more sprinting. The consequences could be dire."

He shook his head. "I don't really know what you mean."

"I'll explain all you're likely to understand, and probably much more. But tonight at dinner, not now."

~ ~ ~

When Keel left I went exploring. I'd seen something in the Telemarch's weave of wards that had intrigued me. I wanted to see if my suspicions were correct.

I knew that, below the four visible floors of the tower, there was a basement that served as larder and kitchen. But the weave suggested there was more to the Citadel, possibly much more.

I didn't bother to take a lantern. The weave of wards and other, still unknown magics was so dense and bright to my magesight that mundane light wasn't necessary. If I needed to see something with my physical eyes—eye—I could always summon magelight in any case.

It was in the great hearth of the kitchen. What looked like a solid, soot-blackened back wall was just illusion. Behind it was a corridor. Where it led to, I couldn't tell from the outside.

I stepped through the wall.

Dust and soot, thick and dry and kicked up by my feet, assaulted my nostrils. I sneezed. It was loud in that cold, silent place. I walked forward, and within a few feet came to a T intersection. Stairs led down in either direction. I chose the left-hand path and descended a short way. The stairs led to a corridor but soon enough that came to an abrupt dead end. I summoned a ball of magelight and took a look.

The passageway had collapsed, and the weave of wards was torn and dead where the rubble began. I did a little mental calculation and came to the conclusion that I was just about where the Riail must have stood, before Amra made it fall down on top of the Syndic.

Retracing my route, I took the right-hand stairs. Soon enough the stairs began to spiral, with a landing here and there, seemingly at random. The stairs went down a long, long way, with the occasional off-shooting corridor, which I ignored for the time being.

Eventually I came to a rough-hewn cavern, featureless and empty except for a massive iron disc set flush into the floor. It was at least four feet in diameter and five inches thick, and had hundreds of sigils carved into its face, all of them whispering of containment and quiescence, torpidity and compliance.

It was the sorcerous equivalent of a prison door.

I traced the weave, found the command, and forced the door. The iron disk floated up and out of the way, revealing a black shaft drilled into the floor. A faint sorcerous whiff of power rose up from it, turning my stomach. It was unmistakably a residue of the same poisonous power that had poisoned my well the night Amra had disappeared.

At first glance I thought the shaft was featureless, but closer inspection revealed more of the same sigils carved into the shaft's smooth wall. They were barely visible to the human eye, so small were they etched. I hadn't noticed them at first because every iota of magic had been leeched out of them, unlike the sigils on the shaft's lid. Closer inspection revealed that they were nearly all still sound, just bereft of power. If it were necessary, they could be renewed.

I summoned a glowing bead of light, gave it weight and enough power to last perhaps a quarter of an hour, and dropped it down the shaft. It fell and fell, and was lost to sight long before its power sputtered out.

This then was what Greytooth called the rift, where Aither had stored his unrefined magic, his unleavened chaos. It was empty now; a very deep, very dark hole in the ground rather than a flawed reservoir of power. I would have given much to know where that power had gone. I had a feeling that, wherever it had disappeared to, Amra wasn't far from it. Which gave me a ghost of a hope.

If I had need of it, I had the world's deepest, most secure oubliette at my disposal. I preferred not to have need.

I'd feared, since I first forced the door to the Telemarch's inner sanctum, that any reasonable approach to locating Amra would be met with disappointment. Slowly, over the course of the last week, as spell after spell failed, I began considering more extreme plans to get her back.

The first that came to mind was finding yet another of the Eightfold's Blades, and using it to find her. I'd put it aside, considering just how powerful, unpredictable and dangerous those Blades had so far proven to be. Put aside, but not discarded. I would do it if I had to. Even if it earned me Greytooth's enmity. Even if it meant I would end up like Aither.

Before I went down that road, however, there was another I could travel. It was equally deadly and equally terrifying, but it was a route that I had much greater knowledge of. The rift, bereft of power as it now was, might still prove useful on that journey. Or at least the residue of the power it had contained.

"Where did you go?" I whispered, and the rift ate my words and gave nothing back.

I sat down on the dusty stone floor, put my elbows on my knees and my head in my hands. Truly alone for the first time in a week, I let my frustration and physical pain and fear for Amra out in a burning shriek. When it was done, my throat was raw. I don't know that it made me feel any better, but at least I felt no worse. Slowly, patiently, I pieced together my self-control and calm reserve, and strapped myself into it, like an armsman his armor.

The frantic worry clawed at my stomach, as it had since Amra entered the Telemarch's sanctum. I made sure no sign of it touched my face.

I replaced the lid and began the long climb back up to the tower.

THREE

"Any unusual pain?" Hurvus asked me as he applied some milky solution to the empty socket. It was cold, numbing and uncomfortable.

"Define unusual, in the context of losing an eye," I replied.

"Sudden headaches? Persistent irritation?"

"No. The pain has lessened, though it still hurts if I glance somewhere quickly."

"The muscles are tied into each other, trying to move an eye that isn't there anymore. The pain will fade. Sit up, lean forward, let it drain into the basin. Have you considered a false eye or sewing the lids shut?"

"I have not."

"Good. Don't. That's just begging for infection."

"Really? I've seen a fair few false eyes in my time."

He grunted. "Vanity always comes at a cost, magus. Why anyone would want to put a foreign object into their head is beyond me. Gods only know what sort of contagion you're likely to stick in there along with it."

He handed me a clean cloth and began packing up his things in a worn leather satchel. I wiped the solution off my cheek and eyelids.

"Don't sleep with the patch on. Disease loves close, damp, dark places. It don't need any more attention from me. I won't miss the walks up the Mount. If you need anything else, you can come see me. I won't be back here."

"Trouble getting through the Girdle?"

"No. The boys on the barricades know me, and the Blacksleeves as well. They make sure the sell-swords leave off. Physicking has its benefits."

"Keel says the Just Men are impaling people down there."

He paused. "Aye. They are. Some of them even deserve it."

"You think anyone actually deserves that sort of death?"

"Sadly, yes. I suspect you know as well as I that some of the worst monsters wear suits of human flesh. But I'll tell you what I told that new leader, Gammond—you can kill a hundred guilty, and it won't bring back one innocent." He shook his head once, picked up his satchel and turned to go.

"What about Keel?" I asked him.

"What about Keel?"

"Anything more to do about that arm of his?"

"I unbound it this morning and re-splinted it. Or hadn't you noticed?"

"I hadn't. I've been rather distracted."

He grunted. "It's properly set and healing well. The splints can come off in a month. No more, no less. Then he'll need to build his strength back up in the arm, but slowly. The muscles will have atrophied. I've told him all this, but Isin only knows if he was paying attention."

I stood and shook his hand. Passed him a few marks. "My thanks, and your payment. Have you eaten? Greytooth will be supping with me in an hour or so."

"I can't. I have a committee meeting."

I raised an eyebrow.

"The Just Men. I've been keeping busy sewing them up after their clashes with the Councilors' troops."

"Have you become a revolutionary, then?"

"I take no part in politics. But their organization regarding casualties is a sad fucking shambles. I decided to give them a little advice, if only to make my life easier and keep people from dying unnecessarily."

"Enlightened self-interest, then."

"Too fucking right."

"A drink before you go?"

His eyes said 'hells yes' but his mouth said 'no thanks.'

I saw him to the door. As he was going down the steep street, he passed another gentleman coming up it. I waited at the door, since anyone who had climbed this far could only be coming to the Citadel. The fellow didn't look like much, but I activated the wards nonetheless. Appearances, deceiving, etc. The man was a mage, that much I could tell with my magesight. How powerful he might be I had no idea.

He was a relatively young fellow, fit enough that the climb hadn't winded him too badly. He was dressed in white hose, black shoes with silver buckles, and a suit that was silk and pale, pale blue. He wore a tri-cornered hat, Isinglas-style. I looked down at my own clothes, and realized I was sorely in need of a laundress. Well. At least black was forgiving of grime.

He stopped a few feet away from the threshold and said "Magister Angrado?"

I nodded.

He doffed his hat and gave me a shallow bow. "Perrick Leed, of Vulkin and Bint."

"Well met, Magister Leed. Would you care to come inside?"

"Your pardon, but no. I was sent to verify your claim, as is necessary before the bank can accede to your request. It will only take a moment, and then I will return to the bank directly to begin fulfillment of your instructions."

"Well enough," I said. I'd set in place the precautions Leed was now following, so it wouldn't have been very fair of me to complain. Being both a thief and a mage, I'd imagined far too many ways to make child's play of a banking house's mundane security procedures.

"Do you submit to the Compulsion, magus?"

"I do."

He summoned up his power, and I felt the Compulsion settle on my mind like a soft cloth. I would notice no further effects, as long as I did not try to lie.

"Are you in fact the mage Holgren Angrado?"

"I am."

"Do you wish to withdraw a sum of forty thousand Lucernan gold marks based on the letter of credit on file with the Bellarian chapter of the bank?"

"I do."

"Does the Lucernan chapter of the bank in fact hold sufficient monies on deposit in your name to cover in full the sum you have requested, including the applicable five per cent accommodation fee?"

THE THIEF WHO WASN'T THERE

"It does, as far as I know and last I checked."

"Are you in any way trying to deceive the bank into giving you monies that you do not in fact possess, or are otherwise spoken for?"

"I am not."

The Compulsion dissipated and Leed bowed once again. "I thank you for your time, magister. Your request will be fulfilled in the morning."

"Why the delay?"

"The current situation in the city is such that we feel it necessary take extra precautions, to ensure that your funds are delivered."

"In other words, the city is a battlefield and you need to gather a small army to make sure I get my gold."

"Precisely, Magister Angrado."

"Well. I apologize for putting the bank out in this fashion."

"Apologies are wasted on banks, magus," he said with a small smile, "as they do not fit in any ledger. But I appreciate the sentiment. Good day."

~ ~ ~

Keel was a dismal cook.

He'd prepared what he said were marsh eels in heartroot sauce, but looked like discs of gristle half-submerged in gray, cold, paste. He'd mistaken pepper for a vegetable, rather than a seasoning. The bread at least was bought from a bakery and palatable, if stupendously expensive, costing nearly as much as the wine. The rebels controlled the docks, but Councilor Steyner and Councilor When controlled the routes into the Bellarian countryside, where virtually all the produce and fresh meat for the city came from. Imported wine was dirt cheap. The price of loaf of black bread was ruinous.

Greytooth, Keel and I ate in virtual silence. Greytooth, I had discovered, enjoyed talking about as much as I enjoyed having one eye. He spooned food into his mouth, chewed mechanically, and swallowed regularly enough to mark time by. The sorcerous tattoos that covered his scalp writhed and tried to lift themselves up from his flesh, as if they were attempting to escape.

Keel could talk all night, but he kept silent, sitting at a table with two mages. As for me, I'd been raised to save conversation for after a meal. Besides, I needed all my concentration to finish the dish without letting on what a chore it was to chew and swallow.

Moc Mien had not yet made his appearance.

I had no idea where Keel had gotten the table. Or the chairs. Or the dishes, or the cutlery. I hadn't seen anything remotely like them when Amra and I had first entered the Citadel, and in the week that followed, I hadn't been paying attention to anything other than trying to find her. Well, that and my eye. I would have been happy to ignore that as well, but the pain, especially at first, had been unignorable.

I finished the last bite and, with a sigh that I hoped sounded like satisfaction, pushed the empty pewter dish away from me.

"Many thanks, Keel. That was..." I searched for a description that wouldn't be an outright lie.

"Horrific," Greytooth supplied.

"...filling," I finally managed.

"I've seen my ma make it a hundred times," the boy muttered. "Not sure what went wrong."

"Cooking is as much an art as the Art," I said. "Perhaps we should hire a professional." I looked around the virtually empty ground floor. "Maybe somebody to dust. Do you know anyone?"

"That would haul themselves up to the Citadel every day, past the barricades? How much are you paying?"

"Whatever you think is fair, Keel. Perhaps a live-in servant I leave it to you. They can do the marketing as well."

He nodded. "I'll find somebody tomorrow." He rose to collect the dishes.

"No, leave them. We need to talk, we three."

Greytooth raised an eyebrow at that, but said nothing.

I filled everyone's glasses and sat back down. "First, I want to thank both of you for all you have done this last week, and for the assistance, and friendship, you tendered Amra before that."

Keel looked down at his lap, embarrassed. Greytooth swirled his wine.

"I have not been able to discover Amra's whereabouts, despite all our efforts. We have done all that can reasonably be done, I believe."

"Does that mean you're giving up the search?" Greytooth asked, voice mild.

"It does not. It means I am preparing to resort to unreasonable means to find her."

"Such as?"

"Well, that depends in part on what you can tell me about the Philosophers' connection to the Eightfold, and Her Blades."

He put his glass down. "I can tell you nothing, Holgren."

"Can't, or won't?"

He avoided my question by asking his own.

"What do you hope to gain by such knowledge? What would it have to do with finding Mistress Thetys?"

"An Arhat was mixed up in the whole sordid affair with the Blade that Whispers Hate. Here in Bellarius, Amra encountered the Knife that Parts the Night—and *you*, Magister Greytooth, another Arhat, another Philosopher. I have learned one thing in the years I have spent with Amra Thetys: Where she goes there is no coincidence, only cause and effect.

"That the Philosophers are connected to the Eightfold's Blades I have zero doubt. That Amra is connected to the Blades, likewise. Therefore you Philosophers are, in some form or fashion, connected to Amra, even if only tangentially. I want to know what that connection is, Fallon."

"Why?"

"Because *anything* connected to her might be something I can use to pull her back from wherever she has gone, or guide me to where she is."

"Holgren. I am sorry, truly. This connection does not offer hope of that sort."

"Tell me, and let me judge."

He took some time to collect his thoughts. "Very well," he said at last. "The Cataclysm was caused by a splinter faction of the Philosophers; this much I suspect you know."

"I do."

"That faction used one of the Eightfold's Blades to... do what they did. The rest of us have been dedicated to collecting Her Blades ever since, to finding them and keeping them out of the reach of anyone who would seek to use them, so that nothing like the Cataclysm might ever happen again."

"Noble," I said, "but not, you'll pardon my saying, terribly effective, judging by the state of Bellarius." Hundreds had died when the power of the rift had begun to breach its containment. Buildings had melted like wax, dark things had been birthed and still roamed the night streets, killing and worse. The Knife that Parts the Night had made it all possible.

"We are few and the Blades are extremely powerful. Until Amra destroyed the Blade that Whispers Hate, we had devoted ourselves for centuries to tracking the Blades down and containing them, believing them indestructible." He tossed back the remains of his wine and set the empty glass carefully on the table.

"Amra Thetys gave us hope that we might accomplish what we all had believed was impossible. She gave us reason to think we could fully discharge the debt that the Philosophers owed the world, for bringing on the Cataclysm. Her destroying Abanon's Blade gave us reason to hope that we need not spend an eternity hunting and imprisoning the mad weapons of a mad goddess, that our quest and our watch might have some end. *That* is the connection between Amra and my order, Holgren. That, and no other. I swear it. I'm sorry that it does not offer you any means to bring her back."

It was the most I'd heard him say at any one time. He looked drained. I poured him another glass.

"How do the Philosophers track the Blades?"

"We do not, as such. We merely look and listen for certain signs that one might be loose, and in the hands of a mortal. We have no direct way of finding them using the Art, or the Philosophy. I do not know where Kalara's Knife is any more than I know where Amra is, nor do I have any special means of finding out."

"What if—" My question was interrupted by a knock at the door. Theiner, I presumed. Or Moc Mien. Whichever. Keel obviously presumed the same, because he was suddenly very busy clearing the table and disappearing.

I went and opened the door.

"Magus," Theiner said with a nod. "Got your invite." He was standing with his arms folded, coat-less despite the cold.

I nodded in return and stepped aside to allow him entry. He didn't move.

"Where's Amra?" he asked.

"That's one of the things I'd like to discuss with you."

"She obviously did what she said she would, or we wouldn't be standing here talking. And I wouldn't be meeting you in the Citadel if the Telemarch still had a pulse."

"Please, Moc Mien, come in." He was Theiner to Amra, not me. I was meeting with a crew chief, not an old friend.

Finally, he did, with what seemed to me a strange reluctance. He wandered around the big, empty room for a moment, sparing a glance for Greytooth, who in turn ignored him completely.

"Where's Keel?" he asked.

"Washing up after dinner."

"Staying out of my sight, you mean."

"I mean he's washing up after dinner." Moc Mien snorted, but let it rest. To my mind, Keel had nothing to prove to anyone. He could have fled the city at any point, knowing his former crew wouldn't be kind at all if they caught him. He'd stayed to help rescue Amra. Moc Mien's opinion of the boy meant nothing to me.

"Care for some wine?" I asked him, and he nodded. I poured him a glass.

"Are you going to answer my question, mage?" he asked as he took the glass from me and leaned up against a pillar.

"As to where Amra is, I don't know. Not here. Not anywhere in the world. But not dead."

"You're going to have to explain that one to me, mage. I'm just a street rat grown up."

I snorted. "So is Amra, as far as that goes. Please don't play the fool, Moc Mien. It doesn't suit you."

"All right, if she isn't dead and isn't in the world, where the fuck is she?"

"That's exactly what I've been trying to find out ever since she disappeared."

"Well. Thanks for enlightening me. Is that all you wanted to discuss?"

"No," I said. "But let's leave the other topics until Keel rejoins us. Amra told me that you were her oldest living friend. How did you meet?"

"I needed someone small enough and with the balls to climb up the inside of a drainpipe. It was a pretty wide drainpipe, but it was long, and as crooked as Kerf's staff."

"What in the world did you need someone to do that for?"

"It was the only way I could find into a place I wanted to get into."

"Did she do it?"

"No. She asked if I was born a moron or became one later, and then picked the lock on a coal chute I hadn't even noticed." He smiled at the memory, briefly. The smile disappeared when Keel came up the stairs from the kitchen, replaced by the stony mask of a crime lord. For his part, Keel ignored his former boss, sat down at the table and sipped at his wine.

I went to the table and sat as well, looking at Moc Mien. After a brief hesitation he peeled his back off the pillar and sat, splay-legged, in the last empty chair.

"Gentlemen. Sitting around this table are the four people in Bellarius who know Amra, know that she saved this city from annihilation, and who have a stake in bringing her back from wherever she has gone."

"Yeah, you might want to explain that part a bit more clearly," Moc Mien drawled. "Where *did* she go?"

"Very well. Here are the bare facts. She entered the Telemarch's inner sanctum. The Telemarch died. Amra, the Knife that Parts the Night, and the power that the Telemarch had summoned, which was rapidly destroying the city, all vanished. The facts and their order of occurrence are what I and Magister Greytooth are completely certain of."

"What in hells is the Knife that Parts the Night?"

"A powerful and deadly weapon made by a powerful and insane goddess. It was what gave the Telemarch much of his magic, and made him insane."

"Fair enough. Next question. Where were you when Amra was facing him down, mage?" Moc Mien's voice had a thick thread of contempt running through it, but I answered calmly.

"Getting my eye ripped out by a monster."

"*He* was protecting a little girl," Keel interjected, pointing to me, eyes hot. "Where the hells were *you*?"

"I'm going to let that pass for now, boy. We'll get to you later."

"Keel," I said quietly, "Moc Mien is here for a parley at my invitation. Don't insult my hospitality." It wasn't really fair to Keel, but he was young and hotheaded. He needed to learn to stay calm when provoked.

"Sorry," Keel muttered. He didn't sound or look the least bit sorry. I wouldn't have either, at that age.

"Moc Mien, Amra isn't dead. Whatever she did, it saved the city and everyone in it. Whatever she did, it caused her to disappear from the world. But she isn't dead."

"How does that work, exactly? How do you leave the world any way other than feet-first?"

"There are an infinite number of planes of existence."

"Oh? Care to give me an example?"

"Certainly. In fact, I'll give you eleven: The eleven hells, to be precise."

"You're saying Amra is in a hell?"

"I don't know *where* Amra is. It's possible she's there. It's equally possible she's wandering around the plane of the gods, stealing fruit from Isin's own garden and complaining about the wine. I don't *know* where she is. I only know she isn't here, on this plane with us."

Moc Mien rubbed his forehead. "Well. Thanks for informing me, I suppose." He put his glass on the table and stood up. Turned to leave.

"I'm going to find her," I said quietly to his back, "and then I'm going to go and get her. And I need your help." I looked at Greytooth and Keel. "I need all of your help."

Moc Mien turned around.

"Just what sort of help is it you think I can offer?" he asked.

"First, I want you to give Keel a pass for the time we will remain in Bellarius. I'll need him to run errands for me. I need him to be able to do that without turning up at my door in pieces."

"How long were you planning on staying?"

"I don't know. Perhaps a week. Perhaps a month. Until I no longer need the Citadel." Which wasn't precisely true, but was true enough. Until I could take, and break, one of the creatures created by the power of the rift, I couldn't leave the Citadel. After that, I could just lock it up to keep anyone else from having it.

"I can probably accommodate you," Moc Mien allowed. "But it won't be cheap."

"I didn't expect it to be free. Second, I'd like for you to arrange quiet transportation for me and mine out of the city whenever I *do* decamp. I imagine you've got ins with the smugglers I've heard of down in the marsh." I did not want anyone knowing when I left or where I was going. Old habits die hard, and usually for a good reason. "Finally, I want to hire your crew. It will be for a very dangerous job."

"What do you want to steal, and who from?"

"I don't want to steal anything. I want to trap something."

"Trap? We're thieves, not hunters."

"Do you see many hunters in Bellarius? I need tough men who know the streets, alleys, rooftops and hiding places in the city. Your crew will serve."

"Not unless I say they will."

"You know what I mean."

"What are you hunting?"

"One of the creatures that was spawned the night Amra disappeared. One of the dark mishaps created by the Telemarch's rift. Which one doesn't really matter."

"So you want me to ignore Keel's existence, and you want my crew to kill something."

"No. Not kill. I need it alive."

"By all the dead gods, what for? Those things are horrors."

"I need it to lead me to Amra."

"How in hells will that work?"

"It's complicated and magical. Just trust me. If I can capture one and break it to my will, I'm virtually certain I can use it to lead me to Amra, or at least very near."

Greytooth cleared his throat. "Have you discovered a way to walk the planes, then?"

"Me? No. But there's a book that might tell me how."

"Oh, really. And where might this book be found?"

"In the Black Library."

Greytooth stared at me, open-mouthed. Finally, he said "You've lost your mind."

"What?" Keel asked. "What's the Black Library?"

"I have to second the kid, unfortunately," Moc Mien added. "Never heard of it. Not that I'm big on libraries."

"The Black Library," said Greytooth, never taking his eyes off mine, "is in Thraxys. The fifth hell. It houses the trophies of the demon Xom Dei, ruler of that realm."

"So let me get this straight," Moc Mien said. "You want to trap one of the nightmares that's been terrorizing the Girdle and house-break it. Then you're going to go to a library in the fifth hell and steal a book that will tell you how to wander around other magical realms of existence. Have I got the basics down so far?"

"Perfectly."

"That's not a plan. That's not even wishing. That's pure, impossible madness."

Greytooth cleared his throat. "I'm assuming you'll be using your new, notional pet as a bloodhound of some sort, to lead you to wherever Amra is."

"That's right. It won't have any connection to her, but it will almost certainly have a connection to the power that spawned it. And I'm virtually certain that if I find one, I'll find the other."

Moc Mien looked at Greytooth. "You're not taking him seriously?"

"I am. Unfortunately. It is both the strength and weakness of mages that we deal in making the impossible become the inevitable. Strength, because without that level of self-belief, we could work no magic whatsoever. Weakness, because we sometimes bite off more than we can chew. Holgren is not necessarily mad, despite what I said earlier."

"Are you joking? I'm not even a mage and I can see holes in that plan big enough to put my foot through."

"Nothing Holgren has said so far is impossible. Incredibly dangerous, yes. Almost sure to get him killed, certainly. But not impossible. Though I do get the feeling he is leaving out some rather large portions of his plan."

"Oh?" I asked. "Such as?"

"Such as how you're going to domesticate a monster. Such as how you're going to gain access to the infernal regions in the first place. Such as how you intend to battle your way past the endless hordes of demons hungering for a taste of living human flesh, rather than the pale, wispy sustenance of a human soul. Such as how you plan to withstand the sorrowind, should you be caught out in it. Such as—"

"Details, magus, merely details."

He snorted. "Does that mean you don't yet know how you're going to deal with those details, or does it mean you don't want to discuss them?"

"Mostly the latter, a bit of the former," I admitted.

Greytooth shook his head. "And what is it you'd like me to do, Holgren?"

"Just research, Fallon, and advice."

"I'll help you to that extent, certainly. My first piece of advice is to find another way."

Silence crept into the room. Keel finally broke it.

Michael McClung

"So does all that mean Holgren is rats-in-a-bag crazy, or not?"

~ ~ ~

The 'party' broke up a short while later. Greytooth and Moc Mien left thinking I was probably insane, but in the end Moc Mien was convinced to help by the promise of large amounts of gold, and Greytooth by simple hope. Keel was also leaning towards crazy, but he was too young and inexperienced to make a final judgment. Even if he became convinced I'd lost my mind, I was fairly certain he'd stick around out of loyalty.

Gold, hope, and loyalty. Powerful enough motivators to convince three people to help me attempt what seemed impossible. Explaining that I didn't need any of them to accompany me on my trip to Thraxys hadn't hurt either.

I knew more about the eleven hells, in all probability, than anyone else alive. Well, anyone who wasn't a daemonist, at least. I'd studied them in depth after I'd sold my soul, looking for some way out of the bargain. Then I'd died, and gone to the third hell. What I'd discovered there wasn't something I could talk much about; some sort of compulsion had accompanied my resurrection. But one thing I'd learned before my resurrection gave me hope that my plan to raid the Black Library might have a chance of succeeding.

The hells were empty. Or at least the third one had been. I was willing to bet my life and my soul that the others were, as well.

Oh, there were still damned souls pouring in, but there were no demons or daemons there to receive them, to torment them, to feast on them.

They were all gone. From demon lords, to daemon foot soldiers, to the hellish daemonette fauna, they'd vanished.

Where they'd gone and why, I hadn't a clue. Whether they would be back, the same. But their disappearance gave me at least a hope of success. If they were still disappeared, I would not have to battle my way across the third, fourth and fifth hells to reach the Black Library—a battle I would have had no chance of winning. Even without their native denizens, trekking across three hells would be a perilous journey.

I would have to enter at Gholdoryth, the third hell. It was the only one with a gate I had relatively easy access to. From there, I *might* be able to avoid the fourth hell, if I could gain access to the Spike. But there was no avoiding Thraxys, and Thraxys, though the smallest of the eleven hells, was in some ways the worst of them all.

First things first. Trap a rift spawn, and test my theory. If it *could* sense the rift, break it to my will. Once I'd accomplished that, I could leave Bellarius behind and return to Lucernis.

I wouldn't be spending much time in Lucernis, however, if all went well. Just long enough to drop Keel off safe and sound at home, visit a powerful, unpredictable being, and reopen the hell gate that the mad sorcerer, Bosch, had created just off the Jacos Road.

Inspector Kluge would be very unhappy about that, if he found out. Best he didn't find out.

From there....

Well. Step by step.

I left Keel by the fire with a nod and climbed the stairs, magelight guiding my way. I passed, once again, the cloth-covered easel on the second level. I was as utterly uninterested in the Telemarch's artistic endeavors then as I had been when Amra and I had first climbed the stairs to his inner sanctum.

I stopped off at the library on the third floor and took a book at random from the dusty shelves, not bothering to look at the title, if it even had one. Most of them did not. It didn't matter. If I did not read to distract myself before sleep, I wouldn't sleep. Facts and suppositions and memories and plans and fragments of plans would parade themselves endlessly across the stage of my mind, and soon enough it would be dawn and I would not have slept a wink. I could function without it, but I would never be sure I was as sharp as I needed to be. Especially if I needed to cast a spell extemporaneously.

Magic was an unforgiving art, and failure due to inattention could mean sudden death; mine or others'. That much Yvoust, my master, had beaten into me early. He hadn't been wrong in that, though he had been in too much else.

I went to 'bed' in the inner sanctum, as I had every night since Amra had vanished. Keel may have felt uncomfortable there, but I found it peaceful. I hardened the magelight, propped myself in a corner and started to read what seemed to be a treatise on the measurement of time, written by some dead Gosland philosopher. It was all rubbish and nearly impenetrable, which was exactly what I needed.

    I got almost two solid hours of sleep. Hurvus would not have been happy with me. I forgot to remove the patch.

FOUR

"Mag—uh, Holgren, there's a bunch of soldiers downstairs," Keel told me. "Again."

"The same as yesterday?" I asked, not really paying attention. I was working out a trap for whichever rift-spawn we could corner. Lacking basics such as paper, ink, or pen, I was writing in the air, the silvery notations visible only to my magesight. Likely I looked mad to Keel, but he didn't comment.

"No, these ones are mercenaries. They've got four iron chests. They look heavy. Say they're from the bank."

"Ah. Yes. I'll be right there." I hardened my notes and stepped out of the chamber. Keel was looking pensive.

"What is it, Keel?"

"Promise you won't get mad?"

"No. But I promise I won't kill you. What?"

"*Are* you crazy?"

"No more so than any mage, and far less than many I have met."

"That's not really comforting."

"I'm sorry, I thought you wanted truth, not comfort."

"Before I met Amra, I'd never met anyone with power like you and Magister Greytooth have. I guess I don't know what's normal for you lot."

"What I'm going to attempt isn't what you would call normal, any more than the civil war tearing your city apart is normal for Bellarius. Both situations are born of circumstance and desperation. You should judge them accordingly."

He thought about that for a second. Nodded. "Well, at least you've got magic," he said.

"Keel, I'll tell you a secret that only Amra knows: I detest being a mage."

He gave me a look that said he was now convinced I was insane. "But you are really good at it. Really, really good. Scary good."

"How would you know that? You've only seen me fail."

"First, because Amra told me so. Second, because I heard about what you did to Fisk. Third, I was there yesterday morning when Steyner's man tried to bash his way in. If you aren't powerful, I don't think I know what the word means. And I really don't see how anybody can not like having power."

"Some people are masters of arithmetic. Doesn't mean they want to spend their time doing long division."

"But we aren't talking about numbers. We're talking about magic! Power!"

"All power comes at a price," I told him, but he shook his head.

"You don't agree?"

"From what I've seen, it's the powerless that pay while the powerful do whatever they want." The bitterness in his voice was unusual, for him. But I did not press. Besides, he wasn't wrong from where he was standing.

"Well, let's go down and receive my delivery," I said.

"What have they got?"

"Another kind of power."

~ ~ ~

Perrick Leed was wearing pale yellow this time, and had traded his tri-cornered hat for what looked like a velvet sack. But then I knew as much about fashion as I did about the Emperor of Chagul's favorite aunt.

"Magister Leed. You'll have to introduce me to your tailor," I said by way of greeting, and he smiled politely.

"Magister Angrado, good morning. May we enter?"

"Of course," I said, and brought down the wards and moved aside so that they could haul in four iron casques, each with an imposingly large lock.

"If I could impose upon you gentlemen to bring them upstairs?" I said to the armsmen. There were a few grimaces, but no muttering. The bank must have been paying them well. They were a mixed lot; Camlachers, Lucernans, Nine Cities men. I wondered where Leed had hired them from, and asked as much.

"Bellaria is at war with itself," he replied. "Such conflict draws mercenaries. You'll find a ready pool of them, wharfside, and many more at Jedder."

"Jedder?"

"A small town half a day's sail south, beyond the marsh," he explained as we climbed the stairs to the second floor. "Those who do not have an inclination to fight for the rebels wait there to be hired by the would-be Syndics. Those who prefer the rebel's cause, or knew no better before taking ship, end up wharfside here in Bellarius."

"Just set them against the wall, if you would," I told the armsmen, and they complied. Then they retreated back downstairs, leaving only Leed, Keel and myself in the dusty second floor of the Citadel.

"I very much regret to inform you that Vulkin and Bint was able to accede to your request only in half-measure, magus."

I raised my eyebrows. "Explain, please."

"By this time tomorrow the bank will have ceased operations completely in Bellarius, owing to the instability that currently holds sway. It is an indelible stain on the honor of the bank that they could not honor your letter of credit completely, and in recognition of the fact, they have reduced their transaction fee by one half of one per cent."

"I would say that their regret was boundless, but...."

Leed had nothing to say to that.

"Is there something I should sign, magister?" I asked him.

"Of course. After you've counted the coin, sir."

"I'm certain that won't be necessary."

"Sadly, I must disagree with you, magus. Vulkin and Bint does love its procedures, and abhors any anomalies regarding them. I would be let go in an instant were you not to count the coin in my presence and confirm that all is as it should be."

I sighed. "Very well, Magister Leed. I wouldn't want to be the cause of any disturbing anomalies."

Keel snickered, and I gave him a questioning glance.

"Do mages always talk like that when they get together?" he asked.

"Like what?"

"Like there's a prize for whoever uses the fanciest word."

Leed gave a slight smile. I considered the question.

"Pretty much," I finally decided, and turned to Leed. "The keys, sir?"

~ ~ ~

So there it was; twenty chains of Lucernan mint. Twenty thousand marks. I signed and Leed and his entourage departed.

"Holgren?"

"Yes, Keel?"

"That's a shit-ton of money."

"Yes, it is." Though it should have been more.

"What are you going to *do* with it?"

"Some of it goes to Moc Mien to keep you from getting knifed by his crew while we're in Bellarius. A bit more goes to him for arranging transport out of Bellarius. A *lot* more goes to him for assisting me in trapping a rift-spawn."

"You don't need twenty large for that," Keel said.

"Correct." Most I would keep on hand in the event I needed to buy my own army. I sincerely hoped it would not come to that. I scooped up a double handful of marks and handed it to him.

"First, find and hire two armsmen who can be trusted."

"How do I know if they can be trusted?"

I smiled. "I trust your judgment." I'd also be putting them under a Compulsion. "One stays here, one follows you everywhere."

"I can take care of myself."

"Did your arm heal itself while I wasn't looking? You need a bodyguard, Keel. Bellarius is far from safe, and I've already made an enemy of one of the warring factions. You will be a target."

"All right," he said, not liking it. "What else?"

"Go to Moc Mien and tell him to come see me to collect his fee. After that, find us a housekeeper who can cook and can be trusted, and send them to me, here. Then order some decent furniture for all of us, and get a tailor for you and me. Have them come this evening. I also want a fisherman's net, as strong and big as you can find. Better make it two. Do you need to write this down?"

"No. Can't write anyway. Or read, for that matter."

"We'll have to rectify that at some point, but there's no time now. What else? Best if the housekeeper is male or a very old woman. Everyone will be staying at the Citadel for the duration of our stay, and since there's a distinct lack of privacy here I don't want to bother putting up partitions. We'll likely be leaving in a few days. Which reminds me. See if there are any ships for sale."

"You want to buy a boat? I thought you said—"

"Not a boat. A *ship*. They're generally much bigger than boats. And I have no intention of buying one. I just want those who are bound to be watching my every move to have something to report."

"All right. Does it matter what kind of ship you aren't buying?"

"I'm not sure yet. Find out what's available, and then we'll discuss it."

"Anything else?"

"Yes. How are you passing back and forth between the Girdle and the gentry-controlled portion of the city?"

"Sneakily."

"That will no longer do, after today. Like it or not, I am now a power in Bellarius. You, as my representative, cannot be skulking about. It will lessen my honor and my status."

He looked at me as though I'd suddenly started speaking Chagul.

"I'm completely serious. There's no chance any of the factions will learn to love me in the brief time I'll be here, so that leaves fear."

"Love? Fear? Status? You said we're probably leaving in a few days, but you're talking like you want to rule this place."

"We are in the middle of a three-cornered civil war, Keel. We are in possession of the Citadel, the *only* physical symbol of authority left in this midden of a city, since Amra pulled down the Riail. You know very well what I want, and it isn't to become a despot. But the three factions assume we are a fourth, I guarantee you, and it won't matter what I say to the contrary. So I won't bother."

"All right, I guess I can understand that. But why not just ignore them until your business is finished?"

"I would do just that, if there was any hope they would return the favor. There isn't. You saw that yesterday. If I was content to stay in the Citadel, it wouldn't matter, but we have business in the city below, and so we must play the part." As much of a stupid, monotonous waste of time, energy and money as it would be.

"Yeah, but what part, exactly? I'm still not clear on that."

"I will play the part of a dangerous, inscrutable archmage whose motives are unknown, but undoubtedly dark and arcane. And dangerous. And inscrutable. You will play the role of my trusted servant, who speaks with my voice." I looked him over. "Hmm. You'll probably need a haircut to manage that. Add a barber to the list. Also, a cobbler. Your big toe is sticking out."

"You look pretty shaggy yourself."

"Shaggy?"

"It sounds nicer than 'homeless.'"

"Fine, send a barber and a cobbler up for both of us, then. Go, the day isn't getting younger."

He turned to go, then turned back.

"You need a symbol."

"Come again?"

"If you're going to play the part of a power. You need a symbol."

"I do?"

"Absolutely. The Gentry all have their heraldry nonsense. Even the crews have got their versions of 'em. If you want to *mark* your territory or your property, you have to *have* a mark. It'll be expected, Holgren. Seriously."

"All right. What do you suggest?"

"You remember that one thing you tried, where fire shot out of all the windows and almost cooked me along the way?"

"I already apologized for that."

"People are still talking about that in the Girdle. Not me getting burned up, of course; how would they know about that? But they're still talking about the night the Citadel burned."

"And?"

"They think that's when the Telemarch died. Your symbol should be a burning tower. If you're serious about making people think they should be scared of you."

"That's... that's not a terrible idea actually. I'll work on it. You get going."

~ ~ ~

Keel was gone for perhaps an hour before my first visitors of the day announced themselves by trying to break down the front door with cannon fire. I knew I would not be left in peace; still, it was disheartening to be proven right so quickly.

I felt the intense, if fleeting, pressure on the wards at the same time I heard the hollow boom of the cannon ball striking them.

"Imbeciles," I said aloud and got up from the table where I'd been working on Keel's burning tower badges. I opened the door.

In the street below, Steyner's halberdiers were back, this time joined by a three-man cannon crew. They were wearing the emerald and jet of Isinglas mercenaries. I couldn't see the cockade they wore that would tell me which free company they served. Not that it mattered.

They had a short, stubby little bronze perrier that was still smoking. They were perhaps twenty yards away, and a few of the halberdiers had obviously been struck by shrapnel when the stone ball had shattered against the wards and then been flung away at high velocity. Two men were screaming. A third wasn't, his head being mostly gone. The idiot captain in half-plate was, sadly, unharmed.

I stepped outside, waited until I caught the captain's attention, then said "I warned you."

Then I summoned up my well and disincorporated him. Or, as Keel would have put it, I made him go 'splat.'

I do not kill lightly. I take no enjoyment from it. But I have no qualms about ending a life. Life is cheap, cheaper than it ought to be, perhaps. But it is what it is, and there isn't a mage alive that would countenance the sort of disrespect the fool had shown by assaulting my sanctum. Most would have slaughtered every man present, but I had made my point, and was content.

I have never claimed to be a good person. I'm not. But I do try not to be more monstrous than is necessary. If I'd wanted to, I could have tapped into one of the many lethal traps the Telemarch had sown throughout the city. I'd found a dozen, and there were more. There was one almost directly under them. The ground would have turned to acid beneath their feet. Any who managed to survive and flee would have been pursued by corrosive tendrils.

The Telemarch had been a nasty piece of work, with a nasty turn of mind.

I considered telling the others not to come back, but that seemed pointless. Either they would or they wouldn't and telling them was far less effective than showing them. Finally, I just shrugged to myself and went back inside.

~ ~ ~

My second caller was a big, beefy sailor, his thinning hair pulled back in a club. He only had one hand. If he noticed the remains of Steyner's captain on the way up, he said nothing.

"Magister Holgren, then?"

"Yes?"

He tugged on an imaginary forelock with an imaginary hand and said "Name's Marl. I've come to cook and keep house."

"Keel told you the position's requirements?"

"Aye. Marketing, cooking, cleaning. I'm to lodge here. The position will likely be temporary."

"Come in then, master Marl." He entered, and I sat at the table. When I invited him to do the same he declined. I asked him a little about his background, learned he had been a navy man until he'd lost a hand in a boarding action, and that he had no family to speak of. I liked him well enough, and it seemed he could tolerate me.

"Keel explained the basics," I concluded. "I'll let you know the finer points. Then you can decide whether you still want the position."

"As you say, Magus."

"You're well aware the city is unstable. Many think I wish to become its ruler, or hope to use me to make them ruler. Anyone who serves me should be aware that this means they may be targets, for those hoping to extract information if nothing else."

"People might try to pump me for information, or worse. I understand."

"You'll be doing the marketing, so you will be in danger. Keel is also hiring armsmen. One will accompany you whenever you leave the Citadel."

"All right."

"I will lay two spells on you. The first is a Compulsion not to betray any secrets you may learn while in my employ. This Compulsion is voluntary; you have to agree to it. The second spell is simple tracking magic; if someone takes you or you get into trouble, I'll know where you are and can come collect you. These two spells are non-negotiable requirements of your employment. Are you agreeable?"

"Will they hurt?"

"Not in the slightest."

"Will they let you read my mind?"

"Not a single stray thought."

"How much is the pay, Magus? Your boy was somewhat vague about that. He said 'at least double whatever you're making now.'"

"What are you making now?"

"Nothing, being unemployed at present." He smiled.

"What were you making before you became a man of infinite prospects?"

"Two gold, six silver a month."

"Then I'll pay you eight."

"Two-and-eight?"

"No. Eight gold."

"That's too much, Magus."

"Three gold for your services. Five for your hazard." I scooped out a handful of marks from my pocket and counted out twenty. "Your first month in advance. The rest is for marketing. If you need more just tell me, but I'll expect a weekly accounting."

"As you say, Magus."

"Any other questions, Master Marl?"

He looked around. "Where's the kitchen, then?"

~ ~ ~

The third caller was an old man pulling a hand cart. The steep incline had obviously worn him out. Inside the cart were two fishing nets, reeking of the sea. I foolishly hadn't specified to Keel that they should be new.

Live and learn.

I tipped the man a couple of silver for his trouble, and brought the nets inside. If I hadn't needed a bath and a change of clothes before that, I certainly did after. I dumped them on the floor and called out for Marl.

"Aye, magus?" he replied, half-climbing the stairs and poking his head up from what I just knew he would refer to as the galley, if only to himself.

"Any idea how to make these less rank and less slimy?"

"Aye, I can do it, magus. Will you be needing them today?"

"Tomorrow will serve."

"D'you need 'em dry?"

"No. Just not sopping wet."

"I'll have 'em ready by morning. But I'll need to buy a tub. Among many, many other things."

"Noon tomorrow is soon enough."

There was another knock on the door.

"Would you like me to get that, Magus?" asked Marl, and I shook my head.

The furniture had arrived.

Five beds, five smallish wardrobes, three silver-backed mirrors in wooden frames, another table and six straight-backed dining chairs, a couch whose pastel embroidery made my eyes want to bleed. Bedding. Linens. Chamber pots. Pitchers. A coat rack. A boot scraper. A porcelain flower vase. Pewter tankards and stamped iron utensils. Other things I didn't bother to unpack and identify.

Keel was having entirely too much fun.

I had them dump it all there on the first floor. Keel could have fun setting it all up, as well.

I tipped them well. Bellarius, being dishearteningly vertical for the most part, couldn't boast much in the way of draft animals. Human toil was the norm.

"D'you want me to get started on all that, Magus?" Marl asked me, face impassive. Here was a man unafraid of work.

"No, let's leave it for Keel, shall we? I asked him to buy a few necessities, for a few days. It looks like he cleared out every furnishing shop in the city."

"Well, to be fair magus, the shopkeepers are hurting. Like as not he paid a pittance for all these goods."

"Speaking of which, have you worked up a list of what you'll need for the kitchen?"

"Aye. I'll be going marketing now, with your permission. And I'll pick up my kit while I'm about it."

"Of course."

~ ~ ~

By the time the next knock on the door came, I'd fashioned four burning tower badges. It was intricate work, and being practically frivolous, I rather enjoyed it. I rarely had a chance or a reason to be artistic with the Art. The exacting work required a level of concentration I was familiar enough with. The consequence of failure was nothing at all; a feeling I'd almost forgotten.

I'd transformed a few marks into the shape of the Citadel, then tied and hardened tiny little flickering flames of green witchlight to come licking out of the windows. The effect was somewhat gaudy, and I'd need to renew each of them every few days. But I was pleased with the result.

There was another knock, more insistent this time.

I got up from the table, expecting Moc Mien. I went and opened the door.

It wasn't Moc Mien.

The man at the door was a hulking brute with a scar that ran up his face and creased his shaved, tanned scalp. His eyes were a dirty green, small, and rather evil-looking. The teeth he exposed with his insincere smile were very, very white, though. He was dressed in woolen trousers and a leather jerkin that was too small to go all the way around his barrel chest. A silver amulet on a chain gleamed between his overdeveloped pectorals.

"Did Keel send you?" I asked, thinking it was one of the mercenaries.

"No. Gabul Steyner did." And then he punched me in the face. Through the wards.

Through the *Telemarch's* wards.

I staggered back, momentarily stunned, and he followed me in, as if the wards simply weren't there. He punched me again, and I fell to the floor, ripping power from my well as I went down. With a flick of my wrist I released it, regretting for Marle's sake the mess of blood and tissue that was about to coat the room.

Nothing happened.

"They all do that," the man said, standing over me and waving his hands in a parody of a mage casting a spell. "And then they all get that stupid look on their faces when nothing happens." He smiled. "I never get tired of that."

He picked me up by the front of my shirt and threw me onto the table. Everything on it went flying. I bounced once and tumbled to the floor. I landed hard and awkward on my side, with an awful wrench to my shoulder, one hand twisted behind my back.

"Sorry I didn't introduce myself. I'm the Magekiller."

He flung the table aside and squatted down, reaching for my neck.

"What do you want?" I asked, and then his hands were squeezing the breath out of me. Hard.

"I got what I want; Steyner's money. Now he gets what *he* wants. You dead."

The muscles in my shoulder shrieked in abused protest as I pulled Amra's knife out of my belt, where I kept it at the small of my back, and plunged it into the side of his neck.

He fell back. I kept the knife. He put his huge hands to the wound, but it was pointless. I'd hit the artery. He looked at me in shock.

I worked myself up to a squatting position, spat blood out of my lacerated mouth. A piece of tooth went with it.

"They all get that stupid look on their faces, when a mage sticks steel in them instead of waving his arms around," I panted, an ugly, oily hate possessing me. "You should have run me through with a sword as soon as I opened the door," I continued, over his dying grunts. "But no, you had to make it personal. You had to dominate before you destroyed. You had to mix business and pleasure, you miserable, twisted shit."

Then I leaned over him and, with a violence-shaky hand, reached out and took the amulet from his neck, snapping the chain. Then I sat back.

As soon as I'd touched the thing, I'd become completely cut off from my well. I knew what it was. For whoever touched the thing, and for as long as they touched it, magic simply didn't exist. I'd heard of such things before, but had never actually seen one. They were rare artifacts even before the Cataclysm, and completely impossible to fabricate nowadays. How this murderous thug had gotten hold of one was a mystery.

"Thanks for the magical sink," I told him as the spark faded from his eyes, slipping the amulet into my pocket. "It might prove useful."

Then, with a groan, I got up and dragged his carcass out to the street.

FIVE

"I want two thousand," said Moc Mien when he finally showed up.

"Done," I replied. I wasn't in the mood to haggle.

"Maybe I should have asked for more."

"Too late now. The first thing I need is all the information you can get on the rift spawn; where they've been sighted, what they look like, what they do, what they eat. Anything and everything, including the deranged mutterings of back alley drunks. But I'm especially interested in anything we can determine about their movements. Think your men can handle that?"

"Collecting rumors? It's not the most arduous of jobs."

"That's only the first step. We'll meet back here tomorrow at the same time, go over what you've found out, and then plan the hunt. Clear?"

"Perfectly. Where's my money?"

"Did you bring something to carry it in?"

His smile was answer enough.

"By the way, you wouldn't happen to know where Gabul Steyner lays his head of a night, would you?"

"In the Steyner House. Where else?"

"Care to point it out for me?"

"Can't miss it. It's the one with the giant bronze hammer topping the weather vane and all the soldiers milling about below. Planning on visiting him?"

"Planning on killing him."

"Maybe you want to talk to the Just Men first, or Councilor When. Or hells, both. I'm sure they'd pony up some coin to see it happen."

"Tempting. But I'm intent upon getting all the various factions to leave me the hells alone, not getting sucked further into their maneuverings."

He shrugged "Up to you, of course." And without a further word, he left.

From the time he showed up to the time he left, he never once mentioned the corpse outside the front door, or the blood on the floor. Perhaps in his world they were unremarkable sights.

~ ~ ~

Keel, on the other hand, seemed excessively preoccupied by such things.

"You can't just leave a dead body outside the door, magus!"

"Why not? Are Blacksleeves going to come knocking? Afraid of getting arrested?" There were plenty of bodies made along the barricades on a daily basis, or so I'd been informed. Most of the Blacksleeves, the local constabulary, had either quit the city or been conscripted into one or the other of the Councilors' armies. The rebels certainly wouldn't have them, as brutally corrupt as they'd been for so long. More than a few had been strung up from the eaves of houses in the rebel-controlled areas of the Girdle. And if Keel was correct, many more were sitting on spikes wharfside.

"It's a dead body, Holgren."

"No. It's a warning."

"It's going to start to smell."

"The weather's fairly chill. That'll take a while. When it does, you have my permission to do whatever you want with it. Meanwhile, there's a whole lot of furnishings there, waiting for your special touch."

He threw up his arms, one expressively and the other awkwardly, and walked away. The two armsmen he'd returned with looked as though they were having second thoughts.

"Gentlemen," I said to them, "Welcome to the Citadel. I am going to pay you an exorbitant amount of money. In return, you are going to make sure my young friend Keel and our chef and housekeeper, Master Marle, do not suffer from any of my unwise choices. Any questions?"

They appeared to be brothers. The younger of the two cleared his throat and said, "When you say exorbitant, that means what, exactly?"

"How much would you normally get a month for your services?"

"Three-and-two. Plus the odd city-sacking, of course. And room and board, and physicking," said the elder of the two.

"Sorry, I've no plans to sack any cities. But you'll get room and board and medical when you need it, and I'll give you five Lucernan gold. Per day."

They started to smile a little too broadly, so I said "But," and the smiles went away.

"But," I repeated, "I'll be putting a Compulsion on you to make sure you aren't working for someone else, and I want to make it very clear that if Keel or Marle are killed on your watch, I expect them to have died *after* you did, defending them. Still interested?"

The younger one, whose name was Chalk, looked at the elder, whose name was Thon. Thon said "Aye, magus."

~ ~ ~

When Marle returned, he cleaned up the blood without comment, and had a word with the armsmen, who then proceeded to help Keel setting up the furnishings while he went down and started dinner. He didn't even give me a reproachful glance.

I never said I was particularly likeable. And two attempts on my life in one day had made me rather ill-tempered.

When the tailor showed up, I had everybody kitted out in black, Gosland-style military coats, stiff collared and completely unadorned except for emerald green sashes, Fel-Radoth style. I ordered matching trousers and white linen everything else. When the cobbler arrived, everyone got measured for Imrian cavalry boots. I may not know fashion, but I know uniforms. I made it known to both tradesmen that I expected everything to be delivered first thing in the morning.

The barber arrived. He decided I needed a goatee. I didn't care. He decided Keel needed to have the wispy patches of hair he called a mustache eradicated. I cheered. On the inside. Everybody else apparently already had some sense of personal grooming, and got away with trims.

Then it was time to eat.

Master Marle could cook. Not much talking got done around the table. When everyone had finished, Keel handed me a sheet of paper.

"What's this?"

"List of ships for sale. Got it from an agent wharfside. He said he can come talk to you, or you can come to him. He made it sound like the second option was his personal favorite. Felt a bit bad, getting his hopes up like that."

"Thank you, Keel." I stood up.

"Gentlemen, I have something for you." I passed out the burning tower badges I'd fashioned. "These are a symbol of this house. They're also your key to passing the magical wards that protect this building, so don't lose them." I paused for a moment, and decided to take a cue from Marle and be a little less reticent.

"I would much rather be about my business in a quiet, unnoticeable fashion, leaving Bellarius to get on with its own. That isn't going to happen, unfortunately. The principal players in the conflict happening in Bellarius have decided I figure in their power struggle, so figure I shall. They have armies. I have the Citadel, and magic, and now you. For the short time that I am here, you each have a role to play in assisting me."

"Assisting you in what, exactly, magus?" asked Thon, the elder armsman.

"Eight days ago, a woman named Amra Thetys saved Bellarius and everyone in it from being completely destroyed by the Telemarch. In doing so, she disappeared. I'm going to find her, and bring her back. For the time being, I need the Citadel to do so. Others, especially Gabul Steyner, want the Citadel for their own reasons. Steyner has been particularly annoying about it, which is why I'm going to go and kill him." I stood up and put on my coat.

"What, you mean right now?" Keel asked.

"No time like the present."

"Begging your pardon, magister, but you can't go and kill a Syndic-Elect wearing that," said Marle.

"And why is that?"

"Forgive me for imagining, but I imagine you killing Steyner has somewhat to do with the dead fellow outside the front door. Steyner sent his message, and you replied, is how I reckon it. You killing Steyner will be a message to everybody else." He rubbed his chin with his stump. "Again, begging your pardon, but if you go and end Steyner looking like that, it'll lack a certain level of dignity, of... gravity. Your message won't carry the full measure of its weight. Or so I believe."

"Seriously?"

"Seriously, magister."

I looked down at my coat. So it was a touch dirty. And blood-stained. And charred. I looked up at the others. "Do I look that bad, then?"

The armsmen kept quiet, obviously not wanting to offend. Keel had no such reservations.

"You look better after your barbering, but you still look like you've been sleeping in a ditch."

I sighed. "So be it. Steyner gets a short reprieve, while I wait for clothes more fitting to kill him in."

"And a bath," Keel chipped in.

"Speaking of which, where are we getting our water from?"

"A cistern, magister," Marle replied. "No worries on that front. It's deep and nearly full. Bellarius at the end of autumn does not lack for rain."

"Very good, Master Marle. Baths all around in the morning. Keel will of course assist you in heating all that water, it being his idea."

~ ~ ~

Sleep was long in coming, and when it finally claimed me I dreamed of Amra. She lay atop a mound of knives as high as the walls of the Necropolis; hundreds of thousands of them. She was unmoving, face as pale as alabaster.

I cut myself to bloody ribbons climbing to her, trying to reach her, never getting any closer.

SIX

One thing about the Citadel. It was bare as a barn and as cheery as a prison, but it had the best view of Bellarius in Bellarius. Not that Bellarius is picturesque, but if you're going to be stuck in a midden, you might as well be sitting at the top of the mound.

Amra had told me once that the difference between a good burglar and a dead burglar was, essentially, mental balance. The ability to ignore distractions such as fear, nervousness, anger, and get on with the job. To be able to retain the ability to think, analyze, and act without undue haste whatever the pressures at hand. Magic wasn't all that different, really.

I looked down on the ugly city that had taught her that hard truth, and realized that Gabul Steyner had managed to rob me of my own mental balance. His multiple provocations had nearly goaded me into doing something I would likely regret. Could I walk into his house and kill him? Certainly. Could I also kill all the armsmen between him and me, and then make my exit unscathed?

Possible, even likely, though the risk of me being taken down by sheer numbers was real enough. And if Steyner had a mage on his payroll, which was not inconceivable, I'd simply be overwhelmed by mercenaries while the greater threat distracted me.

Looking out from the city-facing window of the library, or rather what was left of it after Greytooth had apparently made an abortive attempt to assassinate the Telemarch, it didn't take long to find the bronze hammer weather vane Moc Mien had mentioned. Two towers down, three to the left.

I wouldn't have to walk far to pay my respects to Steyner, if I had a mind to do so. If he was even there.

That was really the deciding factor. Either he was holed up behind layers of protection, or he was in hiding, for he *had* to know I would come for him, after his failed assassination attempt.

I might slaughter my way into his house, only to find him gone.

I rested my forehead against the cold, rough, broken stone of the wall beside the gap. My eye was bothering me, little sharp, spearing twitches of pain. I consciously kept my hand from going up and rubbing futilely at the patch.

I had planned to just walk in and start killing my way towards Steyner, if you could call that a plan. I might have been a little angry the previous day. Considering how close his residence was, and how reckless my original plan was, I decided it would be far more reasonable to kill Steyner from the safety of the Citadel. Less satisfying, certainly; nothing will provoke a mage more than violating his sanctum. But the job at hand was to kill Steyner, not risk myself needlessly. Nobody else was going to bring Amra back if I went and got myself killed.

So.

Steyner's hired killer had surprised me with his magic-nullifying trinket. I decided to return the favor, in a way that would no doubt surprise Gabul Steyner greatly in the moments before he expired. More importantly, it wouldn't matter in the slightest where he was. I wouldn't have to know his location beforehand—such knowledge normally being crucial to the success of a spell. I *would* have to form a connection to him, true; but it wouldn't be a normal one, and it certainly wouldn't be one that any mage had a hope of blocking. A bloodwitch might, but I very much doubted Gabul Steyner had a bloodwitch in his employ.

I went downstairs and stepped outside. The assassin's corpse was right where I'd left it, which rather surprised me. I was half-certain Keel would make it disappear overnight. I suppose he took me more seriously than I took myself. Or maybe he was just at a loss as to what to do with the corpse. I certainly was.

I stepped back inside, called the younger of the guard brothers to help me drag the corpse inside and lay it on the table.

I peeled back the thug's eyelids and stared into those dead, dirty green eyes; or rather, at the dull reflection on the skin of them.

My mother was a bloodwitch, and a rather powerful one. She'd also had the skill to make the dead speak, though none for prophecy. She'd passed on some of what she was capable of to me; unusual if not unheard of, for a male to inherit such power. Much more unusual, she'd actually trained me to use the powers I'd inherited from her. To a degree, at least. Enough for the task at hand, certainly.

Blood magic wasn't as straightforward as the usual variety, however. Sometimes it worked, sometimes it didn't. Emotion seemed to up the chances of success, so as I stared at those cold, going-milky eyes, I summoned up the hate I'd felt when this hired killer had bled his life away in front of me. Then I leaned in, close enough for our noses to touch. "*Show me,*" I hissed. "*Show me Steyner.*" And those dead eyes began to glow ever so faintly.

Slowly, reluctantly, a picture formed in them as they continued to brighten. Or at least the left eye. I couldn't see his right one of course. I saw a hard man in rich clothes. Short hair, going gray. A mouth that seemed set in an ever-so-slight curl of disdain. The picture began to move.

The man spoke, but of course there was no sound. He handed me, or rather the thug, a heavy velvet purse. Then he turned away, clearly dismissing me/him.

The light in the corpse's eyes had been growing steadily stronger all the while. Now it flared white and hot, and the image burned away along with those dead orbs. I backed away hastily, the smell of burnt flesh strong in my nose. I had what I needed.

I had Gabul Steyner's image, now, collected from a dead man's eyes–and so I had enough to kill him without ever leaving the Citadel, and without having to resort to a locating spell that I could not cast anyway, without Steyner's blood or hair or tissue. I wouldn't have to chew my way through all the mercenaries he'd have about him in order to finish him.

That's one I never learned from my late, not-in-the-least lamented master. Nobody mixed blood magic and the Art. Very few had access to both. If anyone else did, it wasn't something that I'd ever heard tell of. Not anyone living, at any rate. But I'd experimented enough to find a few very useful and very dangerous combinations. It was one of the reasons Yvoust had despised me so. He'd called me an abomination, but really, he'd abhorred me having powers he himself did not. Enough to try to break me, and when he failed at that, to set me up for failure, and disgrace.

I shook my head to clear my thoughts of old, bad memories. Working with blood magic called for emotion, and it also called forth emotions. They were not so easy to dispel.

"Magister?" asked the armsman. "Are you all right?"

"Quite. Let Keel know he can dispose of this now," I said, indicating the corpse. "I'll be occupied for the next several hours. Please make sure I'm not disturbed before lunch."

~ ~ ~

It took a dozen gold marks and two hours of casting, and at the end I had a golden spike as long as my hand and as thick as my little finger, needle sharp at one end and flat at the other. It hummed in my hand. As it got closer to its target, its pitch would increase. By the time it got to Steyner, the wail would be deafening. Once it had found his heart's blood, its song would be complete, and it would self-destruct. Which meant that anybody around Steyner at the time would also probably 'kark it' as Keel liked to say, depending on how far the barb had to fly before it reached its target. A little dramatic, perhaps, but I wasn't going to bother building in a sub-spell to safely channel any excess, residual power. I wasn't making a Gate; I was making a weapon. Weapons kill people. And anyone in close proximity to the Syndic-Elect wasn't someone whose welfare I was concerned with.

Also, I was exhausted. This working had brought me to the edge of my limits with the Art. I wasn't up to adding any unnecessary frills.

I broke the circle with a swipe of my hand. I levered myself up from the floor, arms and legs trembling, and stumbled my way downstairs to the library.

I went to the window and flung it overhand towards the stupid, oversize bronze hammer that topped Steyner's tower. I had no idea whether he was actually there, but it made a convenient target.

The spike flipped end over end out over the city, defying gravity and winking in the sun, and then suddenly it plunged downward, a needle pulled to a lodestone. The humming went louder and higher, then suddenly cut off as it drove its way through the masonry of Steyner's house.

He was home after all, then.

Stone was no barrier to it, of course. That was part of the working. If he happened to be in the bath, I might have a problem. Such a quick working demanded trade-offs. The barb would dissolve at the touch of water, and the backlash of power would likely kill me. Nothing ventured and all that.

Nothing for one second, two, three...

Then an ear-splitting wail, swiftly rising up into registers impossible to hear, but somehow still felt. Which meant it had found Steyner's blood, and would presently explode.

It did. Gabul Steyner's house fell in on itself. I saw the idiotic bronze hammer fall into and be swallowed by the boiling masonry dust that billowed up to meet it, just before I passed out.

I'd scraped the bottom of my well to make that little show come off, and the bill had arrived.

~ ~ ~

"Gabul Steyner is dead."

I opened my eyes, beheld a bleary image of Greytooth. My head was pounding, and my mouth was as dry as the Broken Lands.

"He'd damned well better be," I croaked, "after what I just went through to make him that way." I was lying in the newly erected bed, in one corner of the library. The one I'd ignored the night before in favor of sleeping upstairs in the inner sanctum. I sat up, put my feet on the floor. Swallowed a wave of bile that tried to make an escape.

"Have you turned political when I wasn't looking?" Greytooth asked.

"Not that I've noticed."

"Then why did you assassinate Steyner?"

"It wasn't politically motivated, Fallon. It was completely personal. That's what happens to someone who invades my sanctum."

He frowned. "And just how did Steyner manage to bypass the Telemarch's wards and violate the Citadel, may I ask?"

I dug the magical sink out of a pocket. "He hired somebody who had this." I tossed it to him.

He caught it, then dropped it as if it were hot. Pushed it back toward me with the toe of his boot. I leaned down to pick it up and nearly lost my balance, and the breakfast I hadn't had. My skull felt as if it had turned to chalk.

"I don't suppose you've got anything for a headache?" I asked.

Without a word he stepped around the amulet and over to me. He laid a hand on the top of my head, and then whispered something. It felt as if the top of my skull had been ripped off, spun in a full circle, and slammed back down. I nearly vomited from the pain, but when the dust settled, my headache was gone.

"Thanks, I think," I said through gritted teeth.

"You might not have meant it as a political statement, but Steyner's death is having consequences. The bulk of his forces have shifted over to Councilor When, being suddenly unemployed. What was a more or less evenly matched, three-cornered affray has now become a contest between When and the Just Men. When will win."

"Ah, but when will When win?" I said.

"This is not a joke, Holgren."

"Fallon, the fate of Bellarius is up to the Bellarians. I'm here for one purpose only, and once I've got what I need, I am gone."

"And how are you going to get what you need, when virtually the entire population of the Girdle believes you either wish to rule or are supporting When's claim? It will be a neat trick, hunting a rift spawn through the neighborhoods of thousands who are baying for your blood."

I sighed. "Great Gorm, it's always something."

"What are you going to do?"

"Why should I do anything? All of this is just a distraction, and I find myself in short supply of patience. Amra is out there, somewhere, and every moment I'm forced to deal with the ugly, monotonous child's play that is Bellarian politics is a moment I'm *not getting her back!*"

A silence stretched between us, then Fallon cleared his throat. "Got that out of your system, now, have you?"

I sighed again, then held up a thumb and forefinger, about half an inch apart.

"So what are you going to do?"

"I suppose I'd better go talk to whoever's in charge of the Just Men, hadn't I?"

"Send Keel. He's got some credit with that lot."

"No. I'll go myself, and alone. I'm sick of this cold pile of stone, and I'm sick of sitting on my hands while others do my bidding."

"Up to you, of course. If they don't kill you on sight, you'll want to speak to Gammond. But I didn't actually come here to strategize." He pulled a folded piece of paper out of his pocket and held it out to me.

"What's this?" I said as I took it.

"All I could find in my own library that was relevant to your quest."

It was in Old Imrian, and more or less intelligible:

> *And sodeinly that lord of lordes*
> *the greet hell-duke, Xom Dei,*
> *rase up and took the wickid swerd*
> *And smyt the neck of Laghne.*
> *And Laghnes heed, with swiche glarynge open eyen,*
> *rolled acrost the floor.*
> *And Xom Dei, laughyng, gat him thene the book, and the key,*
> *And smylyng bar them awaye.*

"It's from 'Lagna's Reward,'" said Greytooth. "I found it interesting because it mentions not only a book, but also a key."

"It didn't happen to mention what either one did, by chance?"

Greytooth shook his head.

I put the paper in my own pocket and extended a hand. Greytooth shook it.

"Thank you, Fallon."

He shrugged. "It's little enough."

~ ~ ~

I walked down the mount in cold but golden afternoon light. Half of the houses of the gentry were deserted, and the other half armed camps. I walked down the center of the street, garnered a lot of hostile looks, and not one challenge.

I wondered how the mercenaries were finding their way up the mount, considering the revolutionaries held the docks and the Girdle. A moment's thought gave me the answer. Of course, Mount Tarvus went all the way around, as the saying goes, and there had to be routes into the city from the hinterlands of Bellaria to the north and east. Not good routes, perhaps, but obviously good enough. And every border is porous. I couldn't help but think that, if the rebels had made a push earlier, they might have cleared out the gentry before the gentry could gather the mercenary strength they now had at their disposal. That mistake might well cost them their revolution.

"Not my problem," I muttered.

When I finally came to the barricade, I was distinctly underwhelmed. I also understood how Keel managed to sneak back and forth at will, even hampered by his arm. It was just barrels and crates and furniture piled up at choke points created by the narrow streets. If anyone was half-determined, they could find a dozen ways around the barricade–roof to roof, through a window and out a door. The roofs weren't sentried from what I could tell, and while some doors and windows were blocked or boarded up, many above the ground floor weren't. I wondered if anyone was actually in charge of the Girdle's defenses, or if it was all just ad hoc, disorganized volunteerism.

"Not my problem," I reminded myself once again.

"It's the fucking mage," said one of the rebels manning the barricades, his bald head poking up over a chest of drawers perched on top of a pile of broken bricks. "What the fuck do we do?"

"How do you know it's the mage?" asked his companion, who was out of my line of sight.

"He's got the badge, don't he? He's missing an eye, ain't he?"

"I'm half-blind, not half-deaf," I told them.

"You stay right there!" the first one called.

"Hanger," said the second, "We should send a runner to the Chop, ask for instructions."

"Send a message to Gammond," I said. "Say I want to parley. Now."

"You don't get to be bossing anyone around, uh, around here," said Hanger. "Stay still, now, or I'll have to be arresting you in the name of the People's Committee."

"I thought you were the Just Men."

"Well there's a whole lot of Just Men who're women, ain't there? We changed it."

"Cussed women did go on and on about it," I heard the other one mutter.

"Are you going to send my message or not?"

"And if I don't?"

"Then I'll turn that sorry excuse for a barricade into a bonfire and go looking for Gammond myself. Your choice."

THE THIEF WHO WASN'T THERE

He thought about it. "Send the runner," he told his companion.

Michael McClung

SEVEN

Gammond, as it happened, was a woman.

"Let me guess," I said as climbed stood atop the barricade and frowned down at me. "You were behind changing the name to the People's Committee."

"Hells no. I don't give a dead god's piss what we're called. What do you want? If you're here to assassinate me like you did Steyner, it won't do any good."

"Why? Are you magically protected?"

"Not even a little bit. But killing me won't kill the revolution. Not even a little bit. Another will just take my place."

"I'm not interested in killing you, or in politics."

"What do you want, then?"

"Many things. Chiefest among them being leaving your fair city and never, ever coming back as long as I live."

She gave me a long, hard, unblinking look. Without taking her eyes from mine, she pointed her thumb behind her in an offhand gesture. "Docks are that way. Have a safe trip."

I smiled. "If only it were that easy."

"It is. Just put one foot in front of the other until your boots get wet."

"I require something before I can go. Something in the Girdle, as it happens."

"I think your kind have taken enough from those of us in the

Girdle."

"My kind?"

"Gentry."

"I'm not a member of the gentry. I'm not even from Bellaria."

She sucked her front teeth and spat at my feet. "Let me explain in a fashion that will leave you without a doubt as to my meaning. There are those in the world who produce, and then there are those who consume. 'Gentry' is the generic term for those who produce nothing and consume the product of the useful members of any society. Another term would be parasite, or thief."

"I'm not really int-"

"At the end of the day, magus, there are only two sides: production and consumption, creation and destruction, promulgation and ruin. Birth and growth, or decay and death. Tell me, you with your Art—how much destruction have you caused, compared to what, if anything, you have created?"

"I'm not getting into a philosophical debate with you, Gammond. I haven't got the time."

"You haven't got a chance of winning, you mean."

"Fine. Put succinctly, your position is fundamentally flawed and dangerously simplistic. First, every producer is also a consumer, or did you dine on air and sunlight this morning? Second, without the forces of death and decay, any system would eventually become a hell due to the demands of an infinitely expanding population and a finite set of resources. Third, any philosophy that takes as its core tenet an 'us versus them' proposition of any sort is doomed to become a totalitarian nightmare. If this is what your People's Committee truly believes, then all you're doing is reshuffling the haves and have-nots. I find it sadly apt that you've eliminated the word 'just' from your name."

She nodded. "Excellent points all, and as succinct as anyone would have wished for. Now lie down on the street, there, if you will, and put your hands on the back of your head."

"Why would I do that?"

"Because if you don't, the bowmen that surrounded you while we had our little debate will pincushion you, and there's no way you could take them all before one or more of them takes you down."

I raised my magesight, and even then, I could only just make out the veil of illusion that wove its way in and out and around and through all the nearby buildings. As for pinpointing the bowmen, I couldn't beyond an occasional blurred movement in a window or on a roof. I looked back at Gammond and the barricade, and saw that Gammond was a mage, an extremely subtle one, and that the barricade wasn't nearly as pathetic as it seemed.

"Well played, Magus," I said, and she nodded.

"No duel, though," I continued. "That's not very sporting." Mages generally respected the ancient tradition of duels of the Art, but not in a battle setting. I was just talking, trying to stall for time just as she had done.

"We already had our duel. You lost. On your stomach, Magus. I won't say it again."

I got on my stomach.

EIGHT

"I really should just kill you and be done with it," Gammond said as two of her fellow citizens bound my hands and feet. "But as it happens, I've got a problem I think you can help me with."

"I'd love to help, really. But, well, I think I'll tell you to go to hells instead." I started pulling power from my well as they hoisted me up.

"Release your well, magus, or we'll have to knock you unconscious."

Reluctantly, I let it go.

"The Chop," she told my two guards. One hoisted me onto his shoulder, head down and staring at the stained canvas that covered his posterior. Lovely. The other followed a pace or two behind, cudgel in hand. I hoped briefly that Gammond would go elsewhere, leaving me free to call up some magic, but she wasn't anywhere close to being that stupid, alas. She walked along with us, next to the cudgel-bearing fellow.

"Out of curiosity, why did you kill Steyner?" she asked.

I decided to be truthful, and avoid being provocative. "He violated my sanctum."

"You claim the Citadel as your sanctum? And here you were just telling me your fondest wish was to show Bellarius your heels."

"Oh, come now," I said to the backside of the man who was carrying me, "you know as well as I do that a sanctum is as permanent or as temporary as a mage decides it will be."

"And you just decided to 'temporarily' put down your stakes in the Citadel. Uh-huh."

"I'd rather be a beggar in Lucernis than the ruler of Bellaria. Believe it or not."

"I don't."

"That's because politics has narrowed your world-view, I suspect."

She had nothing to say to that, and I've no idea what her expression was, since even with considerable physical effort, all I could see of her were her scuffed boots.

Soon enough we arrived at what, presumably, was the Chop. It turned out to be a sprawling wooden building that, in some former incarnation, had been a public house, at least in part. Or so the old, deep odor of spilled ale and burnt sausages told me. Now it seemed to be the command center of the revolution.

Lots of people were wearing the red and yellow cockades of the Just Men; or rather, the People's Committee. There was a lot of noise, and an abundance of movement. From my unenviable physical position, it was all just a swarm of revolutionary fervor, caught in stuttering snatches and upside-down glimpses. Then I was finally stood up straight, and could see that everyone seemed to be moving with purpose. Runners coming and going at speed to one of a half-dozen paper-strewn tables, delivering and taking messages across the city. Heated arguments burned in corners, infants napped under tables in other corners. An old man was sharpening knives on a pedal-powered grinder in a rickety mezzanine overlooking the large front room, and sparks rained down through the skewed wooden railing, dying and disappearing before they touched the floor. It all looked like controlled, purposeful chaos, if that isn't an oxymoron. And the unselfconscious blend of domesticity, military alertness and revolutionary fervor was something that took me aback. I'd never seen anything like it.

Along one wall, a group of children had stacked up several chairs in an approximation of a post coach. Two of them had apparently agreed to or been forced into the role of horses and were hitched to the jumble, galloping in place; three more scampered around the precarious assemblage, urging them on. Gammond went and appropriated two of the chairs, to the children's loud consternation. "For the cause!" she shouted, smiling.

"For the cause!" they shrieked back, fists in the air. Well, three of them did. The horses neighed loudly, committed to their roles.

Gammond put one chair behind me, and my own mount pushed me

down into it. Gammond set the other facing me, and sat down herself, smoothing out her long brown skirts.

"Now, Magister Holgren Angrado, late of Lucernis, current tenant of the Citadel, let us palaver."

"What, no dank cell?"

"We both know that without constant supervision by another mage, you'd be out of any hole I put you down inside five minutes. So we palaver now, or I kill you. Now."

"Palaver away, then."

"When you killed Steyner, you shifted the balance of power. Councilor When is the one who benefits from your action. Are you working for him?"

"I work for no one."

"Really? Then who was it sent you those four heavy chests from Vulkin and Bint?"

"I sent them to myself."

"Of course you did. Because that's just what a man intent on leaving a city does; he withdraws thousands in coin, in case he needs to buy some sundries for the journey. Sundries like furniture."

"You are well informed."

"Forewarned is forearmed, as they say. Of course we've been keeping an eye on the Citadel."

"Look, Gammond, we can go back and forth all day, you asking me questions and automatically disbelieving my answers. Or I can agree to submit to a Compulsion of truth."

She gave me a hard look. "Why would you do that?"

"Because I have no reason to lie about anything, and I have urgent matters to attend to. The sooner you're satisfied that I'm no threat to you and yours, the sooner I can be about my business."

She kept staring at me.

"What?"

"Nothing." She put her work-roughened hands against my temples. I felt her magic spring up to do her bidding, not as strong as my own, but subtle, subtle. And confident. I did not resist.

"Speak truth, or be silent," she muttered. It was an archaic, unnecessary phrase; I wondered who had taught her the Art. She leaned back again, still giving me that hard look of hers.

"Well?" I said.
"Are you in league with Councilor When?"
"No."
"His daughter?"
"What? No."
"Did you kill Gabul Steyner?"
"I did."
"Why?"
"Because he sent an assassin after me, one who breached the Telemarch's wards."
"How did the assassin manage that?"
I smiled, and remained silent.
"Did you know killing Steyner would shift the balance of power in Bellarius?"
"No. I hadn't considered the possibility."
She tssked and shook her head.
"Do you want to rule Bellarius?"
"I'd rather have my other eye clawed out."
"Do you care who rules Bellarius?"
"Not particularly, though I suppose you could say I have some slight leanings toward you lot."
Gammond snorted. "Oh, thanks so very much for that. How can you possibly be so self-involved as to not care who wins this war?"
"Because I'm trying my damnedest to get the hells out of Bellarius and rescue someone, and this Gorm-forsaken civil war is interfering at every turn. Time is not on my side. You have your cause, Gammond, and I have mine."
"Yes, about that. You keep saying you want to leave, and yet everything you've done that we can see indicates you setting up shop indefinitely."
"I'm going to pretend that was a question. It's complicated."
She indicated my ropes. "You're not going anywhere anyway. Just tell it."
"Take these damned ropes off and I will."
She did. So I did, in abbreviated form. Amra's escapades, and her disappearance. What I needed from the Girdle to track her—the rift spawn. When I was finished, she got up and whispered something to one of the

horses, who was now apparently a gray urdu, stalking several shrieking toddlers. He pumped a fist in the air and piped out a 'for the cause!' and then disappeared out the door. She sat back down, and I felt the Compulsion dissipate.

"All right, Magister Angrado. Your partner made this revolution possible, by taking down the Riail and the Telemarch. That much isn't in question. I suppose you could say I have some 'slight leanings' towards not seeing her dead.

"I'll make you a deal. You can have the run of the Girdle while you try and snare your rift spawn, on one condition."

"Which is?"

"Do to Councilor When what you did to Councilor Steyner."

"Happen to have any hair or blood from When?"

"I do not. But you didn't have any of Steyner's, and still he is dead."

"That's what you would call a special circumstance, actually. In addition to being a mage, I have some powers in respect to blood magic."

"Rare. Should I believe you?"

"As rare as a female mage?"

"More, for a man to have both powers, and you know it."

"I wasn't consulted about my parentage any more than you were about your gender. Would you like me to prove it? A drop of blood should suffice."

"Ha. No, that won't be necessary." She drummed her fingers on her knee, and her brow creased. The silence stretched.

"All right," she finally said. "Here's the problem. Councilor When is a ghost. We've put considerable effort into finding him, and failed. He never visits his headquarters, and his house is impenetrable. He might be there, or he might not. Finding out the hard way would cost a lot of lives, possibly for nothing, and it would leave the barricades vulnerable to a counter-attack."

"How is he directing his troops?"

"All his orders come through his daughter."

"Where was he when the Riail came down?"

"You're thinking the daughter is running a bluff. We also considered that. He wasn't there. He was with Steyner that night, no doubt taking the opportunity to plot against Meyrich while Meyrich attended the Syndic."

"Meyrich?"

"The late third of the Council of Three."

"So perhaps Steyner did him in."

"No. If the daughter wanted to pretend When was still alive, all Steyner would've needed to do was produce a body. Or even just say When was dead, and dare her to prove him a liar."

"Gammond, at the risk of repeating myself, I don't have time for all this. My partner is out there, somewhere, and I'm her only chance of rescue."

"Angrado, you're talking about one person, however special she might be to you or even in general. I'm talking about the fate of an entire nation at a minimum. Perhaps the world, if our revolution takes hold. The very course of history could hinge on what happens in the next few days."

"While I'm no fan of despots, I'm not convinced your revolution will make things all that much better, if what you said on the barricade is really what you believe."

"I believe the aristocracy must be thrown down. I don't care how bloody it gets."

"Yes, I heard you'd brought back impalement."

"It makes the enemy fearful. Fear is a weapon, and we need all the weapons we can get."

"You're honest, at least. But I don't see a lot of nuance in your position. Life isn't so cut and dried."

"Well, it's hard to be nuanced when your face is in the mud and there's a boot stomping the back of your head."

The horse-urdu-boy returned then, followed by two very large men dragging a much smaller, much more bedraggled man between them. Their prisoner was shackled and manacled. He looked as though he'd been beaten regularly for a week, and worse. Someone had taken hot metal to his ears. What was left wept pus pinked with blood.

"Magister Angrado, may I present the piece of shit known as Gentry Froy Besdil. Besdil was When's personal secretary. We've gotten everything useful we can out of him. He's yours now. Maybe you'll think of something we haven't; something that will help you in your chore."

"I'm not in the market for pets, slaves or prisoners."

"But you *are* in the market for information. Somewhere in the slimy corridors of Besdil's brain, there might be a nugget of information that proves useful." She stared at the man, who stared down at the ground. He seemed thoroughly broken.

Finally, she shrugged. "I think we've squeezed him dry, but you never know. Maybe you'll be able to shake something loose. He's been sentenced to death by the People's Committee. We've no further use for him."

I rubbed my forehead, keeping my hand from the patch with an iron will. My eye socket was killing me. Maybe from being hauled around upside down. I forced my hand back down to my side and took a better look at Besdil.

Small, wiry, slightly balding. Covered in bruises and filth, his once-expensive clothes were so many reeking rags, now. He wouldn't raise his head.

"What did he do to deserve a death sentence?"

"The list is long. Longer if you include the words 'accomplice' and 'accessory'. The personal secretary of one of the Council of Three is, often enough, the one who orders the dirty work that a Councilor wouldn't want to see sticking to his own name. Trust me, this one deserves no sympathy. When you're done with him, we'll want him back for the execution."

"No."

"Beg pardon?"

"No. I'm not a jailer, nor am I a torturer." The thought turned my stomach, frankly. I'd begun to like Gammond despite myself. Looking at Besdil, that incipient feeling curdled. "Do your own dirty work, Magister Gammond."

"The impaling stick has been ready for this one for days," she replied. "Either he goes with you now, or he goes to his death tomorrow."

"That's vile." Impalement was a brutal a way to die as I could imagine.

"That's justice."

Besdil let out a shuddering sob.

A sick sort of anger rose up in me. I wanted nothing to do with this. Not with the revolutionaries, or the gentry, or Bellarius in whole or in part. But I couldn't just walk away. The only way out was through, but by all the dead gods, I would do it my way.

I put a hand under Besdil's chin and lifted his head up.

"Look at me," I told him. Slowly he did. He was broken, his eyes full of terror, on the edge of madness.

"Do you want this to end?" I asked him in a quiet voice.

He looked at me for a long time. I saw him intuit my meaning, and watched the resolve coagulate in his bloodshot brown eyes.

"I do," he grated out of his scream-torn throat.

In half a heartbeat I pulled sufficient power to form a brightblade, and punched it into his heart. I released the blade, but not my well. The guards, already holding him up, stood in dumb shock, reflexively compensating for his suddenly dead weight, while Gammond sprang back, summoning her own well.

"Good day to you," I told her, and started out the door.

"Come up with a way of locating When's sorry carcass," she said to my back after a moment, "and you'll have leave to seek out your rift spawn. Until then, don't even think of coming back to the Girdle. You won't enjoy your reception."

I walked out of the Chop, wondering if she'd change her mind and try to stop me. Subtle her magic might be, but I had the measure of her now. I waited for her to start casting as I walked. I half-hoped she would.

She didn't.

NINE

"You're not so good at making friends," Keel observed once I had related my meeting with Gammond.

"I don't give a damn about making friends. I'm losing what little patience I possess."

"Are you going to hunt down When for them?"

"I am not."

"Then how are we going to hunt down the rift-spawn?"

"We're just going to go and do it. Has Moc Mien shown up yet?"

"Not yet. They won't like it if you defy them, Holgren."

"If we're careful, they won't know. If they find out and try to stop me, they'll regret it."

His face scrunched up in anxiety. "But—"

"Listen to me, Keel. If I get dragged into this morass of a civil war, I gain nothing and potentially lose much, up to and including my life. Which would mean *nobody* is going Amra's rescue. Do you know what I say to that? I say I'd sooner see this city burn."

"I really don't want to fight them," he said, face glum.

"Perhaps it won't come to that," I replied. "To that end, I'd like you to deliver a message to Gammond for me."

"What do you want to tell her?"

"Say that if she gives me leave to hunt the rift spawn, I'll agree not to ally with When."

"And if she doesn't agree?"

"She's smart enough to read between the lines."

"You wouldn't really do that."

"I certainly would, if it were necessary. But it won't be. Even if she says no."

"Um, what? I don't understand."

"The Citadel might hold a back door into the Girdle. I'll tell you about it later, though; I've got things to do, and so do you. Go. And don't forget to take one of the brothers with you."

I stood up from the table and went down into the kitchen. I was tired of talking. I was tired of being around people, even ones I liked. I am not what you might consider gregarious. It was one of the reasons I'd chosen to live beside the charnel grounds, before Thagoth. A minor reason, granted, but a reason. My neighbors might well have stunk to high heaven, but they were very quiet about it, and left me to my own business.

Amra was the only one whose presence I never seemed to feel the need to retreat from.

Master Marle was peeling cloudroot; an impressive feat for a one-handed man. I nodded to him and stepped through the illusory back wall of the hearth over an unlit stack of cord wood. Behind me, I heard him grunt in a 'well what do you know' kind of way. I smiled slightly. I was beginning to like Marle.

I took the right-hand set of stairs down. I was certain one of the branchings I'd ignored on my first excursion down to the oubliette would take me where I wanted to go.

Gammond would be watching the barricades, waiting for me to try and slip past. But she couldn't keep the whole of the Girdle under surveillance.

As I descended, I also berated myself for all the missteps I'd made since washing up in Bellarius. After I'd killed Steyner's assassin, I should have just ignored him. I certainly doubted he could have had any other arrows in his quiver. But mages will be mages. I also should have ignored the Just Men, or rather the People's Committee, and gone about my business. Instead I'd tried to calm the waters.

I should have realized such an attempt was pointless. The gentry had been too harsh for far too long, and they were reaping now all the bitter discontent they'd sown. I'd gone down to the Girdle to try and reason with a scythe. All in all, I'd gotten off lightly.

Lessons learned. I would not be drawn further into the sucking bog of Bellarius's self-destruction. I would get what I needed as quickly as I could, and be gone. And I would not be gentle with anything that stood in my way. So resolved, I quickened my pace.

The first branching led to a closet of horrors.

The room itself was small, no more than four paces long and wide. There was no door. I felt something in the weave, something foul, and summoned magelight.

I've no idea who the mummified corpses might have been, but they were all women with long, blond hair. There were at least a dozen deaths on the black marble floor, limbs twining about each other, positioned in such a fashion as to suggest an especially vile sigil. They were all positioned within a circle that had been inscribed into the floor. The meaning of the corpse sigil teased at the edge of my consciousness, something full of dread import and power, *power*, **pow-**

I tore my gaze away before the sigil could draw my consciousness down into whatever madness waited. Then I summoned magefire to burn the corpses, a vomitous, sour feeling sucking at the pit of my stomach. This went beyond necromancy as I understood it. The Telemarch had been dabbling in what even I would consider evil; and I do not use that word lightly. I didn't even want to contemplate what sort of horror he had been about in that room, lest I start to understand. I vehemently did *not* want to understand anything about it.

Good riddance to him, then.

Before I released the magefire, something moved in the room, the barest shadow rising from one of the corpses. Then another, and another. A dozen in all, one for each of the corpses. They quickly took on substance.

Each of them looked exactly the same. Each was a perfect replica of the thing that had taken my eye.

They looked drowsy, sated. Slowly they drifted towards me, but stopped at the sorcerous circle that contained the corpses. They smiled at me, revealing teeth any gray urdu would be envious of. They slithered across the surface of their containment, spectral flesh merging and parting, merging and parting.

Suddenly I had the intimation that interfering with what the Telemarch had created in that room would lead to terribly unhealthy consequences. I dropped my hand and released my well.

I retraced my route to the main stairs and continued my descent. I refused to look back on general principle, but the skin on the back of my neck didn't stop crawling for a long time.

The second branching went on for quite a long way. I walked for an hour or thereabouts before coming upon ascending stairs and a massive iron door which wept rust. I forced it open with some difficulty, and found myself on a scree-littered slope. It took me a few seconds to get my bearings, but when I did, I smiled. It wasn't what I was looking for, but it was potentially useful nonetheless.

I'd found a passage to the far side of Mount Tarvus. Below me lay a patchwork of fields, gray and brown in the twilight, and made even darker by the shadow of the mount.

This was likely why Steyner had wanted the Citadel so badly. He would have been able to move mercenary troops up from Jedder in numbers sufficient to win him the Syndicacy in a matter of days.

Too bad for him.

I walked back into the mount, shutting the door after me and setting a binding on it.

It was a long walk back to the central stairs, and hunger had started to gnaw at me. I'd missed both breakfast and lunch.

I descended.

The third branching yielded up what I needed.

It was a relatively short passage, and at the end of it was a damp-swollen wooden door. I lay a silence upon it, and with more effort than I liked to admit, pried it from its frame with muscle and the Art.

It opened on a root cellar; one that had not been used in decades for anything other than breeding spiders and centipedes. A decrepit set of stairs ascended to a trap door. I crossed to it and listened. No sign of any sort of movement.

The trap door had a bolt on my side of it. I shot the bolt and slowly lifted the door. The room above was in darkness. The dust of years coated the floor. Jumbles of rubbish were just barely visible in the thin, reedy light that managed to leak in past closed shutters. I opened the door fully and began to climbed up.

I heard it a bare moment before it attacked me from behind, just the softest scrape of chain along the wooden floor.

TEN

It was a thing of rusted wire, warped wood and broken chain; splintered bone, saw-teeth and magic. It sprang at me from a night-dark corner. It was a construct; a golem set to watch the way and eliminate anyone who didn't do what they were supposed to do upon arriving at the far end of the tunnel. I flung myself back down the stairs, shifting to my magesight, searching for the filament that must connect the construct to the Telemarch's greater wards.

Its tail, a length of rusted chain whose links were as thick as my thumb, clipped my ear as it lunged through the space I'd just vacated. That was painful, but not nearly as painful as the back of my head meeting the bottom stair. I scrambled back, dizzy, senses momentarily blurred and magesight lost, certain the construct would be on me in less than a heartbeat.

Nothing happened.

My vision cleared, and I saw its dark bulk motionless at the head of the stairs.

"You must be bound to that room," I told it while calling up my magesight once again. It didn't respond; I hadn't expected it to. Constructs intricate enough to speak hadn't been made since before the Cataclysm. The fact that the Telemarch had managed to create one at all was a testament to his skill and power, if nothing else.

I could see the filament now, a dirty yellow thread that stretched from the thing down into the tunnel and, certainly, all the way back to the

Citadel. It was a subtle thing, impossible to see unless you knew it was there. Which suggested it was meant to be a magekiller. Or perhaps the Telemarch had just been paranoid. Or an obsessive craftsman. I supposed I'd just have to live with the mystery.

Whatever the case, I wasn't going to trek all the way back to the Citadel to sort out whether the node I'd co-opted was the one that controlled this thing. I took hold of its filament, and with a slash of will and power, I *cut*.

The construct went berserk for a few moments, throwing itself violently around the room. I could have let it just wind down on its own; eventually the Telemarch's hardening would dissipate and it would collapse into its components. But it was making an awful racket, and I might have a use for it at a later date. So as quickly as I could, I fashioned a simple set of commands, a little node of my will, and began to splice the severed ends of its filament to it. The cellar was cold, but sweat was running into my eye. Impatiently I wiped it away, though it wasn't mundane sight I was working with.

At first the filament wanted to reject the graft I was imposing on it, but I had enough familiarity with the Telemarch's very particular, very driven personality as it applied to his use of the Art to persuade the severed ends to accept this new, unwelcome addition. It had no choice really, since the will to exist had been leavened into it at its inception, and I held its continued existence in my hands.

The construct suddenly became still once again. The filament had been re-knitted. That did not necessarily mean I had succeeded.

If my extemporaneous casting had worked, the construct would now simply do nothing in my presence. Later I could revise and expand the commands it would obey. I ascended the stairs once again.

If my casting hadn't worked—if I'd botched it, or if the Telemarch had been prepared for someone such as me—the construct would once again try to make me a corpse.

It was sprawled on the floor, motionless, perhaps a yard from the trap door. I climbed the last step, and set foot on the floor proper. It shuddered once, and went back to motionlessness. I frowned. It shouldn't even have done that. But good enough for the present.

I summoned up magelight and took a look around. There wasn't much to look at. A long-abandoned building, it seemed, littered with detritus and smelling strongly of the black mold that covered much of the walls and ceiling. The plaster had mostly fallen, exposing brick walls. The entire building seemed to be just this one room and the cellar below. There was one shuttered window hard up against one door that led, presumably, to the street outside.

I put an eye to a gap between the shutter slats and saw a narrow, rain-slicked cobbled street and a darkened, shuttered shophouse opposite. It certainly looked like I was in the Girdle, at least.

I turned my magesight and my attention on the door, discovered a simple binding there and took a few minutes to dismantle it. Then I opened the door and stepped outside.

It smelled of rain, and pungent fried fish. There were few lights, and the sky was overcast, but none of the great cities of the Dragonsea are ever truly dark. Bellarius might only just qualify as one of great cities, but it did qualify.

I needed to know exactly where my new-found route into the Girdle terminated. So I walked up the dark street until I came to a rather dismal little public house. An old man sat on a stool outside, chewing determinedly on some sort of seed or leaf and spitting regularly into the street. Inside there wasn't a single patron.

"Excuse me," I said to the spitting gentleman. "What street is this?"

The old man continued chomping and spitting as if he hadn't heard me.

"You won't get anything out of that one," came a voice from above. I looked up, and across the street a heavyset woman looked down at me from a tiny balcony. "Hellweed, you see. Took it up after his wife died."

I looked back down at the old man. On closer inspection, I could see his pupils were tiny as pinpricks.

"I do see, thank you. Could you tell me what street this is?"

"You don't know?"

"I'm afraid not."

"Where are you from?"

"Gosland."

"What are you doing here?"

"Trying to leave."

"You don't need the name of the street for that."

I sighed. I'd obviously just met the local gossip. "True, true.

Goodnight then. Thanks for the help." I started back down the way I'd come, feeling her eyes on me the entire way. I found it vaguely amusing that I could survive magical attacks and political maneuverings, but I couldn't manage to learn the name of the street I was on.

Of course, she might well be more than a busybody. It was entirely conceivable she was the People's Committee's version of the local watch. There were no Blacksleeves in the Girdle anymore, certainly, and the People's Committee wore no uniform, it seemed, beyond what appeared to be a wholly optional cockade.

I also realized I didn't have to know the name of the street; a landmark would do. I looked back at the pub, and took note of the signboard—an improbably pink pheckla holding a tankard in each tentacle. I counted the number of doors between it and the Telemarch's bolt hole. Fourteen, as it happened. I knew the gossip was still staring at me. It was too late to become unobtrusive via magic, so I gave her a little distraction in the form of an aural phantasm instead: I made it sound as if the old man chewing hellweed had begun barking furiously. Then, when her gaze had lifted from the back of my head, I slipped into the bolt hole, reset the binding, and started the long walk back up to the Citadel.

ELEVEN

Upon my return, which startled Marle more than he liked to show, I ate a hasty meal of beef stew and black bread. Keel passed on Gammond's response: 'Mistakes have consequences.'

I grunted and ran a hunk of bread around the bowl to sop up the last of the gravy. Master Marle's fare was simple and excellent.

"Any word from Moc Mien?" I asked.

"Not yet." He stifled a yawn. It was late. I was tired myself, but I wouldn't see sleep for hours. I still had work to do.

"If he hasn't shown up by morning, I'm going looking for him. We need to get out of this city before I level it out of sheer irritation."

I drafted the guard brothers to help me haul the nets up from the kitchen to the inner sanctum on the fourth floor, much to Marle's obvious if silent relief. They were more than a little in the way down there.

It was the brothers' first look at the room. They didn't like it any more than Keel did.

"What in hells happened here?" asked Thon.

"That is the question I've been trying to answer," I replied.

"It doesn't feel right in here," Chalk said. To which I had no response. He was right. Reality had been twisted out of true in that space. Or rather, a portion of reality had been ripped away. But it didn't bother me the way it seemed to bother everyone else. Perhaps I should have been worried about that. Certainly, it didn't say anything comforting about me. But I had a sufficiency of worry as it was.

"I'll be busy 'til morning," I told them, "but let me know if Moc Mien shows up."

They left me to my own devices with alacrity and I settled down to the tiresome, tedious and critical process of turning the fishing nets into something capable of trapping a rift spawn without being torn to shreds.

~ ~ ~

Call it a weave, a strand, a filament of purpose. Or of desire.

It doesn't really matter what you call it; magic frustrates ordinary speech. Any word you might apply to any facet of it is only an analogy, a dull metaphor devoid of the spark of meaning that makes magic *magic*. Words, in the context of the Art, are merely an attempt to contain a concept that, by its very nature, is change, is changing, is changeable, has already changed, and has never changed, all at the same time.

Magic is the slipperiest of scale-bright fish, quicker than the here-and-gone-and-back sunscalds in the Bay of Bellarius, and language is a net with gaping holes. When I write of magic, understand that I am sharing a comfortable lie, a useful approximation; for the precise truth is simply inexpressible.

In the chamber where whatever had happened to Amra had happened, I wove a filament of my will through the fibers of the still slightly damp nets Keel had procured for me. As my fingers followed every inch of cord and squeezed every knot, I muttered in Kantic the words for strength, passivity, and immobility. Kantic is a beautiful language, the syllables liquid, the lexicon deep and rich, the grammar stunningly logical. It is the language of magic, though it is not magical. It is the language of instruction, because it lends itself to precision of meaning. It is also a dead language, Kantos having been devoured in the Cataclysm. Superior grammar is no defense against chaos. There is probably a lesson to be learned from that, but I'll be damned if I know what it might be.

Magic can, of course, be cast without speaking, or even moving a single muscle, come to that. But words can be a great aid in concentration, in precision. They helped to prevent careless mistakes, especially when it came to repetitive magic such as I was casting.

The last thing I needed was a weak spot in the weave for the rift spawn to exploit.

Trapping the thing, while sure to be dangerous, was the easiest part of my plan. Forcing or convincing it to do my bidding would be much more difficult. It would be a creature born of chaos, the likes of which had not been seen since the Cataclysm. Unpredictability would be bred into its bones—if indeed it had bones—and rationality would be a foreign concept to it, as like as not. Its intelligence might be no greater than a dog's, or it might make me look like a simpleton. Indeed, its intellect might shift from one extreme to the other depending on the phases of the moon or what it had for dinner. There was just no telling.

I had finished the first net, and was contemplating starting on the second with a distinct lack of enthusiasm when a knock came at the door. Gratefully I summoned up a magelight, rose, and opened the door.

It was Keel, looking sleep-rumpled, freshly barbered hair sticking up at odd angles.

"Moc Mien's here," he yawned into a fist. "He looks like he tangled with a gray urdu."

"You don't seem especially upset about that," I remarked.

"I'm deeply concerned." He smiled a not-nice smile. "On the inside."

He followed me down to the first floor, where Moc Mien was slouched in a chair at the table, trying to look nonchalant. The effect was spoiled somewhat by a fresh black eye that was blossoming, and the freshly stitched claw marks on his forearm.

"Now I know why you didn't haggle over the fee, mage," he said by way of greeting.

"I asked you to find me a rift spawn, not find out if it was a good kisser," I replied.

"Funny. Two of my crew won't be laughing."

"I'm sorry about that, truly." I sat down opposite him. "Tell me what happened."

"We sorted out the general location of three of the fuckers in short order, based on what folks had to say. I set a watch on the areas, three men each. Three wasn't enough, on Halfmoon Street." He shifted in his chair and winced.

Keel appeared at the table, silent and stone-faced, with a bottle of wine in one hand and two glasses in the other. He plunked them down on the table without a word and went back to his bed. The wine might have appeared by magic, as much notice as Moc Mien gave Keel. Which I supposed was an improvement. It was a step up from not-so veiled threats of bodily harm, in any case.

Moc Mien poured for both of us, and took a long drink. Set the glass down.

"Halfmoon Street is full of buildings that got slagged the night the Riail fell. You know? Melted like wax?"

I nodded, and he continued.

"Most people who lived there didn't survive that night. Those who did found somewhere else to doss down soon after. This rift spawn hunts that area pretty regular-like. I figured it must lair there as well. I set three sharp-eyed fellows up on a rooftop that looked safe enough, told them just to watch, see if they could find out where it crawled out of, where it crawled back into.

"A couple hours ago, one of them came stumbling back, torn up something fierce. The thing had snuck up on them, climbed a sheer wall, attacked silent as you please. The fellow that made it back to me got knocked from the roof in the fight, fell two stories to the roof of another building. He got lucky, landing just right. The thing didn't chase him. He said it sounded like it was too busy making a meal of his mates. I rounded up the rest of the crew and went to see what was what. And to collect the bodies. A decision I'm now regretting."

"What happened?"

"It was still there." He shrugged. "I told the boys to wait downstairs while I took a look. I climbed the stairs and had a gander through the door to the roof. Looked like it was taking a nap. Maybe full after a good meal. It woke up sharpish for no reason I could tell and started sniffing the air. I backed down the stairs as quiet as I could, but I guess it got my scent, because it followed with a shriek like you've never heard. It caught up with me on the ground floor, we tussled a bit. I lost some skin and blood and it lost some of whatever it is that's wet and runs through its body. I got out, shut the door. It didn't try to follow." He thought for a moment, shrugged. "That's it."

"What did it look like?"

"Like nothing I've ever seen."

"Try and describe it."

He sighed. "If I had to? Like a rock ape from hell, with tentacles in place of its mane. Almost as big as a man. Spider's eyes. No fur, rubbery blue-black flesh. A long, long muzzle, and black fangs. Agile as a lizard. And a smell. Like burnt sugar and bile."

I sat silently for a while, considering what he'd told me, trying to determine the best way to approach the thing's capture. Considering what he'd told me of its behavior, I thought getting it to enter a trap would not be impossible. It seemed quite territorial.

But the fewer the people involved, the better. Then I realized something he'd said might make my life much easier.

"You wounded it?"

"I stuck it. It didn't seem all that inconvenienced."

"Do you have the knife you cut it with?"

He gave me a hard, considering look. Then he smiled. "That's not part of our bargain."

"You'd charge me for looking at your knife?"

"No. But after you look at it, I have a feeling you're going to want to borrow it, may be even keep it. And it's suddenly become my favorite knife, a family heirloom in fact."

"Dead gods, you and Amra really did grow up together."

"My great grandpa's knife. Great sentimental value. Also, my lucky charm." He patted the knife affectionately, where it rested in a thigh sheath.

"Fine. How much?"

"Three hundred."

"That's absurd."

"Great-Gran saved Great Gram from a fate worse than death with this knife. Three fifty."

"Stop. You win. I'll get the coin for you before you go."

"Now's good."

I knew when I was beaten. I went up and dug the marks out, returned to the table and stacked them in front of him. He laid the knife on the table.

"I'll need the sheath as well."

"My lucky sheath?" he replied, false amazement in his voice.

"Don't push it," I said. "You're already ahead."

He chuckled and took the sheath off as well. I sheathed the knife and put it in my pocket. I'd see what sort of nastiness I could impress on the blade later.

"Do you know an inn with a signboard sporting a pheckla with a beer in each tentacle?" I asked him.

He nodded. "It's called 'Good News, Bad News.' The News for short. It's a fucking shithole. Why?"

"I'll meet you there just after dark tomorrow. Just you. No need for your crew."

"I should charge you extra for having to be seen there." He downed the rest of his wine and left without another word.

TWELVE

It was perhaps an hour before dawn when I finished with the second net. I'd also come to the conclusion that I didn't have to do much trickery with the incredibly expensive knife Moc Mien had sold me. What I had planned wasn't tricky, but it was fairly nasty. I didn't do anything in preparation beyond verifying the fact that there were indeed traces of the creature's bodily fluid remaining on the blade, and inside the sheath.

I was deeply tired; too tired to sleep. I have been prone to insomnia for most of my life, and using my power always made it worse. Working with the Art as much as I had over the previous ten days or so was taking its toll. I had a real fear that I would not be mentally acute enough to make sound decisions soon, if I didn't manage to get something resembling sleep.

You can't magic yourself to sleep. Or at least I can't. The Art has strange limitations; limitations unique to each practitioner. Another limitation of mine was the inability to heal, myself or others. Perhaps that spoke of a regrettable lack of empathy on my part, that I could explode flesh but not re-knit it. Or perhaps it simply reflected the truth that it is easier by far to harm than to heal.

My thoughts chased each other down dark corridors and twisting pathways, and refused to come to hand and be still, no matter how firmly I recalled them. Chief amongst them was a longing for Amra. I missed her terribly, and selfishly. She reminded me without even knowing it that the world did not exist solely for me to inhabit it; that there was a reality beyond the confines of my own thoughts and desires, prejudices and peccadilloes, preferences and passions. She reminded me I was part of something much vaster than the contents of my own skull, and that it might actually be meaningful. She kept me from becoming, eventually, something that might well resemble the Telemarch.

In other circumstances I would have gone for a long walk. Sometimes fresh air and stretching my legs helped. But that wasn't really a sensible option, given the state the city was in and my place in it. And I had no desire to wander the Telemarch's dry, claustrophobic tunnels and steep stairs again that night.

I went down to the library, picked another book at random from a bottom shelf. I read almost an entire closely-packed, punctuationless page of scribbled madness before I realized it was probably one of the Telemarch's own journals. It was gibberish. I recognized the individual words as words, but none of it made the slightest bit of sense. It might have been written in code, but somehow I doubted it. I had a suspicion that Aither had believed he was writing down deep thoughts, when in reality he was simply inking unintelligible ravings.

I put the book back in its place and took up the next one on the shelf. It was more of the same. As was the third, and the fourth. Even the individual letters were degenerating into nonsensical shapes in that one. Had he always been mad, I wondered, or had the Knife driven him to the brink, and beyond?

It must have been the latter. A madman could never learn the Art, certainly not to the degree of skill the Telemarch had. I was intimate with quite a few of his workings at this point, and the precision and insight he'd brought to bear on his Art were undeniable. Madness often accompanies genius, true enough, but the scribbles I held in my hand showed no intellect or sense greater than that of a dog's bark. Perhaps less.

The Knife had twisted his mind until it broke.

Wherever Amra was, the Knife was there was well. Amra, the rift, and the Knife that Parts the Night.

"She destroyed one of the Blades," I told myself. "She will not be easy meat for this one." But too much time was passing. Ten days already, and it might be weeks more before I had all I needed to find her. Assuming I survived the gathering.

What would she be like by then, exposed to the Knife?

I looked back down at the leather-bound journal in my hands, and was not in the least comforted.

I put it back in with the other inmates and wiped my hands on my shirt, not wholly because of the dust. I went down to the second level, which, aside from the cloth-covered easel and all my coin, was open and empty enough to pace in without getting dizzy from constant turns.

I paced for perhaps half an hour, thoughts wandering. I wasn't really conscious of my surroundings, or even my own pacing, in any meaningful way. Not until I bumped against the painting on its easel, and knocked it down.

The way it fell kept the canvas on the easel, while the painting itself slid off the cross member and skimmed along the floor for a short distance. I sighed, bent to pick the painting up—and froze.

Amra's face looked up at me; those clever, expressive hazel eyes, the furrowed scar that made testament to an injury that had nearly half-blinded her, and the other, lesser scars that surrounded it, that looked to me to be remnants of some deliberate, prolonged torture that she never, ever spoke of. That long, straight nose, those lips that were full and soft in sleep, but almost always compressed into a thin line otherwise.

She stood in a doorway. The same skull-shaped doorway that belonged to the Telemarch's inner sanctum. She was looking out, directly at me. Behind her, in the background and less visible, stood a girl child. A child with the same bronze skin tone as Tha-Agoth, the same black, curling hair, the same starlight eyes.

It—for some reason I could not bring myself to think of that figure as she—was smiling an unpleasant, knowing smile.

Why had Aither painted this? Did he even know that he'd done so? Had it been the Knife, rather than the Telemarch, who'd actually guided the brush? Too many questions, and not a single answer.

I summoned magelight without really thinking about it, and studied that painting, returning again and again to Amra's face.

I was still doing so when morning, and Keel, found me.

"There's a lady at the door," he informed me.

"Gammond?" I asked, putting the painting away under the canvas again.

He snorted. "Gammond's no lady," he replied, and I couldn't disagree. "She says she's Lady Gwyllys When," he continued. "Councilor When's daughter."

"What does she want?"

"To see you, if I'm guessing," Keel replied with a smirk. "Maybe she heard you'd started bathing again."

"Sarcasm in one so young. What is the world coming to? All right, I'll let her in, then, if she agrees to come alone."

~ ~ ~

She was dressed impeccably, the deep décolletage and narrow, corseted waist of her embroidered, pastel green silk dress drawing looks even from phlegmatic Marle. She was handsome rather than pretty; strong jaw, sharp cheekbones. Her hair was piled, pinned and powdered, exposing a pale neck. She was perhaps thirty, and her eyes were clear and green and cunning. Behind her a small contingent of armsmen stood, obviously uncomfortable, wariness practically radiating from them. They were no sell-swords; probably family retainers.

"Magister Angrado, I presume."

"Lady When."

"I assume it is polite to invite a lady caller in, even in far Lucernis?"

"Indeed. You are welcome to enter. Your lackeys, however, are not."

Without hesitation she turned to the men behind her and said, "You will wait here." Then, ignoring their protests, she stepped past me and into the Citadel. I couldn't decide if it was brave, foolish, or desperate of her.

"Please take a seat," I said, indicating the table. For a moment she stood still, then gave a small shake of her head and sat in the chair at the head of the table. I realized she'd been waiting for someone to pull her chair out for her. She'd come to the wrong place for that.

I sat to her left, nearer the door, and Marle made wine and glasses and a tiny plate of delicate pastries appear. The man was more of a magician than me. I hadn't even suspected we'd had anything like pastries.

When's daughter didn't touch them, probably because there was no finger cloth. I poured both of us half a glass and helped myself to one of the pastries. Almond. Delicious. I regarded her silently, except for the chewing.

"I would like to discuss private matters with you, magus. Mightn't your servants make themselves more discreetly available?"

"No."

She raised a carefully shaped brow. "Very well. I come to you today to sound you out. Soon enough my father will have the low town rabble pacified, and take up the Syndicacy."

"About your father. Where is he?"

"Indisposed. Rest assured I speak with his voice."

"Oh, I don't need assurance. It doesn't matter to me whether you or your father command your forces. I asked only out of curiosity." Of course she would take my frankness as deliberate rudeness, which I suppose it was to a degree. The truth is often insulting.

She plowed on, though, despite what she must have seen as provocation. Mentally I put her motivation into the desperation category. Provisionally.

"I see you prefer to speak plainly, sir, so I shall oblige you. Once my father's forces have pacified the rebels, there will only be two powers of note in Bellarius—him and you. I am here to discuss what happens at that juncture."

"What would your father like to see happen?"

"He sees no reason why the old accords between the Riail and the Citadel should not be renewed. He will rule, and you will do whatever it is that magisters do to pass the time. And neither shall interfere with the other."

"So in essence, Councilor When is suggesting I sit in the Citadel and do nothing, and that I ignore him, in return for which he will ignore me."

"To be perfectly plain, magus, we want you to sit out the coming conflict, and subsequently refrain from interfering in the politics of the city and the country. We can certainly discuss what sort of remuneration you wish in return. The Telemarch eschewed monetary consideration in favor of more personal services rendered by the state."

"Such as?"

"The use of the Blacksleeves in killing and abduction. Or so I am informed."

"And such an arrangement would be open to me as well?"

She waved a hand, clearly disinterested. "I paint a picture for you in bold strokes, sir. The fine details can come later."

"I see." I bit into another pastry. Decided I did not like this woman any more than I liked her opponent, Gammond, down in the Girdle. Less, in fact. I changed my mind regarding her motivation in coming inside the Citadel unguarded, as well. It wasn't desperation. Or bravery, or foolishness. It was just that she couldn't imagine any danger. In her world, human lives were just various bargaining chips, markers to be pushed back and forth in the great game of power, some worth more than others. Game pieces did not, could not offer any threat to the players of the game. They simply existed to be manipulated. I was just a game piece with a relatively high value.

As I finished the pastry, I decided I did not want to be manipulated.

"You can tell your father that I find myself utterly uninterested in his offer," I said, and stood. "Good day to you, Lady When."

She looked at me as though I had begun speaking Chagan. Then her pale cheeks flushed and her eyes narrowed. In that moment, her aristocratic mask cracked for the briefest moment, and I thought it likely she'd killed her father herself. Or perhaps locked him, shackled and gagged, in a closet. She seemed wholly capable of it. Then the curtain came down again and she was just a spoiled, haughty member of the ruling class once more.

"If I bring that message to him, he will have no choice but to view you as an enemy, sir. Reconsider your reply."

"That won't be necessary. My response is firm."

She flounced out. I'd never seen a real flounce before; I suspect it was because a true flounce required the type of dress she was wearing. Something to do with full skirts.

"Was that really for the best?" Keel asked after I shut the door.

"Almost certainly not," I replied, "but it felt good." And I hadn't felt good about much of anything since Amra had left for Bellarius on Halfa's Night.

If the gods were kind, When and Gammond would tear each other down to their foundations, and other, less brutal souls would pick up the pieces. But the gods are rarely kind.

"Gentlemen," I said to the three men who had taken my coin and the boy who'd taken my cause, "leaving the Citadel through the front door has just become a dangerous proposition. Lady When will almost certainly either put the Citadel under siege or detail assassins to ambush any who come or go."

Thon cleared his throat, and I gave him a look inviting him to speak.

"Why would she do that? She'll need all the arms she can muster to assault the Girdle. Town fighting is dirty business."

"She came here to try and take me out of the game. I'm willing to wager it's because she has no magic of her own, but that's immaterial. She's weighed the odds and decided, now that Steyner's dead, she has the strength of arms necessary crush the rebels, so long as I do not interfere. She tried to induce me to remain neutral, as you heard, again because of Steyner, or rather what I did to him. Now that I've refused, she has no choice but to try and contain me. Either directly via siege, or indirectly by taking one or more of you hostage."

"We're not provisioned for a siege, magus," said Marle. "Water is no problem, but food is."

"Don't be concerned," I told him. "The Citadel has a back door."

Marle smiled. "It wouldn't be located behind the kitchen hearth, would it?"

"Indeed. I think it's time to show you all the Telemarch's basement," I replied. "Or at least a portion of it. There are places you won't want to wander. Chalk, would you help Keel bring down the two nets from the top floor?"

~ ~ ~

We had only a few candles and no other means of illumination, so I called up magelight and led us all down into the bowels of Mount Tarvus. Keel had wrapped the nets up in sheets to make them more manageable to carry. They were still obviously burdensome, more for their bulk than their weight.

When we came to the first branching corridor, where the Telemarch had played with his vile sorcery, I stopped.

"Never, ever go in there. No matter what you hear, or think you see. Do I make myself clear?"

"What's down there?" Keel asked.

"Evil, and madness, and death," I said, and left it at that.

When we came to the second corridor, I stopped again.

"This corridor leads, ultimately, to the far side of Mount Tarvus. If we find it necessary to flee the city for whatever reason, we have the luxury. Master Thon, have you or your brother ever been to Jedder?"

"Once."

"It is possible, but highly unlikely, that I might need for you to go there and recruit some fellow armsmen. This would be the route you would take."

He nodded. "I can do that, magus. If it comes to it."

"Good. I'd show you all the door, but it's a long walk, and I haven't got all night."

We continued our descent.

Outside the cellar door I told Keel and Chalk drop the nets, which they did with a will. Then I gathered them all close and altered the weave I'd crafted into their burning tower badges, so that the construct would ignore them. Mindful of the resident busybody up the street and Gammond's threat, I also layered on a hasty disinterest spell, to keep any dangerous eyes from taking any real notice of my people. It wasn't in any way an invisibility spell—as far as I know such magic is impossible. It just kept observers from getting curious about the bearer. It was quite like what I'd made for Amra after Guache Gavon had inked a contract on her life. Gods, that seemed like ages ago.

"Beyond this door is a cellar. Above that, a ramshackle building somewhere in the Girdle. I don't know enough about the Girdle to tell you just where, but it will serve us well as an entry to the city. Master Marle, you'll be able to do marketing whatever When's daughter tries.

"Inside the building above, one of the Telemarch's workings is active," I told them. "It is a construct, a guardian. It is not alive, but it is deadly. It should ignore you so long as you wear your badge. Do *not* attempt to enter the building above without your badge, from either direction, unless you've grown tired of breathing."

"What happens if we lose the badge?" Keel asked. "What should we do?"

"It's a good question. There's a tavern up the street, called the News, according to Moc Mien. If any of you are outside the Citadel and lose your badge for whatever reason, wait there. Someone will eventually notice you're missing, and when we come looking for you, that will be the first stop.

"Now, gentlemen, go on back up the stairs. I'm off to meet with Moc Mien. If all goes well, we'll catch a rift-spawn tonight and be measurably closer to getting the hells out of Bellarius."

"We should be going with you, magus." said Thon, indicating his brother as well as himself. "You can't mean to go alone."

Keel said, "I'm going too." Marle just frowned.

"More is not better, gentlemen, not in this case. I'm baiting a trap, and you would only frighten off the prey. Or be eaten by it. Moc Mien will not be bringing his crew, for the same reason."

"But—"

"This is not negotiable, Keel."

Marle cleared his throat. "What if you don't come back?" he asked.

"Don't talk like that," Keel told him.

"If I have an unfortunate evening, Keel takes over your employment. Keel, if something happens to me, go to Magister Greytooth. He'll be able to give you the key to the casks on the second floor." Meaning he'd be able to open them using the Art. "I hope he will also help in continuing the search for Amra. What happens next would be up to you."

"Don't talk like that!" Keel said, more loudly.

"Everybody dies. I very much doubt it will be my turn tonight, but it's good to get such talk out of the way, in the event. Master Marle has the right of it. Now go, all of you." I tethered the magelight to Keel, and opened the cellar door. I didn't look back.

Michael McClung

THIRTEEN

Moc Mien was right. The News was a shithole.
  I had an hour or more to kill before night fell, so I left the nets there in the corridor and went up past the motionless construct, out the door, and through a miserably cold drizzle to the tavern.

The old man outside was there again, or had never left. He certainly hadn't bathed or changed his clothes since last I saw him. The sentry was sitting on her sagging balcony, buttoned up against the chill wind. She took no notice of me, of course; I'd come ready for prying eyes this time. I watched her scan the street, making a mental note of what little foot traffic crossed her view. Her eyes slid over me half a dozen times as I walked up the street towards her.

The tavern itself reeked of fried onions, sour ale, and layers of vomit. The floor, recipient of years of spilt alcohol and bodily fluids left to gel, sucked at the soles of my boots like a bog. There were three patrons. None of them were conscious, and I was convinced that only two of them were breathing. The barkeep had a lazy eye and no personal experience with bathing. He also didn't seem to understand the word 'wine' so I took a mug of something semi-liquid and retreated to a corner table facing the door and watched the late afternoon light bleed out of the sky through tiny, grimy leaded glass windows while I waited for Moc Mien.

I'd wasted too much time the first few days after Amra's disappearance, I admitted to myself. I'd ignored important events going on around me and obsessed over increasingly unlikely strategies for retrieving her. The reward for my shortsightedness was the infuriating entanglements I now dealt with. Skulking about the Girdle to get what I needed, lest I be forced into a running battle on its streets, irritated me to no end. It was more than just my pride, though; it was that every additional risk and delay lessened Amra's chances in some non-measurable but real way.

And I had no one to blame but myself.

I'd made bad choices at the outset, and then I'd allowed myself to be provoked into making my situation considerably more complicated and risky not once or twice, but three times. Steyner, Gammond and When's actions had all been predictable, given the context of the situation in Bellarius. I'd failed to predict them because I'd considered them unimportant in relation to my own goals. And so I'd reacted in ways that were at best unhelpful, and at worst, stupid.

Why?

I sat there at that filthy table for a long while, pondering the question. I didn't much like the answers that suggested themselves. They all spoke of a certain level of selfishness, and misaligned priorities. Fortunately, Moc Mien arrived in time to distract me from any serious foray into soul-searching.

He seemed to just appear at my table, which either said much for his ability to move quietly, or my distraction.

"Ready, then?" he asked, and I stood.

"Not going to finish your drink?"

"I'm not even going to start it," I replied. I was fairly sure I'd seen things moving in the depths of the mug. "You're welcome to it."

"And I thought we were starting to get along."

"I'll go and get my equipment, it will only take a few minutes, if you don't mind waiting."

"I mind just breathing the air in here. But I'll wait."

I returned to the bolt-hole, retrieved the nets, and returned to the News, silently cursing my bulky packages. Moc Mien was staring idly at his fingernails when I entered. He looked up, noticed the bulky sheet-wrapped bundles of nets. I put one down on the table in front of him.

"What's this?"

"A net, to catch the rift spawn."

"And what have you got?"

"A backup net."

"Mages really are wise," he replied, and I couldn't tell if he was being sarcastic or not.

He stood up, took up his net, and led the way to the back of the tavern, where an intentionally-almost-unnoticeable door, half-hidden behind a moldy cloak hanging from a hook on the wall, opened onto a very narrow, refuse-choked back alley that was all stair steps. The tap man pretended we weren't there right next to him.

"I thought you didn't want to be caught dead in this place," I said.

"I don't."

"Then how did you know that door was there?"

"The News is mine. I own this shit shack."

"That's—you—never mind."

He squeezed himself through the narrow door, and I followed. The alley, or stairwell, was so narrow that my shoulders brushed both filthy walls.

"Storm channel," Moc Mien commented. "Quite a few in the city. Keep the place from flooding and buildings washing away down the slope. Most folks use 'em to toss their rubbish. Also, useful for getting about without attracting attention."

"Picaresque," I commented.

"Whatever that means. You'll want to avoid 'em when it rains."

"What do you call what's happening now?"

"This ain't what you'd rightly call rain, though it'll freeze by morning, I warrant. That'll make moving around on the mount an exciting proposition, storm drains or streets." He moved off down the storm channel, and I followed.

"So why do I want to avoid places like these in the rain, then?"

"If you manage to keep your feet in the flood, the rats'll find you a convenient piece of higher ground."

"Rats don't bother me."

"You've never been swarmed by hundreds of 'em, obviously."

~ ~ ~

Moc Mien led me a long, torturous route through storm channels so narrow we had to walk single file and sideways, and through real alleys and near deserted streets. Once or twice we crossed low roofs, me cursing the bulk of my burdensome net. Finally, we came to one of the areas that had been affected by the rift. Halfmoon Street, I remembered him saying. One of the slagged areas, as he called it.

And he was not wrong. Stone is not supposed to run like wax left in the hot sun.

We climbed a set of flimsy, groaning metal stairs that led to a high, flat roof, and from there looked down on ruin, on the aftermath of chaos. Whole buildings had slumped over, some almost to the point where their eaves touched the street. Others leaned against and melded into each other. A few had only been partly ruined; a portion standing perfectly normal, while the rest of the building, brick and glass and wood, had pulled away from it, sagging and stretched and distorted.

It was a cityscape out of a nightmare, or a madman's dream.

"Did any of the residents survive?" I wondered aloud.

"A few," Moc Mien replied. "They got put out of their misery quick enough. Or did it themselves, if they were still able." He shifted the bundle to his other hand and pointed to one of the partially 'slagged' buildings on the periphery of the damage. Only one corner of it had been changed. "That's where it waylaid my boys."

"All right. Wait here, please. I'll need your help in dragging it back to the street the News is on."

"You're going in there alone?"

"Not exactly," I replied, and took out his 'lucky' knife. I couldn't argue that it had been lucky for him; it had earned him a small fortune, after all. I squatted down, cut the fleshy pad below my thumb, and let the resulting blood drip onto the knife's blade. From there it pooled on the grimy stone.

Making a blood doll wasn't something I enjoyed. To give it enough substance to die convincingly, I had to put entirely too much of myself into it. The connection would exist until my doppelganger was murdered, which meant I got to feel it. Not the full effect, but enough that I didn't go around creating blood dolls just for the fun of it.

The first time I'd ever created one for myself had been during an especially vicious vendetta season. I was very young then, before I went to study under Yvoust, and the only sort of training I'd been given was in blood magic, by my mother, in secret. Theyoli House had assaulted and overrun the family compound in the middle of the night, and were going room to room, slaying everyone they could find. In a frenzy of desperation, I'd summoned up a doppelganger and commanded it to lie down on the bed while I hid in the wardrobe.

They'd had a mage with them. He disincorporated the blood doll. The blood link between me and the doll insured that I knew, intimately, what it felt like to be turned into a bloody mist. Which is, ironically, why I find that particular magic so easy to cast.

At any rate, making blood dolls never ends up being terribly amusing.

Add to that the fact that I could cast almost no other magic while the doll was an entity, and you can see why it's something I do only when necessary. Pain and debilitation are not my two favorite things to experience.

Once, in the ruins of Hluria, I'd cautioned Amra not to mix her blood with mine when I'd made blood dolls for each of us, to sacrifice to the nightmare Shemrang. Now I was doing it deliberately with the rift spawn's ichor. If I succeeded in what I was about, the rift spawn would get an unpleasant surprise when it attacked my doll.

I worked the blood, balancing the passionate certainty that fed blood magic and the cold clarity that the Art demanded. It was a chill night and getting colder, but sweat ran down the back of my neck and along my ribs soon enough.

I was lost to my physical surroundings as I wrestled the two powers and the two bloods, bending all to my will, forcing an amalgam at finer and finer degrees—until the final acquiescence, when reality itself could no longer deny the change I had forced upon it.

That is the seduction of magic, for those who long to dominate. Even I, who care nothing for power or mastery, was not immune. When you can take the very stuff that makes up your world and force it to change according to your desire, you cannot just pretend that you are the same as the butcher, the lamplighter, the tailor. But instead of thinking myself as *better*, or *more*, I came to the realization long ago that I am simply *other*.

Which has had its own pitfalls.

I only realized I had closed my eye when I opened it, and my own face looked back at me. Or a fair approximation, at least. My doll's features were coarser, and it still had two eyes. I hadn't consciously decided to make it so. They were vacant.

"I've never seen anything like that," Moc Mien commented. "Not sure I ever want to again."

"I'm going in to lay the trap. I'll be back out soon, or not at all," I told him, wrapping my lacerated hand in a less-than-fresh handkerchief. "Do please keep an eye out for the thing, and give a shout if you see it."

I lifted one of the nets onto a shoulder. I gave the doll a mental instruction to do the same with the other, and then follow me down the rusting back stairs and out to the street.

FOURTEEN

I might have made a locator for the rift-spawn using its blood, if I'd had the time or energy. I'd had neither, and really didn't think a locator was necessary anyway. The creature seemed to take intrusions on its territory in a bad way. If it was as belligerent as Moc Mien had described, I thought it safe to rely on it showing itself without me having to hunt it down.

The doll followed me silently up the street to the place where two of Moc Mien's crew had met their end. The door was shut.

"Here's the uncertain part of the plan," I told my creation. While it had a convincing-looking brain, it did not have a mind of its own and so of course did not respond. If the creature was still waiting on the other side of the door, I'd have no time to set up the trap.

I commanded the doll to drop its net and open the door. When nothing jumped out to rend it limb from limb, I ordered it inside the pitch-black interior. When bad things failed to happen a second time, I followed and got busy laying out the nets on the ground floor, one atop the other, by magelight. It was work that was too manually dexterous for the blood doll to do quickly, so I had it wait out of the way. The interior of the room was unremarkable, except for one corner. While the outside portion of the structure had, in some fashion, melted, the interior area that had been affected looked as if it had been put on a slow boil.

There was a wholly unremarkable stockinged foot attached to a body sitting in a rocking chair in that corner. Neither the body nor the chair were something my eye wanted to linger on. Unnatural, impossible things had happened to both. Wood and flesh and clothing had become indistinguishably intertwined in places, and had bubbled like a gravy left unattended on the fire in others.

When I was satisfied that the nets had been laid out in a useful fashion, I ordered the blood doll in, had it stand in the center of the nets, and retreated up the street, leaving it to its fate. I could do nothing more, magically, until it had expired.

I didn't want to retreat all the way back to Moc Mien's position, but neither did I want to be too close to the trap, for fear it would scent me instead of my double. It was impossible to judge how far, or how close, I should position myself, so I split the distance and waited halfway down the street.

I took up a position with a good view of the door, leaning against a badly plastered, un-melted wall, in the deeper shadow of an overhang. Patience is no more common among mages than it is anyone else. I was irritated, tired, sleep-deprived and nervous. As the minutes stretched out and grew into an hour and beyond, I focused on the bond between myself and the blood doll, and foolishly let my mundane senses, and my attention, wander. If I had been alert, I might have noticed the slight, strange scent of burnt sugar and bile that had slowly built up in the still, cold air.

"'Above you!" I heard Moc Mien cry, and without thinking hurled myself towards the building where I'd set my trap. The rift spawn threw itself down from the wall above me, crashing down with a screech on the space I had just vacated. I didn't bother looking back. Either I would be fast enough, or I wouldn't. I did get my knife in my hand, though.

I ran for the door, holding nothing back. I could hear its talons scrabbling along the paving stones behind me, and from the sound of it, it was definitely gaining. I gave a mental command for the blood doll to open the door, which it might or might not be capable of actually doing without me there inside with it. I did not want to have to stop and open the door. The rift spawn would almost certainly close the distance between us in the time it took.

I was coming up quickly on the door. It wasn't opening. The thing behind me let out a hoot that rolled into a growl, and then I heard an explosion of breath from it as it lunged. I threw myself flat on the street, earning a few scrapes and bruises. The rift spawn sailed over me.

The door opened. I got an instant's look at my blood doll, just before the rift spawn crashed into it, hurling it back into the interior of the room. Then I had the joy of experiencing the rift spawn disemboweling it and biting into its face. My only consolation was that the monster also got to feel it.

That was why I had paid Moc Mien a hundred times the value of his extremely unremarkable knife. With the blood that had been present on the blade, I had made *it* a part of the blood doll as well, and subject to the same debilitating, painful consequence.

The blood doll felt nothing, and had no trouble following my command to hold on to the rift spawn until it had perished. Gritting my teeth against the agony of second-hand death wounds, I climbed to my feet and leaned against the door frame, watching what was happening inside as best I could in the deep gloom of the room. When my magic returned, I would have to act quickly.

The rift spawn was in pain, and maddened by it. It kept trying to hurl itself away from the blood doll where it lay bleeding on the floor. For its part, the doll held on with a perfect tenacity, which seemed to infuriate the beast. It would then savage the doll for hindering it, which of course meant it inflicted more pain upon itself, which it would then react to by trying to escape....

Half a dozen times the cycle repeated itself before the blood doll finally expired with a sigh, and I was able to draw power from my well again. I immediately activated the weave of commands I'd laid on the nets, pouring power into them at a reckless pace.

The nets came alive, wrapping themselves around the screeching rift spawn and then contracting, whispering their enjoinders to be calm, to be passive, and to cease struggling. With every movement of the monster they twisted themselves tighter around it, fibers creaking as they swiftly immobilized it. I had to bolster the strength of the nets twice in a handful of seconds, or else they would have burst in the struggle. I was perilously close to draining my well. If that happened, I would fall unconscious. Which meant that I would be dead.

Finally, the creature could do no more than shift slightly and mewl and grunt through its bound muzzle. What I could see of its hide kept shifting from blue-black to muddy gray in an effort to blend into its surroundings, as it must have done when sneaking up on me.

Drawing so much power so quickly had left me physically unsteady. The world was starting to tilt. I hardened the spells on the nets, staggered back into the street and sat down heavily. My heart was racing, and I was perilously close to vomiting. I forced myself to take long, slow breaths of the cold night air. Getting the beast's stench out of my nostrils seemed to help somewhat.

"You're still alive," Moc Mien observed as he walked up the street towards me.

"More or less," I managed to reply.

"That thing can turn invisible. I didn't see any sign of it until it just appeared, ready to jump on your head."

"Not invisible, just a color changer. From a distance, it's as good as, though."

He shrugged. "Whatever. What now?"

"Now we need to transport the creature back to the street the News is on."

"It's called Squareshank."

"My lifelong quest for knowledge has been completed. What do I do with myself now?"

"Your sarcasm, it cuts. Are you going to magic that thing there, or what?"

"I'm going to drag it, and you're going to help."

He took a long look at me, then peered into the building and gave an appraising look at the rift-spawn.

"Yeah, well, I think a cart would be more efficient, don't you? Should have told me before. I'll be back."

I waved a hand vaguely, and concentrated on managing a fresh wave of nausea. Overall I was not displeased, though. The rift spawn was finally caught, and more easily than I'd feared.

But my struggle with the creature had only just begun.

Michael McClung

FIFTEEN

The journey back to Squareshank Street took approximately forever, and pushing a cartful of rift spawn up the steep slopes that passed for streets in the Girdle was as pleasant as one might imagine, but the rest of the night was uneventful. Moc Mien and I took turns pushing the hand cart and steadying it, and with various colorful curses on his part and mine, we eventually fetched up at the Telemarch's back door.

For its part, the creature hadn't made a sound after we left Halfmoon Street.

"Best you go no further," I told Moc Mien. "The Telemarch left a rather dangerous sentry inside that's still active, and I don't think I've recovered sufficiently to keep it from attacking you." Which was a lie. I just didn't want Moc Mien to have unsupervised access to the Citadel. That he knew where a secret entry was located made me uncomfortable enough. He might have been Amra's oldest friend, but he'd still been prepared to duel her to the death. Likeable or not, he wasn't getting a key to my house, the more so because he was both clever and competent.

"I suppose that concludes our business arrangement, except for the matter of transport that we discussed," I said.

"Recon so."

"There is one more thing."

"Yeah?"

"I find myself in need of a diamond. It doesn't have to be big, but it must be as flawless as possible." Now that I'd secured the rift spawn, my mind had begun to consider what I would need in hells.

"I'll find you something suitable. For a price, of course."

"Of course."

To my surprise he stuck out his hand. I shook it. "If you find yourself in the market for another knife, I've got one almost as lucky. And mage?"

"Yes?"

"Vosto's own luck to you. Hope you really can bring her back." And with that he walked down the dark street, without a glance back.

~ ~ ~

The construct wanted to attack the rift spawn, which came as no surprise. I stilled it while I shifted the creature and the handcart down into the cellar, but otherwise left its desire unaltered. If the rift spawn somehow escaped captivity and tried to escape in this direction, it would find itself opposed at the very least.

But it would not escape the confinement I had planned for it.

I trundled the beast and the cart down the corridor to the central staircase that ran down the spine of the mount, and as exhausted as I was, my heart was considerably lighter than it had been at any time since I'd first entered the Citadel. Capturing the creature was only the first step in a series of suicidal steps, but after days of obstruction and delay, I had finally managed to *take* the first step.

My next step was considerably simpler. I believed the rift spawn would have a connection to the source of its creation—the rift. In fact, I was virtually certain of it. But I needed to make sure.

At the staircase, I tipped the beast out, and pushed it down the stairs. It rolled down to the landing below, still not making a sound, and I followed it. I shoved it into position, pushed it down the next flight, and in such fashion eventually arrived at the chamber that had once allowed access to the rift.

As soon as the thing bounced into the chamber, it went berserk, which caught me off guard. It shrieked and writhed, furiously assaulting its bonds. The nets began to weaken and tear, and I quickly poured more power into them.

"Well, then. I suppose you do have a connection to that which birthed you," I said, pleased that the first, crucial part of my plan had born fruit. I was surprised when the creature responded.

Kill... you. Eat you.

"You already tried that. You failed. And suddenly you've gotten smart." This creature had shown only animal intelligence. Now it spoke, and mentally at that?

Before... no need. Now, need.

"To speak?"

Intelligence.

Born from chaos, from possibility. Perhaps I should not have been surprised that it could morph and evolve. But I found the idea extremely disturbing. What were its limits? Did it indeed have limits? How long might it take to evolve an intelligence that equaled or surpassed mine?

Let me go. Or I will kill you and eat you and shit you out.

I walked over to it, squatted down, and regarded the visible few of its faceted eyes. I had to break this thing to my will, or it would be no use to me. If I couldn't break it, and quickly, I'd have to kill it and try to take from it what I needed; and I did not have sufficient confidence that the extraction would be successful. The Art requires confidence virtually indistinguishable from egomania, or delusion.

"None of those things are going to happen," I told it.

It howled and struggled. I let it, for a time.

"Be silent," I said, and it ignored me. So I summoned up a wave of force and pressed down on the thing, harder, harder, until it had no breath with which to howl.

"You will do as I say, when I say," I told it.

Kill you tear you eat your eye—

I flicked my fingers, and sent phantom pain down the nerves of its monstrous face. Especially its eyes. It shrieked. And writhed. And shrieked. I let it go on for a long time. When I finally dispelled the pain, it lay still, except for panting.

"You will not threaten me again. You will do as I say, when I say, or I will remove your limbs so you can never escape, and your teeth so that you pose no danger."

You... are monster.

"And now we finally begin to understand one another."

THE THIEF WHO WASN'T THERE

~ ~ ~

I left the creature bound in the rift chamber. I strengthened the nets once again, and I found, activated and augmented many of the wards the Telemarch had installed in the room.

I could never trust the thing, which I decided to call Halfmoon after the street it had hunted on. It was a man-eater. It was chaos-spawned. It was dangerous. Make it afraid of me, yes. Completely break it to my will?

Never.

It would always look for a way to break free. It would not rest until it found a way to destroy that which had turned it from hunter to hunted, monster to victim. But until it believed it saw such an opportunity, it would bide its time.

And that was good enough for now.

The satisfaction I'd felt upon trapping it had been suffocated by the cruelty I'd been forced to use on the thing. I felt very, very tired, inexplicably dejected, and more than a little soiled as I slowly climbed the stairs up to the Citadel.

Ah, well. It wasn't the first time I'd done something I found repulsive. I am not overburdened with morals, but I have at least a general grasp of right and wrong, and torture is something that refuses to be chalked down on the light side of the slate however you try to justify it.

Halfmoon had to be forced to help me rescue Amra. Halfmoon was a man-eating monster who would happily bite off my face and lick my brains out through my nasal cavities. That didn't justify torture, because it wasn't about the rift spawn, ultimately—it was about me. What *I* was prepared to do. How far *I* was prepared to go to get what I wanted.

And of course I was prepared to go as far as I had to, however vile that made me.

I'd been here before. Different situation, different consequences, same self-reprehension. Those who do not shrink from dark deeds should at least be clear-eyed and honest, with themselves if no one else.

There was nothing wrong with the eye that remained to me.

~ ~ ~

Marle was snoozing in a cane-backed chair in the kitchen when I walked through the hearth. Though I made little noise, he woke almost instantly.

"Magus," he acknowledged, rubbing at a sleep-bleared eye with his stump.

"Marle," I replied. "What keeps you up?"

"You were right about the When woman. She's set troops all 'round the tower. We thought it best you know as soon as you returned."

"Have they tried anything aggressive?"

"No. They seem content just to stand around with their thumbs up their arses."

"Then I'm content to let them. Get some real sleep, master Marle. That chair looks likely to produce nightmares."

He nodded and I left him, passing the others in their beds on my way up to the inner sanctum.

Gods, but Keel could snore. I was surprised one of the others hadn't yet smothered him in his sleep.

As I lay myself down in my bed for once, I felt at least some of the tension of the last few days slough off. I wasn't concerned about Lady When's move. Unless she had a mage on her payroll, she might as well be shouting at clouds for all the harm she could do me or mine. And now that I'd secured Halfmoon, Gammond was much less of a worry as well. In a few days at most, I'd either have the creature sufficiently broken to leave the Citadel with it, or I'd be forced to try and take from it what I needed. Assuming I succeeded, I could leave Bellarius behind, thank all the useless gods. Or I could just leave, and try to break Halfmoon during the voyage. The more I thought about it, the more the idea appealed. I was beginning to hate Bellarius as much as Amra had always claimed to.

For the first time since I had arrived in the City of the Mount, I drifted into sleep without a single twitch, startlement, or horrific nightmare waiting for me right on the other side of those misty gates. It was a good, solid, dreamless sleep.

So of course the next day everything went straight to hells.

THE THIEF WHO WASN'T THERE

SIXTEEN

I've never had much talent for or interest in illusion. It takes a certain kind of mind to spin convincing lies using the Art, and a level of subtlety and precision that I found maddeningly tedious. Oh, I could throw up a decent enough seeming, something that would stand a moderate amount of visual, and even tactile scrutiny if I had to. I could project a noise, or cover a stench. Most mages can. But I've never pretended to be any sort of master when it came to illusory magic.

Gammond was a master.

A mage is damnably difficult to hold against his will. He will break chains and bend bars, rip doors from hinges, turn stone walls to dust. He will burn guards to cinders, and melt their arms and armor to shining puddles.

But not if you blind him, and deafen him, and take away his ability to tell up from down.

I woke because I was suddenly falling, spinning, with a rushing roar of air pounding at my ears. I opened my eye, and saw nothing but a riot of kaleidoscopic colors. I called forth my magesight, and it appeared as if I was falling endlessly into a vortex of power.

"Good morning, magus," came Gammond's voice from everywhere and nowhere, cutting through the howling wind.

"How did you breach the wards?" I asked, forcing my voice to a level of calmness I did not feel. I scrabbled at the magic that bound me, but could find no purchase, no loose thread to pull. It wasn't a weave, it was a fog.

The level of subtlety she was capable of employing was frankly frightening.

"We found your mouse hole on Squareshank. I'm surprised you didn't bother to disguise yourself that first night. It's not as if there are many tall, one-eyed men who speak with a foreign accent wandering around the Girdle. At least, not ones who are obviously not sell-swords."

So, the nosy neighbor had indeed been an informant. All my subsequent precautions had been a case of too little, too late.

"I hope the construct didn't give you too much trouble." By which I meant I hoped it had mauled her and hers badly. I still had access to my well. But unless I could kill her, it didn't really matter. I couldn't negate her clever trap. And to kill her, I needed to be able to locate her. Which was why her magic placed her voice everywhere and nowhere.

"The golem? Bit of a nasty shock, but we took care of it in time. Your bindings were much more formidable a barrier, I'll give you that."

"You overcame my bindings and the construct without alerting me?"

"If it makes you feel better, I probably couldn't have managed it if you'd been awake."

I could lash out randomly, and hope to get lucky. I could destroy everything in the room with me. I could probably bring down big chunks the Citadel, if I really gave it all I had. But there was no guarantee she was in the same room, or even the same floor as I was. I wouldn't have been, in her place.

"What do you want, Gammond?"

"When's going to attack today. Soon, actually. No more probes, no more skirmishes along the barricades. She's got the numbers, and her numbers have the training, and she means to break us."

"You've known this was coming. I'm sure you've prepared the Girdle appropriately."

"Oh, aye, we've turned our homes and shops into a slaughter yard, and we're waiting for the stock to arrive. I don't give them good odds of finishing us quickly, if it comes to house-to-house fighting. But I'd rather not see my parlor turned into an abattoir, if you take my meaning."

"Well who would?"

"Right, I'm glad you agree. So when the trumpets sound, and When's troops are engaged along the barricades, we're going to give them a nasty shock. I've got armsmen and women pouring into the Citadel, coming from the Girdle and up that long set of stairs down in your basement, and when the time is right, we're going to fall on them from behind and hack them to pieces."

"Which leaves me and mine where, exactly?"

She was silent for a moment. Then, "In the way."

And there it was. She didn't dare let me go, even after she'd got what she wanted. No one holds a grudge like a mage. She thought I'd come for her, and she was right.

"I did tell you not to return to the Girdle," she continued. "This isn't personal. I don't hate you like I hate the gentry."

"But I'll end up just as dead." Except I wouldn't. Because I still had the silver amulet Steyner's assassin had used.

"Aye."

"Would large amounts of money help to change your mind?" I asked, questing blindly for the pocket the amulet rested in. Which sounds easy enough, but is in fact somewhat difficult when you can't see and all your other senses tell you are falling from an endless height.

"You want to bribe me with money I already have possession of?"

"You have possession of four casques. Not what they supposedly contain." I rarely lie, because I rarely have need to. I was sure she hadn't yet been able to open them. My hand finally found the pocket it sought, and I drove it in.

"You expect me t—"

As soon as my bare flesh made contact with the magical sink, her voice and her magic were cut off instantly.

I was still in bed. I was alone on the second floor. Downstairs I heard Gammond curse. I realized two things at once: That I had more or less trapped myself, and that, if Keel and the others were still alive, they had just become hostages.

It was still better than whatever Gammond had had planned for me.

I couldn't stay cut off from my well indefinitely. She had troops down there, lots of them by the sound of it, and without magic I'd fall to a sword or an arrow sooner rather than later. I'd broken her hold on me, and hopefully made her cautious. That was about the extent of the amulet's usefulness.

Two choices lay open to me now: try to escape the Citadel, or fight to take it back.

I've never been terribly good at running. Not because I'm

particularly brave. I'm not. But I am stubborn and possessive. In certain situations, the difference is negligible.

And so I dropped the amulet in my pocket and put into effect what little I had learned of Gosland battle magic from my reluctant father. What I lacked in experience, I tried to make up for with sheer force.

Confusion. An enemy confused is an enemy defeated. I put my hands on the floor and willed the magic through my palms, to flood the lower levels. I heard it pour down on them, men swearing in annoyance, dropping weapons, crashing into each other. When I felt Gammond begin to counter, I switched abruptly.

Distraction. I dropped the Citadel's now-useless wards and, with a painful mental shove, forced the main door open. I threw in a hellish howling for good measure. I doubted When's troops would take the invitation and come rushing in, but that wasn't the point. The point was what came next.

Panic. I was intimate with pain. I shared that intimacy with everyone below. By shared, I mean I projected it downstairs, whether they liked it or not. I summoned up a perfect recollection of what it felt like to lose an eye, and let it rain down on my unwelcome visitors.

Their screams were satisfying. Someone shouted "Hold fast!" and I knew that at least a few of the intruders had availed themselves of the open door.

After a few moments, Gammond managed to blunt my casting, but she could not dispel it completely. I switched tactics. I summoned up the terror I'd felt when, as a boy, the Theyoli had overrun the family compound and I'd heard death methodically coming for me, room by room.

Again, Gammond was able to blunt the worst of it. Emotional magic was a form of illusion, after all, if only just. But her troops weren't battle-hardened veterans, most of them. They were shopkeepers and chandlers and tinkers. Many were fleeing now, by the sounds of it, either out the open door or back down the secret passage in the kitchen.

But not all of them.

Half a dozen armed and armored men rushed the stairs, two at a time. The first pair had shields and swords, the second pair had crossbows. I don't know what the third pair were armed with, because nothing below their heads made it above the level of the floor before I sent my Art scything into them.

I can only disincorporate one person at a time. I can, however, cast a blade of force as long as a wagon and thin as a razor through as much flesh and mail as you please, though it drains my well alarmingly.

The various pieces of armsmen tumbled back down the stairs in a riot of blood and a fair amount of screaming.

I summoned up a little enhancement for my voice, making it a little lower and much louder, and spoke to those below:

"I'm going to kill all of you."

I could sense Gammond working feverishly to put some steel back into her troop's collective spine, but she was much better at sensory illusion than she was at emotional magic. And my well was deeper than hers. I let them all taste the despair I'd felt when the Shadow King forced me to make Amra feel as though molten lead were being poured into the marrow of her bones.

This was not the sort of magic I preferred, or was particularly good at. But you don't have to be a trained carpenter to hammer down a nail with a sledgehammer. You don't have to be a minstrel to scream. I could swing harder and scream louder than Gammond, and subtlety be damned. Gammond didn't have the well to stand toe-to-toe with me, and she knew it.

"If you want your servants to live," she shouted up the stairs, "you'll stop right now."

"You say that as if they weren't already dead."

"Two are more or less unharmed. One might survive, if he gets attention soon."

"I've only got your word, which you'll admit doesn't carry much weight."

I heard her mutter something. Some furniture shifted. Then I heard Marle's voice.

"She's not lying, Magus."

Gammond was perfectly capable of mimicking someone's voice.

"Tell me everyone's state. By name please, Marle."

"Chalk's still alive, but took a blow to the head that put him out. Thon didn't make it. Keel is breathing, but he's got a foot of steel pinning him to his wardrobe, through the thigh." He paused. When he spoke again, his voice was lower. "There's a lot of blood come out of him, magus, and it ain't slowing much."

Dead gods. I couldn't give in to Gammond. She'd just kill me and *then* kill them. She had to. She'd gone too far by invading the Citadel, my stated sanctum, and she knew it. She knew, soon or late, I would force a final reckoning on her. Even if I swore I wouldn't pursue her, she'd never believe me.

The silence stretched. Through the big barred window I heard a low roar, a distant thunder of open throats and clarions. I stole a cautious glance down the mount.

When was assaulting the barricades. Virtually all the armsmen who had been loitering around the houses of the gentry were now streaming down the mount, dressed for battle. Hidden from view, steel met steel and rang echoing up the hill, along with screams of agony and battle fever.

"Gammond," I called.

"What?"

"You're about to lose your war. When has begun her assault, and I very much doubt it will go well for your side if I keep your reinforcements pinned and disorganized here."

I heard her move, presumably to take a look for herself. Then I heard her curse.

"Send me up my men," I told her, "And I swear by my name and my power I will not interfere with your forces leaving the Citadel. Or don't, and watch me make damned sure your cause will fail."

It was her turn to let the silence stretch.

"Your time is leaking away, Gammond."

"Damn you to all hells," she said. Then I heard Keel scream. Then he started using the kind of language I'd been beaten for as a child. Then he and Marle appeared on the stairs, Marle supporting him.

"He'll need a tourniquet," Marle told me as he lowered Keel to the floor. "I'll go back and collect Chalk." And he did.

Blood was indeed pumping out of Keel's thigh at a steady pace. He was already pale, his lips chalky. I ripped off my belt and wrapped it around his thigh above the wound, but couldn't get it tight enough with just my hands. I needed a stick or something else long and stiff enough to twist the leather tighter.

I looked around the room, which was bare except for the casques, the bed—whose wooden posts were far too thick—and the Telemarch's cloth-covered easel.

Perfect.

"Hold tight to the belt," I told Keel, and went and smashed the easel apart, knocking the covered painting to the floor. I broke one of the easel's legs in half, then returned to Keel and jammed it between the leather and his thigh, and twisted, hard and tight.

"Gorm on a stick!" he swore.

"Don't be a baby," I told him, and he gave me a look that said he'd happily murder me in my sleep. Then, eyelids fluttering, his eyes rolled up into the back of his head and he slumped forward, passed out from blood loss and pain.

Marle stumbled awkwardly up the steps then, carrying Chalk across his shoulders. As soon as he'd cleared the last step I wove a binding over the stairwell. It wasn't particularly strong, since only air was being bound, but it would serve.

Marle laid Chalk in my bed and stood back up. I could see he'd taken a beating about the face. He'd have some ugly bruises soon enough.

"Are you well?" I asked him.

"Well enough. Better than Thon, and better than these two. How did they break in, magus?"

"It's my fault. A moment of carelessness on my part led them to the Girdle entrance. Gammond was mage enough to take advantage." I moved to the window and watched Gammond's strike force boil out of the Citadel's front door, take a few casualties from the bowmen among the troops When had left to pin me in the Citadel, and then overwhelm them with sheer numbers. It was more than a hundred against a dozen. When that slaughter was done, they took a moment to regroup and then set off down the mount to where the true battle was raging. Gammond's illusions began to draw around them, I saw with my magesight and my eye. Silent and flickering, mostly hidden by a sorcerous mist, they would fall on the rear of When's battle line, wreaking havoc.

"What do we do now?" Marle asked.

"We wait for the last of them to clear out. And then I get our injury-prone young friend here some help."

"And after that? Seems everyone in the city has it in for you now. No offense."

"It does, doesn't it? Well I've got what I need now, more or less. Time to take our leave." But before I left, I'd give both Gammond and When something to remember me by, and sooner rather than later. The memory would not be a fond one for either of them.

I am not, sadly, a live and let live sort of person.

SEVENTEEN

Keel needed attention as soon as possible. I waited another minute or so, then went down the stairs behind gale-force winds I summoned to clear my path. Good thing, too. Gammond had left two crossbowmen behind to try and finish me. They weren't able to draw a bead on me, having to fire into a gale, though one got off a quarrel before I disincorporated him.

There wasn't anyone else on the ground floor. I closed the door and raised the wards once more, then investigated the kitchen. It was free of assassins. I wrestled the splintered kitchen table up against the hearth and set a binding on it, so that the troops who had fled back the way they'd come couldn't reenter. It wasn't the best binding I'd ever managed, but it would hold while I went for help for Keel.

Before that, I went and looked for Thon in the mess of bodies and body parts in case Marle had been mistaken. There were quite a few more corpses than I could personally account for, so Thon and Chalk must have had some effect before being overwhelmed. I hadn't seen Thon in my initial sweep.

I found him half-sprawled across one of the beds. He hadn't had time to get his armor on, but reading the battle-sign, it looked as if he'd still taken three men with him. A spear had done for him, and they'd cut his throat just to make sure.

I closed his eyes and removed the blood-spattered burning tower brooch from his shirt. He wouldn't need it any more. I would. I slipped the thing into a pocket and left.

Hurvus, the Hardside chirurgeon, would be practically impossible to find, and wouldn't be dragged away from the stream of casualties coming to him today for one boy in any case. Greytooth was much closer, if he was home. I didn't know for certain that Fallon Greytooth could heal others beyond curing headaches, but he could damned well heal himself, which was more than I could say, and that gave me hope. If he couldn't, then Keel was getting a red-hot poker in his wound, which might or might not stop the bleeding, but would definitely leave him crippled for a long time, maybe forever. If he survived at all.

The temperature had fallen, and the drizzle-slick streets of the night before, while not completely glazed over with ice, certainly sported patches of the stuff. Enough that watching my footing took up too much of my attention, and when I turned a corner, I consequently almost died.

One bowman had been stationed on the way to Greytooth's house, a mercenary. I turned the corner, looked up from the cobbles, and there he was, about twenty yards away, shaft already nocked. I've no idea whose coin he took or why he wasn't down at the main event, nor did I bother to ask.

I tried to dart back around the corner, and so of course my foot went out from under me on a patch of ice, and down I went.

The arrow came perilously close to me. It hit and splintered on the cobbled slope behind me, perhaps a foot distant, with a sound like breaking bone.

I dispatched him before he got his fingers on the fletching of a second arrow, carefully regained my feet, and walked on, through his blood.

~ ~ ~

Greytooth didn't answer my strident knocking, so I carefully sent a whisper of power through his wards. Not enough to activate them; I wanted to live. But enough that he would certainly notice, and investigate.

The door opened less than a minute later.

"I assumed it was you," he said.

"Why is that?"

"I know no one else who would be so insistent, and so cavalier with dangerous magic."

"It's an emergency. Keel's been gravely injured. You know I've no skill in healing. Will you come?"

"Aye. Wait a moment." He disappeared back inside, and then returned with a satchel tossed over a shoulder. We started back up the mount.

"I can't guarantee I'll be able to help," he warned me. "My healing comes not from the Art, but the Philosophy. It has limitations."

"I appreciate you trying, in any case."

The rest of the walk happened in silence. He did not ask what had happened. I hadn't really expected him to. We arrived at the Citadel and I passed him through the wards.

"They're on the second floor. Thank you for your assistance." I took Thon's passkey out of my pocket and handed it to him. "It'll let you come and go through the wards."

He frowned. "It's bloody."

"Sorry." I turned to go.

"Where are you off to?"

"I've got scores to settle."

"I thought you didn't care about Bellarius," he called after me.

"I don't," I replied, and I meant it.

~ ~ ~

When I was born my father took me to the Seer of Dragon's Eye, as was his right as a battle mage and against my mother's wishes. I do not, of course, remember the episode. But I was told that the Seer took one look at me and said that my well was as deep as she had ever seen. This made my father very happy. Then she said that I would either be a ruler or a reaver, the difference being a vanishing one to her old eyes. This made my father distinctly less happy.

"Not a battle mage?" asked my father.

"A mage, yes, of course. And he will see battle. But not a battle mage."

As far as my father was concerned, she might as well have told him I would be a tinker. He loved my mother, but he lived for his duty. That I would not follow in his footsteps and take oath to a border lord, fighting the good and honorable fight against belligerent northmen, or grohl to the west, or the twisted horrors that still lash out at Gosland from the Broken Lands to the south—well.

The Seer was never wrong. So I grew up on my mother's family holdings in Fel Radoth instead of the mossy marches of Southern Gosland. And at sixteen I was packed off and apprenticed to Yvoust.

I sometimes wonder what I might have been, if I'd been apprenticed to a sane master of the Art, rather than a sadistic one. Might I have become, in time, a lord of some demesne; a ruler, as the seer had said was half-possible?

I honestly cannot imagine such a fate now.

So. I had what I needed from Bellarius. I'd taken what I'd come for, just as any reaver would. As any reaver would once they'd secured their spoils, I would depart. But before that, I did what any self-respecting reaver did, once they'd taken what they wanted.

I set fire to the rest.

~ ~ ~

Here is the thing about a magician and his well: You don't know when you've drained it until you do, and you find out because you collapse into unconsciousness. So you learn early to judge when you're in danger of doing so, and you learn early to get a feel for the rate at which your well replenishes.

I didn't have much left, with the serious magics I had been hurling. And it would be hours before I would feel confident in performing much more of the Art without danger of passing out. Gammond had to be in even more dire straits than me. If it were possible to approach her alone, I had no doubt I would mop the floor with her. Unfortunately, she wasn't alone. She was undoubtedly surrounded by troops from the People's Committee, and quite possibly in the thick of the fighting. I wouldn't be sneaking up on her.

That was quite all right. I had no desire to get close to her. And with a little luck, I wouldn't have to pull more than the merest whisper from my well to do her in. Her, and the bulk of the two armies that were engaged in hacking each other to pieces.

The Telemarch had seeded the city with deadly magical traps. Likely they were meant for Amra; she'd said she had triggered two of them. But too, I think they were a product of his paranoia and madness. Some were set in logical terrain; all the gates had one, for instance, as well as the major wharfs. Others were located in areas of dubious usefulness. I doubted, for example, that there was much call for the trap he'd set in just one crypt in the small cemetery that sat on the border between the Girdle and the upper slope claimed by the gentry.

I made my way towards the sounds of battle, growing more confident with every step that I'd be able to accomplish what I intended. When I arrived at the small, stepped, nearly vertical public square that was part of the unofficial demarcation between Girdle and gentry territories, I smiled.

The bulk of When's forces were in the square, fighting on two fronts—down slope, assaulting the barricades that bisected the square, and up slope, fending off Gammond's counterattack. Which meant that the bulk of Gammond's forces were also in the square.

The square was the location of one of the Telemarch's traps.

I called up my magesight and scanned the chaos for Gammond. I caught signs of her workings all around—she'd done a very convincing job of making her forces appear to be double their actual numbers, for one—but at first, I couldn't find the woman herself. Then she cast something, I don't know what, and the flare of her magics to my magesight picked her out.

She was on the very edge of the square, guarded by four men in half-plate. She looked exhausted, her iron gray hair mussed and a red smear of blood on one side of her face. She did not look as if she was having a very good day.

Her day was about to get much, much worse.

I retreated up the mount to what I thought was a safe distance. I still had a goodly slice of view of the square, and the carnage being committed there, though I could no longer see Gammond from my new position. You can't have everything.

I tapped into the Telemarch's trap, and sprung it.

At first it seemed that nothing was happening. Certainly, the combatants didn't suddenly leave off trying to kill each other. But the chalky-white quarried stone that the square was paved with had loosened, slowly becoming the consistency of thick mud. Everyone in the square was ankle-deep within a few seconds.

Then, between one heartbeat and the next, the stone went back to being stone, trapping the living and the dead, the dying and their killers. Everyone except those atop the barricades, where the fighting was at its most desperate and vicious.

A noise of confusion started up. Some shouted out in alarm. And then the next part of the Telemarch's trap swung into action.

There was an enormous roar, and a sun suddenly sprang into being in the square, incinerating everything and everyone within its confines. I'd thought myself far enough away. I hadn't been prepared for just how much power the Telemarch had invested in the working. I was thrown back by the blast, hurled perhaps half a dozen feet. I hit the cobbles and curled into a ball, covering my face and letting the blast roll me even further up the slope. Trying to fight it would have been futile.

When I came to rest, I just lay there a moment. Nothing seemed broken, though I'd lost a bit of skin to the street, and my face felt as if I'd got a sudden sunburn.

I got up and went to look at what I'd done.

The square no longer existed. It had been scoured down to the bedrock of the mount, which itself was smoking. Every building that had bordered the square was a burning ruin, as were many of the buildings beyond them in all directions. It was total devastation.

I'd had a notion to go looking for Gammond's corpse. With mages, it pays to be sure they're truly dead. Once I saw the effects of Aither's magic, I gave up the idea. Hundreds had been in the square. There was nothing left of any of them.

"All I wanted was to be left alone," I said to the devastation.

I turned around and started the climb back up to the Citadel. Behind me, screams had started up. I don't know whose, perhaps residents, perhaps supporters of one side or the other who'd come to watch from what they'd believed were secure locations. It didn't really matter.

Hundreds were destined to die in that square, on that afternoon, no matter what. I'd just made sure that neither side won that particular battle.

I didn't give a damn who won the war.

AMRA: INTERLUDE ONE

When I opened my eyes, there was a little girl squatting next to me. She had long, rich brown hair in tight, natural curls, skin the color of old, old oak, and stars in place of the pupils of her eyes. She wore the rags and scraps any street rat might. She was squatting on her haunches, forearms resting loosely on her knobby knees. Her expression didn't change when I started looking back; intent, but not insanely so.

I turned bleary eyes on my surroundings. Still the same room. The Telemarch's corpse was right where I'd left it, looking dead as ever, but not noticeably decomposed. Which could mean it hadn't been all that long since my lights were put out. Or it could mean in this place, things didn't rot. Hard to say. I looked back at the girl.

"Hello. I'm Amra. Who're you?" My voice came out as a croak.

She just kept staring at me.

"Fine, then. Be that way." I struggled up to a sitting position, and she scooted back away from me a bit. Not like she was scared; more like she just didn't want to be touched, even accidentally. Fine by me. I felt stiff as all hells, and my mouth had a taste I wouldn't wish on my worst enemy. I decided to blame that on the Knife, and not my habit of sleeping with my mouth open. My mind skittered away from thoughts of the Knife. I wasn't ready to mull over that particular violation just yet.

"Right then. I suppose standing is the next thing on the list, since I don't see me getting a glass of wine any time soon." I was talking to myself, but the girl's presence was a convenient excuse not to feel as though I was the crazy street lady who talked to herself.

I made it to a standing position. Looked around again. Same room, plus girl. Same corpse. Same open door, same void and rift beyond.

"Next chore, house cleaning," I told the girl. I pulled Aither's corpse up to a sitting position—no rigor—then let him slump forward like a sitting drunk passing out on the pavement. Then I got behind him and booted him out the door. I closed the door quickly, not bothering to watch his corpse float off. I didn't like staring out into nothing, and I didn't like having my back to the girl. Call me paranoid, but people mysteriously appearing literally in the middle of nowhere without explanation made me suspicious, no matter how cute they were. Especially how cute they were. I turned back to her. She hadn't moved, except to follow my every move with her Athagos-like eyes.

"'That's the house cleaning done," I said to her. "What's next on the list? Oh, right. Waiting for you to say something."

"Did you notice that there's no light, but you can still see?" she asked, voice pleasant and high and absolutely normal.

"Huh. What do you know?"

"Many things."

"That was rhetorical on my part. What I really meant was "I don't really care, because at this point nothing whatsoever could surprise me.""

"'You'd be surprised," she said with a small, not particularly nice smile.

"Oh, a witty retort. We're making progress." At which point she went silent again. Of course.

Time passed. Or technically, I suppose, didn't pass, me being outside time and space. But it certainly felt like it passed. Being in this place put me in danger of turning philosophical. I shuddered at the thought.

Being stared at by the little girl was starting to get old.

"Well, thanks for coming over. Sorry I didn't have any refreshments to offer. Next time maybe send a note first. Let me get the door for you." I opened the door.

The kid didn't take the hint.

"*She* is also trapped in a pocket reality," she said, "divorced from the rest of existence. Of course, on Her part, it was deliberate and intentional."

"Who exactly are you talking about?" I asked her.

"She Who Casts Eight Shadows."

"And how would you know that?"

"I'm one of the Shadows that she casts, of course." She smiled. "Surprise!"

I sighed. "No, no really." Bitter and disappointed, and hating whatever fate had led me to this place, this situation. But I was not surprised, no.

I scraped my fingers through my hair. "Which one are you?"

"Kalara."

"Are there any more lurking about?"

"Abanon. But she won't be making an appearance."

"Oh? Why's that?"

"Because you cowed her."

"Eh?"

"You crushed the Blade that Whispers Hate. Your will overbore hers in a rather thorough fashion."

"Still not following you."

"'She's afraid of you."

"Ah. Why didn't you say so? And what about you?"

"What about me?"

"'You're not scared, obviously."

"I don't feel fear. Or much else."

"Because?"

"Because that would interfere with my purpose."

I sighed. "Look, I'm not going to keep handing you conversational cues. It gets tiresome."

"You fought The Knife that Parts the Night to a stalemate. Well done, and I congratulate you. But it's only a temporary situation. This balanced opposition you've engineered, it cannot last."

"Look outside, Kalara. You see any route back to the world?"

"I don't have to look outside to see it, Amra Thetys. I'm looking right at it."

"It'll be a neat trick, you getting back. Especially without the Knife. It's your body, more or less, isn't it? Without that, you're powerless. So even if you did escape, you couldn't do a damned thing." I was guessing, but it felt right.

"I need a vessel, true. Which is why I left the Knife when it became obvious you were going to send it into the void." She leaned forward a bit, and her face became serious. "The Knife may be gone, Amra, but *I* am still here. And as long as you live, I will remain here. I have not failed. I've simply had to retrench, as it were."

I took Holgren's pistol out of my pocket. It was useless, of course. I had no powder, I had no ball. Reloading couldn't be all that hard to figure out. I should have asked him for all the bells and whistles. Ah, hindsight.

I threw it at Kalara, mostly just to see how she would react.

It passed right through her, hit the wall, and clattered to the floor. She hadn't even flinched.

"If you want to do me harm, Amra, I'm afraid you'll have to root me out of your own soul. Down there beneath all the broken glass Aither mentioned. And of course whatever you do to me, you do to yourself."

Kerf's louse-ridden beard.

~ ~ ~

The Knife didn't go away. I decided three things about it. First, I wasn't going to be talking to it anymore. Second, I wasn't going to call it the Knife, or Kalara, or any damned thing else except Chuckles, even in my thoughts. And third, I was definitely not going to think of it as a little girl. It was an entity, not a person. It was an *it*, and a mass-murdering *it* to boot.

That took all of five minutes or so to conclude. Or what felt like five minutes, anyway. Who knew if it was an age or no time at all?

I looked around my small world. It hadn't gotten any more interesting. Aither hadn't even installed a secret compartment in his throne. It being the only thing in the room other than me, I checked.

I sat down on it, careful not to lean back into the blood spatter, and sighed.

Eternity was looking pretty tedious. I really, really wanted some wine.

"You could just make some," Chuckles said to me. It couldn't read my thoughts before, but that had changed, apparently, when it stowed away in my soul. I wasn't happy about that. But then, I wasn't happy about much of anything at that moment.

But was it right? The rift was still down there beneath my feet. Limitless possibility, just waiting for my will to tap it. That gave me the itch of an idea that I shoved away before it could form.

"What was that, Amra?" It stood and took a few steps toward me. I bit my thumb at it and turned my thoughts back to wine.

Holgren told me when he performed extemporaneous magic, he had to envision the magic he wanted to perform as precisely as he possibly could. The greater the detail, the greater the chance of success. Which at the time had made me wonder about just what kind of imagination he had, to be able to turn people into blood fog.

So I followed his advice. I imagined holding a cup of the wine that I was, sadly, most familiar with–Tambor's. Sour, vinegary, resinous, with overtones of dirt and the mouth-feel of despair. Watery-red, reflecting light as though each bowl came with a drop of oil on top. The earthenware cup's lumpy, rounded bottom in my hand–Tambor was happy if it spilled, it meant you were about to buy another–

I called up the barest breath of power from the rift, and there it was, in my hand.

I took a sip.

"Gah, just as ghastly as the real thing," I said out loud. If I ever got back to Lucernis, I could set up shop across from Tambor and absolutely ruin him. He had to pay *something* for his stock, little though it might be. My cost would be nil.

But of course, I would never be going back to Lucernis. I couldn't.

"Of course you can," Chuckles said. "I can show you how."

I reversed my first decision.

"Listen carefully, Chuckles. I'm not going to make a habit of talking to or acknowledging you, but you need to understand something. I will never, *ever* allow you back into the World. You're a fucking monster, and I've got a grudge against you that beggars belief. You're a tick who's attached itself to my soul, so until I figure out a way to scrape you off and stomp on you, neither one of us is going anywhere. Are we clear?"

It just smiled.

I finished the wine. Yes, it is possible to feel both reluctant and desirous at the same time. Just so you know.

I tossed the cup to the floor, both out of anger over the situation and in curiosity as to what would happen to this thing I'd made from magic. It broke into convincingly real pieces, with convincingly real sounds.

"And now I know. Better check again to make sure."

I summoned up another cup of wine. You know, in the spirit of inquiry. And getting drunk.

And drunk I got, while an abomination in the shape of a child watched with disinterested, endlessly patient starlight eyes.

PART II: LUCERNIS

EIGHTEEN

Words can hardly express how happy I was to see Lucernis's low skyline slowly reveal itself off the starboard bow in the early morning light—the squat, clumsy needle of the Dragonfly Tower, the bulbous Dome of Sighs. The age-stained walls of the Arsenal, marking the southern limit of the harbor. Lucernis was no paradise, certainly; there was as much obscene poverty as there was obscene wealth, and bad things happened to good people as a matter of course. But the largest city in the west had a soul all its own, and its vastness afforded anonymity that, in many respects which were important to me, equaled freedom. I had first arrived in Lucernis as an exile. I'd soon discovered that my exile was a blessing in disguise.

But most importantly, it wasn't gods-damned Bellarius. That city had brought out the worst in me. Also, the weather had been pure misery.

Keel hobbled up to the rail next to me and took his first long look at the Jewel of the West. Greytooth had been able to save both Keel and Chalk, though he had been unable to heal their wounds completely. I didn't pretend to understand what his Philosophy could and couldn't do, and had no reason to believe he would withhold a portion of healing unnecessarily.

"So that's Lucernis?" asked Keel.

"It is."

"It's kinda flat," was all he came up with.

"You'll appreciate not having to limp up and down a mountain to get anywhere. In fact, you won't have to walk much at all. We have these things called carriages."

"You're making fun of me."

"You sit in them, and a horse pulls it. Anywhere you want to go. You'll love it."

He rolled his eyes. "I think I liked you better when you were in a bad mood all the time."

I liked me better away from Bellarius, not being forced to do terrible things as a matter of course. Not having ruthlessness be my default mental state. But I kept it light.

"Not getting homesick, are you?"

"No. I know as well as anybody how awful Bellarius is. I thought once the Syndic was brought down, things would get better. Somehow, they got even worse. Amra warned me about being optimistic. I guess she was right."

"You don't want to go believing everything Amra says. If she was half as cynical as she makes out, there wouldn't *be* a Bellarius anymore. Though I have to admit, the thought of a world without Bellarius has its merits."

He glanced up at me. "As fucked as Bellarius is, it's still all I know. That city there? I don't know anything about it. Nothing."

"Well that's the joy of a fresh start. You know nothing about it, but more importantly, *it* knows nothing about *you*. No dangerous gangs of criminals looking to spill your blood, for example."

"There is that," he said, smiling.

"I predict that inside a week, you'll never want to leave Lucernis again." I put a hand on his shoulder. "There's no other place quite like it. You'll see."

"I guess I'll take your word for it. Oh, I came up to tell you. Marle says the thing in the crate is getting restless again."

"Ah. I'd best go and deal with it, then." And I left him leaning on the rail, trying to imagine what his future might hold. Amra had seen fit to keep him alive at the cost of putting her in deadly opposition with her oldest friend. She must have seen something in him. I admit I valued his loyalty.

Whatever the future held for Keel, I'd support him as best I could. Though I doubted he'd enjoy at least one of the things I had planned for him.

Below deck, Marle was making sure our baggage was ready for disembarkation, for the hundredth time. Actually, he was taking his turn keeping watch on the crate that held the rift spawn, as well as the single casket of gold I'd brought along. The last thing I needed was some light-fingered sailor cracking open the crate in search of loot. Things would get bloody, quickly. And on a ship, there was nowhere to run.

"Master Marle. Our cargo is shifting again?"

"Aye, magus."

I laid a hand on the crate. I could sense at once that it had been stealthily gnawing on the nets again. I strengthened them, and the enjoinders I'd woven into the nets. Halfmoon subsided with a faint growl.

The rift spawn wasn't housebroken yet, not by any stretch of the imagination. Between keeping the creature pacified and the project I'd been working on my every other waking moment aboard the ship, I was constantly treading the edge of exhausting my well.

"How is Chalk?" I asked Marle.

"The same, magus." The armsman had elected to stay in my employ, but after the death of his brother, he had become taciturn in the extreme. His grief, in my opinion, was the worse because he seemed to feel that it should never, ever show. Which made it as plain a day.

We'd laid Thon to rest in Jaby cemetery before we left Bellarius for good, Marle and I, in a crypt whose occupant had gone to dust and bone. Chalk looked on, head bandaged, eyes red from tears he refused to let fall. I'd sealed it up and put a binding on it, and that had been that, for Thon. The rest of the corpses that had been made that day, we dragged out into the street. I burned them with magefire. Then I'd gone to check on Halfmoon, hunting any stray rebels that might still be hanging about the tunnels under the mount along the way. There hadn't been any, and Halfmoon had been exactly where I'd left him.

I'd gone on, re-securing the Squareshank entrance. The construct had done for one or two of Gammond's force, judging by the blood. But it was bound to the room, and didn't know how to retreat. They'd stood just outside, out of its reach, and beaten it to pieces with Gorm only knew what.

Everything they could lay hands on, judging by the pieces scattered across the floor.

Effective.

I'd walked up to the News. I gave the tap man a gold mark and a message for his employer. Moc Mien had shown up an hour later. I'd given him even more money, and by midnight the four of us had boarded a smuggler's boat at the edge of the marsh, Moc Mien's crew acting as porters. We rendezvoused with a proper ship somewhere down the coast before dawn, and then were on our way, finally, to Lucernis.

I'd left most of my coin in the Citadel, not wanting to tempt Moc Mien into doing something we'd all regret. I also made damned sure anyone who tried to enter the Citadel in my absence wouldn't live to regret it. I'd offered occupation of the Citadel to Greytooth, who'd shaken his head and said he'd rather live in a cesspit.

~ ~ ~

"Holgren, does Lucernis send out the army for every ship that docks?"

"Eh?"

Keel pointed to the wharf. Inspector Kluge was waiting on the dock, with a platoon of arquebusiers lined up behind him, looking quite sharp in their crimson and white uniforms.

"No. No they don't." I had hoped to avoid Kluge completely. He knew where the hell gate was, of course, having helped to seal it. He wouldn't be best pleased if he found out I intended to reopen it, and wouldn't believe me if I told him it was perfectly safe. How he knew I was arriving, or even that I'd left, was a mystery.

I told Marle, Keel and Chalk to wait on deck, and once the gangplank was lowered, I went down it, smiling. Sometime smiling helps. Actually it never helps, but you do what you can.

"Good morning, Avrom. Fancy meeting you here."

Kluge inclined his long head. "Welcome back to Lucernis. I'd ask how your trip was, but I've already heard enough to know it wasn't particularly restful, magus. Or should I say arch-magus?"

"Why would you say any such thing?"

"Because your stay in Bellarius resulted in the Telemarch disappearing and you taking possession of his tower."

"I claimed his Citadel, but not his position. And I'm surprised you heard *anything* about my journey, to be honest. I went to assist my companion with a spot of bother she was having. You remember Amra, I assume."

He ignored any mention of Amra. I suspect he held a grudge that she'd been able to talk her way out of Havelock prison. The law rarely enjoys seeing criminals walk free.

"You did quite a bit more than help a friend and take possession of a tower, according to our sources."

I raised an eyebrow. "The sources of the City Watch?"

"Hah. No." But he didn't elaborate.

"Well, Inspector—"

"I've been promoted since we last met. I'm now the Watch Commander."

"My congratulations on your advancement. Now if you will excuse me?"

"Lord Morno extends his invitation to meet with him. Immediately."

Morno. Lord Governor of Lucernis. He wielded more power and influence than most kings. He was utterly loyal to Lucernia's monarchy, and utterly humorless. I suddenly regretted helping Amra steal wine from his cellars.

"Well, I suppose we shouldn't keep the Lord Governor waiting. You won't mind if I drop my compatriots and baggage off at home? It *is* on the way."

NINETEEN

The Governor's Palace was at the terminus of the Promenade, a little less than a mile from the manse that Amra had bought with the gold we'd plundered from the carcass of Hluria. I rode in a gilded carriage with Kluge; Keel, Marle, Chalk and our baggage followed behind in a distinctly less ostentatious rented hack. Kluge stopped, reluctantly and briefly, on the service road behind the manse so that I could unlock the house for them, and then we continued on down the Promenade proper. It was then that I knew that Kluge had been promoted into a position of authority far beyond a mere inspector. Only the Governor's staff would be allowed to take to the Promenade on anything but foot.

Our trip was almost completely without conversation. Kluge sat opposite me, and the carriage being small and both of us tall, our knees tended to brush the other's whenever the carriage took a turn or rocked much.

"You've lost an eye since I last saw you," Kluge observed after perhaps fifteen minutes of muteness.

"And you lost more hair," I replied. He rolled his eyes and looked out the tiny window.

Kluge was content to stay silent for the rest of the journey. I was content to let him. Though I had more than a few questions that cried out for answers, I wasn't about to give him the satisfaction of choosing to answer or withhold answers.

Mages play power games. Games not solely limited to the Art.

We arrived at the huge old pile of pink granite that was the Governor's Palace, and white-gloved servants opened the doors and folded down the steps. I followed Kluge into the ornate but surprisingly small foyer, and while he spoke to some functionary I studied a rather striking painting of the River Ose at dawn, wraith-like narrowboats being poled through the rising mist. You didn't see such boats much anymore. The artist had captured the truly ethereal sense of the setting. There was no signature.

"This wouldn't be a det Gueller, would it?" I asked Kluge, indicating the painting.

"I've no idea," Kluge replied. "Lord Morno will see us now." And so I followed him up a set of marble stairs and down a dim, carpeted hallway. He knocked on an unmarked door, waited two seconds, then entered.

Lord Morno was in his forties, but looked older. He looked careworn, dark circles under his eyes and skin loose on his face, as if he'd lost weight suddenly. He wore rich clothes smothered in embroidery but sported a trooper's sheared, artless haircut. He was sitting at a massive desk that had been carved and gilded to within an inch of its life, and he was writing, pen scratching across the paper. He did not look up. Kluge did not sit down, though there were three low-backed wooden chairs ranged in front of the desk. This went on for a considerable amount of time, the only sound being Morno's pen, the only break in the scratching being when he stopped writing to dip it in a silver-chased ink pot on the corner of the desk.

Finally, Mono finished with whatever he was writing. He set it to one side, and carefully laid his pen down on a blotter next to the ink pot. He rang a little silver bell and an aid came and made the paper he'd been writing on disappear. Morno looked up at me, and his eyes were mild.

"Holgren Angrado. Sit."

"Lord Governor," I replied, and sat. Kluge left.

"I know far more about you than a person with as little interest as I have in the subject should. I tell you this so that you won't be tempted to prevaricate. I don't have the time to waste on verbal dancing."

"I very rarely lie, my lord."

"You are not a Lucernan citizen, therefore I am not your lord. You are Fel-Radothan on your mother's side, and a Goslander on your father's."

"Indeed. You are well informed, lord."

"If you *were* Lucernan," he continued, ignoring my comment, "I could have you executed for treating with a foreign power as a private citizen."

"Oh?"

"Yes. As you are a foreigner resident in Lucernis, I could have you expelled for any number of reasons. And then, as you are a thief, I could of course order your execution more or less any time it strikes my fancy."

"Is this meant to frighten me, Lord Morno?"

"I doubt that's even possible. My aim is to make clear to you that Lucernis is not Bellarius."

"I am acutely aware of that, and deeply appreciative."

"You overthrew the sitting ruler of a nation—"

"Beg pardon, but I did not. The Syndic was dead before I arrived in Bellarius."

"I'll thank you not to interrupt me again. The Syndic and one of the Council of Three died the night you arrived in Bellarius, his palace pulled down around his ears. You took possession of the stronghold of his chief ally, the Archmage Aither the next morning, and it would beggar belief that you did so in any way other than by stepping over Aither's corpse. Days later, you assassinated one of the remaining members of the Council of Three. Days after *that*, you annihilated the army of the single remaining member of the Council of Three. It very much seems to me that you, Magister Holgren Angrado, are a very dangerous person, with a talent for the Art to rival Ardihal Flamehand, and a tendency to make rulers dead and governments fall."

"Well, when you put it that way—"

"Therefore, it falls upon you now to convince me that you are no threat to this city, or to the crown of Lucernia. If you can't, I will give you until dawn to be gone from Lucernis before I issue your death warrant."

So much for my quietly stealing into Lucernis and opening the hell gate.

"Well," I replied, "First I must congratulate you on your information gathering agents, though I do take exception to the rather one-sided view of events they seem to have reported. While what you've said is the truth, it is in no way the whole truth."

"I set out the events that concern me the most. I did not say that they were the extent of my knowledge of the events."

"Lord Governor, if I had any desire to rule Bellarius, I would not be sitting in your office now."

"I never suggested your aim was to rule Bellarius. I don't know what your aim was or is. I do know you were in some way connected to the destruction of the sitting ruler and his dwelling, that you eliminated, directly, two of the four people who could legitimately have laid claim to the rulership after his death, and that you destroyed the army of a third."

"I did not kill the Telemarch. Or the Syndic. Or two of the three Councilors. I *did* kill Gabul Steyner, but only after he tried to have me killed, twice. As for destroying When's army, I'll merely note that I dispatched the fighting force of the rebel People's Committee at exactly the same instant, for the simple reason that whoever won would surely have turned on me next. But since my time is apparently short, Lord Governor, can I suggest you simply *tell* me what it is that will convince you I'm not some rabid maniac, intent on toppling nations for the sheer joy of it? Because I *do* call Lucernis my home, and do *not* wish to be expelled from it."

Morno sat there, looking at me with his mild eyes, and his sallow, worn-down face gave nothing away. Finally, he leaned forward a little and put his hands on the desk. I noted absently that he chewed his nails. Obviously he did it in private; his public persona was far too sanguine.

"Magister Angrado, you have lived in Lucernis for nearly a decade. In that time you've done nothing to distinguish yourself, or indeed call attention to yourself in any way, other than to aid the Watch in dispatching a few daemonettes and in the closing of a hell gate. Yes, we know something of your illegal activities, just as we know about your workshop. But for the most part, you have lived your life in Lucernis as if you were an ordinary soul, rather than a mage gifted with rare talent and ability."

"I am a private person."

"Your privacy is at an end. That is, if you wish to remain in Lucernis."

"I'm not following you, Lord Morno."

"You state that you do not wish to rule. I believe you. If I did not, you wouldn't be sitting in this office; you'd have been executed on the dock. But if you would not rule, then you must serve."

That did not sound at all good. "Serve? Serve who?"

"The Crown, generally, and me more specifically. Or rather the office of the Governor. What you *cannot* do is run around loose, answerable only to yourself. You will enter public service, or you will take ship and never return, on pain of death. You are simply too dangerous."

"So you wish to leash me. Using what? The threat of banishment? I've been banished before, Lord Morno."

"And I'm sure the memory is still a bitter one. But you seem content enough in Lucernis."

"Yes, it is. And yes, I am. I made a new life here, and am well content with it."

"You've traveled extensively I take it?"

"I have."

"Does anywhere compare to Lucernis?"

I shook my head. I had a feeling I knew where he was leading the conversation.

"Let us speak frankly, Holgren Angrado. You made a new life in this city. *My* city, magus. Mine. Twenty years ago I was given Lucernis to govern, a huge cauldron boiling over with vice, anarchy, rage, murder and misery. The Jewel of the West was, in fact, a boil on the ass of the Dragonsea. Riots, food shortages. Disease and starvation. Pirates just off shore strangled trade, and they were paid to do so by merchant cartels right here in the city. Lucernis was a disgrace to humanity. There was a *slave market* not a hundred yards from Traitor's Gate, for Isin's love. It was an open secret. Women, children, foreigners and debtors, tricked and taken and stolen, and sold over the sea to Far Thwyll and Chagul."

He paused, looked out the window. I suspected he was actually looking back into the past.

"My king had had enough. He sent me to clean up the mess. I hanged the previous governor in Harad's square. I broke the power of the merchant cartels. I crushed the gods-damned pirates. I took a broom and swept this city, if not clean, then at least clean of the worst filth. And now, twenty years later, I'm still sweeping. Because the moment you stop sweeping is the moment the filth starts creeping back in."

I waited a moment, but it seemed he had finished. So I said "Forgive me, but what does any of that have to do with me?"

"Sometimes I need a bigger broom."

"Oh. No. I'm no tool."

"Everyone is a tool. At the moment, you are the tool of your own desires, whereas I am the tool of my king. I am also the tool of every resident in this city who wishes to live a life more or less free from the effects of misrule. There is great honor in being a tool used for the greater good. If you object to the term, choose another."

"Then I choose the term 'private citizen.'"

He did not smile. "If you choose that term, you'll have to enjoy the use of it somewhere else."

"What do you want from me? Specifically?"

"You will swear an oath of fealty to the crown of Lucernia. You will of course cease any illegal activities you are now associated with, assuming there still are any such activities. And you will serve as a special adviser to the office of the Governor, at my pleasure and in any way that I see fit."

"So essentially I'll do what you say, when you say to do it."

"I won't be asking you to polish my riding boots, magus."

"Perhaps you could give me an example of what you *would* be asking me to do."

"Certainly. Some eighteen months ago a not-inconsiderable portion of Lucernis was burned to the ground. We know the s were set deliberately, and we know that they were of magical origin. We do not know who or what caused them, or whether it might happen again. You will investigate, and at the end of your investigation, you will advise us that the threat has been dealt with."

"So I am to be your problem eliminator. I think I'd rather be your boot polisher."

"That position is taken."

"Speaking of filled positions. What you're asking me to do, isn't that what Kluge already does for you?"

"Avrom Kluge is in many ways an admirable, upstanding man. He has some skill at investigation, and a middling talent with the Art. He excels at managing resources and manpower. He has been advanced to exactly the level that best fits his abilities."

"So he's already tried to find the arsonist, and failed."

"Indeed."

"Lord Morno, I will accept your 'offer' since I see no palatable alternative. But I must insist on one stipulation."

"What stipulation?"

"I have business of a personal nature that simply will not wait. It will take me out of Lucernis for an unknown amount of time. I plan to leave within two or three days, at most. I cannot accede to your request before this business is finished."

He gave me a level stare. "And if I insist that you take up your duties now?"

"Then I will be forced to depart tonight, ill-prepared, and I will have no choice but to accept all the consequences that flow from your decision."

He kept his gaze on me as he considered, one chewed nail tapping the top of his desk.

"All right, magus," he finally said. "You may take up the mantle of special adviser after your return. But you'll take the oath of fealty now."

Damn. But it hardly mattered. If I managed to survive my trip to hells and return, I'd deal with the consequences then.

"Very well," I said, meaning the exact opposite, and he rang his bell and stood and came around the desk.

TWENTY

There was kneeling involved, and a recitation of oaths in front of three bored clerks acting as witnesses, and a very long sheet of parchment with quite an astonishing number of words writ small that I signed and he chopped. Then there was polite applause and a pat on the back, a quick sip of an inferior Courune brandy after a toast to the king—now my king—and inside of ten minutes I found myself standing on the front steps of the Governor's Palace with a copy of my oath in my hand and a nice view of the Promenade.

I started the short walk home. It was a rather anticlimactic way to formally end my state of statelessness, after a decade. I remember thinking that Amra would laugh herself sick when I told her, and smiled. I stopped smiling when I remembered just how unlikely it still was that I'd ever see her again. With an effort I discarded such thoughts and concentrated on my surroundings. I was in Lucernis, on the Promenade, surrounded by some of the most elegant architecture in the world. It was late autumn, which in Lucernis meant it was gloriously cool and breezy. The trees were just turning, and yellow and gold leaves were everywhere. Even better, it was incredibly unlikely that anyone would try to assassinate me during my stroll.

It's the small, things, I find, that offer the most satisfaction.

The tiny front garden of the manse looked awful. But then it always did. I pushed open the ornamental gate, put a hand on the big blue front door, and whispered to it. It showed me everyone who had come knocking since the last time I asked it. No one that I recognized. I unlocked it with another whisper, and went inside.

Keel was in the front parlor. The chest full of money was there as well. Keel looked bored, to the point of falling asleep.

I tossed the parchment on a dusty credenza and said, "Wake up, Keel. Where is master Marle?"

"Off somewhere cleaning. He took one look at this place and his eyebrows went into this v shape and he started muttering. I think dust is his sworn enemy or something."

"You're not far wrong," I replied. "Master Marle was in the navy."

"Which one?"

"Pinghul, if memory serves. But they're all the same, believe me. And where is Chalk and our other baggage?" Meaning Halfmoon.

"In the building at the back."

"The carriage house."

"If you say so. He and Marle thought it was best not to bring it inside."

"Sensible precaution, but unnecessary. I'd ask if you all had eaten, but I know you haven't. There's nothing edible here. Gather everyone please, while I call a hack. We'll have a decent lunch, and then we've got work to do."

While Keel went to collect the others, I poked my head out the front door and gave a sharp whistle. A boy of about ten, one of the many who loitered on the Promenade waiting for odd jobs, waved his hat at me. I made a circling motion with my finger and he ran off in the direction of the Dragon Gate. A carriage was waiting behind the house in less than ten minutes. If you lived on the Promenade, there was always a hack available.

I made sure of Halfmoon's containment once again, and then we were off to Fraud's. I had the hack wait for us. The meal was excellent as always, and the service was miserable, as always. All of us ate in near-silence, having had no breakfast and having food in front of us worth concentrating on. When all that was left was mopping of gravy and picking of teeth, I spoke up.

"Gentlemen, welcome to Lucernis proper. I wish we could sit back, digest and drink wine for a few hours, but there is a fair amount of work to be done today, and only half a day left in which to do it. Here is what happens next: We secure a wagon, visit a butcher, return to the manse to pick up our cargo, then take a trip to the charnel grounds. Chalk, are you able to drive a wagon?"

"Aye, magus," he replied.

"Excellent. Let's be off, then."

I would have given custom to Amra's wainwright friend in the Spindles, but I simply couldn't face another discussion as to her whereabouts. So I chose another more or less at random of the half-dozen in his neighborhood, paid too much for a two-day rental and for the nags to pull it, and paid a deposit to rid myself of the driver that came with it. Chalk took the reins. I directed him to Traitor's Gate market and we stopped at one of the largest butchers I knew of, where I bought half a dozen pig carcasses, mostly bled out but otherwise whole. We waited while they removed the hearts for me and packaged them separately, at my request. I was given the wax-treated canvas that held the hearts, as well as a dubious look, at no extra charge.

Marle begged leave to briefly explore the market and find something to bring back to the manse for dinner, and Chalk elected to go with him. Keel sat on the wagon's tail and took everything in. His head was on a swivel. Traitor's Gate market was loud, boisterous, and extremely crowded.

While we waited, I poked him in the side to get his attention.

"What do you think of Lucernis so far?" I asked.

"I've never seen so many people. I mean, Bellarius is crowded, but you end up knowing every face, near enough. Here? Impossible. How many people live in the city?"

"I'm not sure, honestly. At least half a million, if I had to guess."

He gave a low whistle. "Easy to get lost here," he said, staring at a pretty young fishmonger across the way, her citrine-toned skin flawless, her laugh loud and honest as she haggled with customers.

"In more ways than one, my young friend."

~ ~ ~

Then we proceeded back to the manse, and loaded Halfmoon's crate onto the wagon. It roused at once at the smell of pigs' blood, and I pushed the creature down again into torpor. It was an effort. I'd have liked to have transported Halfmoon and the carcasses separately, but the logistics just weren't worth the trouble. So I rode in the back, sitting on the crate to keep direct contact with the rift spawn, and to keep everything but my boots out of the slowly pooling blood. They had been bled out, but it would be impossible to remove every drop.

I called directions to Chalk, who was more than competent as a teamster, and by mid-afternoon we had crossed Daughter's Bridge and were rolling along the dusty road that led to my former residence.

"Gorm on a stick!" Keel stood up abruptly, staring at the fields that surrounded us. "Those are dead bodies. They're fucking everywhere!" Chalk and Marle were also wide eyed, if less loud.

"The charnel grounds," I told them. "Or if you prefer the flowery description, the fields of the dead. Corpses on top of corpses on top of untold bones. They're very old, these fields." Older than even most Lucernans knew.

"These people don't believe in burying the dead? Or burning 'em?"

"Burial, yes. Cremation, never. Remember the huge white-walled edifice we passed just before the bridge? That's Lucernis's only graveyard. As big as it is, it isn't big enough. The poor never make it in. The forgotten get removed, to make room."

"Crazy," Keel muttered. "This city is crazy."

"Not really. They're a bit odd about death, certainly, but they have their reasons. Otherwise Lucernans are no more crazy than anyone else."

"Crazy as a box of frogs dancing jigs," Keel insisted.

"Crazier than living on the side of a mountain?" I asked him, smiling.

"At least the view is a sight better than this."

"True," I conceded.

We arrived soon enough at the remains of my former home. A carriage was drawn up at the edge of my land. I suspected Kluge was waiting for me, and was proven right when he stepped out of the carriage as we pulled up.

"Commander Kluge. If I'd known you were going to call on me, I would have at least brought a chair for you to pull up."

"Magus," he replied, ignoring the others. "What's in the crate?"

"Have you been waiting all day to ask me that question? Why didn't you ask earlier?"

"Earlier it wasn't important to me. Now it is."

"What changed in the mean time?"

"Your *position* changed, Holgren Angrado. You went from capable mage and petty thief to special adviser to the Lord Governor himself."

"First, I'm not an adviser yet, as it happens. Second, my *alleged* thefts were never petty. Third, if I am merely competent, what does that make you? And finally, what does any of that have to do with what's in the crate?"

"You cannot be trusted. You are a criminal and, it seems in the light of your actions in Bellarius, an anarchist. The very thought of you being legitimized by the Lord Governor is worrisome in the extreme. I will be your shadow, Angrado. I will dog your every step, and I will scrutinize everything you do, and everything to do with you. And I will start by examining the contents of that crate."

I realized three things then, in rapid succession. First, that Kluge had expected me to be punished in some form or fashion by Morno when he brought me to the palace. While I certainly felt punished, Kluge could not but help to see what had happened in the opposite light.

Second, in his own mind, Kluge was an officer of the law first and foremost. Being a mage came a distant second, which surprised me. Virtually every mage I'd ever met defined themselves by their powers.

Finally, I understood that Kluge bore me a deep enmity, both personally and professionally. He was going to be a thorn in my side as long as I had a side into which a thorn could be jabbed.

I looked around. "Where are your constables, Commander?"

"I need none."

"You mean they would do you no good." If it came down to a duel between us, he would lose. He would need all the help he could get, but a gaggle of city watch wouldn't make a difference.

"Where is your writ of search?" I asked him.

"I need none," he repeated, and he *was* technically correct about that. As an officer of the law, all he needed was suspicion of wrongdoing. But it didn't matter. I had to call him, immediately, and see if it was a bluff.

"I disagree, Kluge. If you're going to be scrutinizing me to death and treading on my heels, you're going to do it with a writ signed by the Lord Governor each and every time. Otherwise you will get no cooperation from me. To make it even more plain, if you want to look inside this box, I want to see a note signed by Morno himself that says 'Show Avrom what's in the damned box.' If you don't like it, you can try to take me into custody, I suppose, but it won't go well for you. Do I make myself perfectly clear?"

He smiled. Or at least bared his teeth. "Yes. Perfectly." Then he turned on his heel and strode back to his carriage. He got in and it rolled off, the coachman looking bored and dyspeptic, the horses and iron-banded wheels throwing yellow-gray dust up into the air.

Kluge wasn't a *good* enemy to have. There are none such. He wasn't stupid, and had a measure of power, both the temporal sort and power in the Art. But he wasn't the worst enemy I'd ever had, not by a long, long measure. I was a little surprised he had tried to strong-arm me in such a fashion.

Keel heaved a theatrical sigh, interrupting my thoughts.

"What?"

"Do you have to make enemies of powerful people in *every* country you go to?"

I snorted. "Kluge isn't powerful."

"Can he put people in prison? Have them hanged?"

"Well, yes." I decided not to mention Kluge also being a mage. It wouldn't help my case.

"I don't know what your definition of powerful is, Holgren, but I think you need to revisit it."

"I believe 'revise' is the word you're looking for."

He squinted at me, and scratched his head. "Also, you should probably try to figure out whatever it is about you that makes people hate you so much, and then be less of that."

"Shut up and help us with the crate."

"With one arm?"

"Fair point. You can clean up all the blood when you get back to the manse, then. One arm's good enough for that."

"It's not *our* wagon!"

"I want my deposit back."

He limped off, muttering something that sounded like 'less of exactly that.'

There was nothing left of my old house except the foundation, a few charred beams, and some broken statuary that had haunted the front garden since before I'd bought it. The wards I'd laid on the house had faded while I'd been away in Thagoth and the Silent Lands, and by the time the great fire had spread, they had not been sufficient to protect the old wooden structure. That my home had been the only one north of the Ose to burn hadn't escaped my notice, but I honestly hadn't much cared after returning from Thagoth. The house was gone, but I hadn't exactly been in love with it to begin with. The location had been the important thing. And I would have abandoned the house in any case, when Amra and I moved to the Promenade.

The *basement* of the house was another matter entirely.

I called up a stiff breeze and blew the detritus off the foundation, scouring clean the stone and the very large iron trap door in the center of it. The wards on it hadn't failed; I would have been very surprised if they had, given what I'd invested in them.

I bent down to inspect the door, and saw with my magesight that someone had tried, and failed, to break in since I last had checked. They had failed to gain access, but they had also escaped with their lives. Pity. Probably it had been Kluge, but that was just supposition.

Chalk and I, being the most able bodied, hauled the crate and the carcasses over to beside the trap door, and then I sent them all back to the manse. Only Chalk had his burning tower badge on his person, so he got to be the key holder.

"Admit no one," I told them, "unless they have a note from me or the Lord Governor. Or an army. I'll be back late tonight." Marle nodded and off they went. I was fairly certain they wouldn't get lost, and anyone could direct them to the Promenade if they did.

Once they were out of sight, I got to work moving the rift-spawn down into the dark of my long-disused sanctum.

~ ~ ~

I had a fair number of dangerous items stored in the basement. Halfmoon was, by far, the most dangerous thing I'd ever kept there. So once I got the crate down the stairs, I shoved it across the tiled floor to the warded circle I had laid out years before. A perfect, unbroken circle of gray-white granite, five feet in diameter, it had cost me a fortune to have carved. It had cost me half as much again to have a portion of the ground floor torn up and the circle lowered down into the basement, and then to have the floor and wall repaired.

Anything could enter the circle, but nothing could come out, unless I allowed it to. I'd installed it in hopes of trapping the demon I'd sold my soul to, but it had been far too canny to step into the trap. So while it had been tested innumerable times, it had never actually been used. Until now.

I strengthened the nets that still restrained Halfmoon one last time, then set about opening the crate, pulling nails one by one using the Art. I hadn't thought to bring a crowbar. I broke the crate down completely, leaving only the boards under the creature. Then I stepped out of the circle, imbued the granite with more than sufficient power, and severed all the knots of magic that held together the nets that confined Halfmoon.

The nets disintegrated into dust and loose fibers, and the rift-spawn exploded into motion, hurling itself at me—only to be slammed back into the center of the circle by its invisible, undefeatable barrier.

It tried that three times, then crouched on the wooden pallet, panting and glaring.

"Are you finished, then?"

It said nothing.

"Are you hungry?"

Always, it said, grudgingly.

I went upstairs and rolled one of the pigs down the steps. It was not light. I shoved it across the floor until one trotter broke the circle.

"You can pull it in the rest of the way."

This is not man, and not alive.

"This is all you'll be getting from now on. And since you don't actually need to eat in order to survive, you shouldn't complain."

It bent down and sniffed the trotter. A pale gray tongue darted out, licking, sampling. Suddenly Halfmoon dragged the pig inside the circle, and set to gruesome work. I sat down on the tiles a careful distance away and watched it, mindful that it would do the exact same thing to me, given the chance. Within ten minutes, the pig was no more.

No blood to roll in, it complained when it was done.

"You'll live."

No heart. The best part, after the brain.

"I'm happy to hear it. I'll be giving hearts to another once we've finished our conversation." In other circumstances I'd be fascinated by the mystery of how the creature was acquiring vocabulary and grammar. And how it could eat something that was rather larger than itself. As it was, I left it at 'chaos is capable of most anything'.

I want more. Hungry. Many days I sleep.

"There are five more of these upstairs. You'll have them all, if everything goes well. But first we are going to discuss what I want from you."

What do you want? You never tell me why you take me.

"You will help me to find what birthed you. The rift. I know you can sense it."

I remember... the fire. At the heart of the mountain. The power. The roar of all creating, all destroying in my ears, in my body, my brains. I remember making and unmaking and remaking. I remember it. I remember it left. I do not know where it went. I cannot hear it anymore. Let me go.

"You sensed it when I took you under the mount." It wasn't a question.

I heard... I heard an echo. I smelled my birthing water. The fire I did not hear. The smell was old.

"Yes, it left. You and I are going to find it, wherever it went. I believe that as we get closer to it, you will hear it once again. That is why I took you."

You cannot have the fire. It will eat you. That would make me happy.

"I'm sure it would. I don't want the fire. I want something that went with it, when it left."

I don't care. Let me go.

"Here is my dilemma, Halfmoon: I need you, but I cannot trust you. I've been picking at the problem since before I trapped you, and I've come up with nothing resembling a comforting solution. I think that the moment you have the opportunity, you'll try to devour me just as you did that pig. Am I wrong?"

Not wrong. Hate you.

"Your honesty is refreshing. Given time, I might be able to break you more thoroughly. But I don't have the time, and I don't have the stomach to devote to it in any case. And I very much don't want to give you the chance to learn guile. So we will just have to go about things a little more expeditiously." Which was a pity, but having Halfmoon romping along at my side through the infernal regions as a loyal pet had never been terribly likely.

I got up and went to a dusty chest in the far corner of the room. I opened it with a whisper, and took out the head of Bosch, the mage who'd dueled me in front of Tambor's and lost.

He was still conscious. I hesitate to say he was alive, or even aware in any meaningful sense. When I pulled up the surprisingly light, amber-tinted clear cube his head was encased in, he blinked and stared at me.

His eyes were pits of madness. Not that he'd been sane before he'd lost his shiny metalwork spider's body, or his real one before that. You had to be mad to treat with demons.

Yes, I know I also technically treated with a demon, but it was just the once, I was very young, and I certainly never tried to open a hell gate on the Jacos Road, or anywhere else for that matter. Stupidity and desperation only look like madness to the outside observer.

At any rate, being locked in a lightless chest for the best part of two years hadn't done anything to improve Bosch's mental balance. Thankfully his lack of a body also meant he lacked a voice. His screams were completely silent. I took him over to the circle and set him down near the stairs, out of the way.

Is it food?

"No."

I could not trust the rift-spawn to not try to kill me. But I needed the rift-spawn. I didn't like my odds of fashioning something from its corpse that would lead me to the rift. Quite a conundrum. Except I knew how to remove Bosh's head from the demon-wrought amber cube. And I knew how to replace it with another head. Halfmoon's head, even with the tendrils, was smaller than Bosch's.

"All right, Halfmoon. Our time is up. I will give you one chance to kill me and escape. If you fail, you will serve me in whatever fashion I desire." All of which was true, if not in the way the creature would take it.

Then release me and die. It rose to all fours and crouched, ready to spring. Its skin began to shift, attempting to camouflage itself with the pattern of the tile floor around it.

The timing had to be perfect.

"On three then. One. Two. Three." It was already launching itself as the last syllable left my mouth. It was a fearsome beast, made more terrifying, to my mind, because of those emotionless insect eyes. I dropped the circle's ward—and instantly raised it again.

Halfmoon's body fell back into the circle, thrashing, its skin cycling through a hundred colors and patterns in a heartbeat. Bluish ichor gushed out of the severed neck, splattered against the barrier and ran down it to pool on the floor. Halfmoon's head rolled to a rest at my feet.

I picked up Bosch. Traced the demonic glyph that opened the cube. Let his head fall to the tiles, then kicked it into the circle. It fetched up against the beast's flank, more or less face-down. I powered the circle again with a thought, just in case, and then replaced Bosh's head with Halfmoon's. I sealed the cube, then sat down on the steps and let my breathing settle down. I'd been more nervous than I'd realized, and now my nerves were telling me how profoundly relieved they were that my plan had worked.

"I told you you would serve," I said to the brutally ugly head in the cube.

Halfmoon didn't need a body to talk. I heard him call me 'monster' perfectly well.

"The good news is, I can put you back together." And I could; the circle would keep the creature's body from dying, and Bosh's head as well, for as long as the power I'd given it lasted. I'd given it enough for a month, more or less. Any longer than that and I likely wasn't coming back, and wouldn't have any use for either.

Do it now.

"Find me the fire, the rift, and I might. Now be quiet."

Of course I had no intention of giving Halfmoon back its body.

I went around my sanctum and put together a pack of items that might prove useful for what was to come, then threw the pack over a shoulder and climbed the stairs. I sealed and warded the door once more, collected the pig hearts and, vaguely regretting the wasting five other carcasses, set off down the road towards Daughter's Bridge and the Necropolis. My land backed onto the Ose, but the little boat I'd kept on the bank had disappeared once the concealment wards had worn down, probably about the time I'd been moldering in a shallow grave in Thagoth.

The late afternoon light was liquid gold, and the wind had a delicious chill to it. It would have been quite a pleasant walk, if it had been anywhere except beside the charnel grounds.

I crossed Daughter's bridge, then took a seat at a dingy but furiously busy eating house across from the Necropolis. I refused food, sipped bad wine, ignored the serving girl's intermittent unhappy stare and watched visitors stream out of the cemetery's huge gate until it was almost time for the gate to close. Then, once it appeared that all those visiting the departed had themselves departed, I picked up my pack, crossed the busy street, and entered the Necropolis. I hoped I wasn't making a mistake.

Michael McClung

TWENTY-ONE

The Necropolis.
It was one of the old, old places of power in the world, and while it looked like a beautiful if crazed park in these modern times, it hadn't always. In fact, it had looked worse than the charnel grounds for centuries.

It had always been a place for the dead; before the founding of Lucernis, before the Diaspora, before the Cataclysm, even. It was the demesne of the Guardian of the Dead, and beneath the manicured lawn and the carefully trimmed topiary, beneath the marble mausoleums and alabaster statues and stone vases full of fresh-cut flowers, beneath the recent dead and their comfortable hereafter were the bones and souls of those who knew the Guardian of the Dead by a different name: Queen of Souls.

All my considerable research had never turned up the name of the mage who had leashed the Guardian, who had bound her within the confines of the Necropolis and forced upon her the agreement that stood to the present day—to protect the peace of the departed, and to hold their souls on this plane for as long as the smallest mote of their physical bodies remained within her territory. Whoever it had been must have been terribly powerful or immensely clever. Or both.

Amra had never asked me why I chose to live beside the charnel grounds, and I'd never told her. The reason was simple. The Guardian was confined within the Necropolis, but her territory stretched north across the

Ose. Those souls dumped across the river were not in fact thrown out of Lucernis's afterlife. They were just forced to live homeless in its slums.

I'd lived beside the charnel grounds because, as long as I happened to die on the Guardian's territory, I was instantly and automatically a citizen of her version of the great beyond, and the demon who held a contract on my soul could go bugger itself. At least until there was literally nothing left of my corpse, which would take centuries. As stopgap measures went, it was the best I'd found. It was also the reason I tended to stay home most of the time. Unlike native Lucernans, if I perished outside her physical sphere of influence her doors were shut, and I got what was coming to me. Which is what had ended up happening—more or less, and temporarily.

When Amra had snatched the Blade that Whispers Hate away from the Guardian's grasp, I'd interposed myself and my magic, to allow Amra to escape. I'd done it knowing the Guardian wouldn't be terribly happy with me, that I couldn't really do more than inconvenience and distract her. I'd done it for Amra's sake, certainly; the Guardian would have done messy things to her to get the Blade back. But I'd also done it because the thought of the Guardian holding one of the Eightfold's Blades was terrifying. There was no conceivable good end, if that had happened.

So. I didn't regret getting in her way, and given the choice, I would have done it again. But as I entered the Necropolis, I will admit to feeling a certain amount of trepidation. She was unlikely to want to give me a big hug, unless it culminated in my spine being cracked.

Which is why I'd brought presents. Never let anyone tell you research is dull or unimportant. It can save lives, possibly even your own.

As soon as I entered the Necropolis, the gate slammed shut with an ear-splitting boom. That definitely wasn't normal.

"You remember me, then, I take it," I said to the air. In reply the shadows, already long in the late afternoon, rushed across the grass and began to drown everything within the walls. The Necropolis was a huge bowl, filling rapidly with inky dark. I looked toward the badly carved weeping mother statue that stood on the little knoll in the center of the cemetery, the highest point in the Necropolis. I wasn't there anymore.

"I will melt the flesh from your bones to feed the grass," came a voice on the wind. "I will give your skull to the worms to frolic in. I will use your ribcage to rake the fallen leaves, and on the rare occasion it snows, I will bring out your lovingly preserved scalp, hair still attached, and brush the cold flakes from every tombstone."

"While it's flattering that you've obviously thought of me so much, you'll do no such thing."

"Will I not?"

"No. I am known to the honest dead. I broke no stricture. I spilled no blood, nor did I fornicate, or litter, or even play the hurdy-gurdy."

Suddenly she was before me, massive, her face a mask of rage.

"YOU THWARTED ME!" Her shriek was so loud I feared for my hearing. She grew larger, larger, until she blotted out half the stars. "You robbed me of the Blade! Without your interference, I would have had that thief in a trice, and had the Blade from her in a second trice!"

"Oh, don't be petty. If you'd gotten hold of the Blade that Whispers Hate, you'd have broken every vow you ever made, and likely the entire world along with them. You'll forgive me if I had an interest in seeing the world *not* destroyed. I happen to live here."

The guardian grew larger still, and her presence loomed over me, blunt-fingered hands now become vicious and bony and talon-tipped. Her huge, pale, unlovely face filled the sky. She ground her teeth, the sound of an avalanche escaping her lips. The very air crackled, and it was hard to draw breath.

"Anyway, I brought you a present," I told her. "But if you'd rather be angry—" I shrugged and turned to go, pretending I had some way to open the gate if she preferred that it remained closed. I got three paces away from it before she spoke.

"Well ...let's see it, at least. Before I ruin you."

I didn't smile. It wouldn't do to smile. I turned around. She was back to her normal self, approximately twice human size. She held out one stony hand. I dug out the waxed canvas package from my pack and dropped it into her huge palm. She plucked open the wrapping with impossibly nimble fingers, and frowned.

"Pig's hearts? Once I feasted on willing sacrifices, a dozen at a time!"

"Well if that's not to your liking, I can dispose of it. Outside. It wouldn't do to litter in the Necropolis."

She frowned. "No. They'll do." And she sat down on the grass and proceeded to snack on the hearts, little finger held out to the side in a parody of daintiness.

"I was told recently that men and pigs are much the same on the inside," I remarked. "Is there any truth to that?"

She grunted. "It's not wrong." She finished the last of her snack, and sighed, and squeezed the wrapping smaller, smaller, until it disappeared entirely. "Less. I am less. The whole world is less, in this lesser age. That was the first half-proper offering I've had in a century."

"Surely not."

"Do you know what offerings they make to me nowadays? Dolls! Dolls with little pink felt hearts sewn on! What do they expect me to *do* with them? Once they served up the hearts of virgins, still beating! They disgust me. I disgust myself. I should kill you just for reminding me. I fucking despair. What do you want, mageling?"

"What do you know of She Who Casts Eight Shadows?"

"I know She makes me look like your kindly old auntie. I know that anything to do with Her ends badly for everyone except Her, be they gods, demons or you lowly, maggot mortals."

"Then why did you try to take one of Her Blades, if I may ask?"

"Because a bad end is exactly the kind of end I was made for, fool."

I could think of nothing to say to that. "Who is She, really? What does She want?"

"As to what She wants, you'd have to ask Her. But I will tell you this: She was born a weapon in the wars of the gods. She is destruction, divinely incarnate, just as Her sister was preservation. If She wanted, She could make an end of everything."

"Everything? Forgive my skepticism."

The guardian of the dead leaned down and poked me in the chest with one huge finger. "Mark me. I do not lie. She could end all existence." A smile. "Who knows? She might yet."

"What a comforting thought."

"Did you mistake who you were talking to?"

"Oh, I don't know. Death can be comfort, of a sort."

She snorted. But she did not contradict me.

"So there is nothing you can tell me of Her plans?"

"I just did, you git."

"What about Her Blades?"

"What about them?"

"What are they, really?"

"How should I know?"

"You seemed to know enough about the Blade that Whispers Hate to want it." Which was the whole reason I'd risked her wrath in coming to the Necropolis. Any source of information regarding the Blades was invaluable.

She smiled. "Very well, little mage. Each of Her Blades is the vessel of one of Her eight aspects, each a goddess in and of themselves, distinct and separate from all the others. You ask what She wants. I do not know. But tell me, if you found yourself fractured into eight pieces, what might you want?"

I thought about it. Far too rapidly to trust, I came to the obvious conclusion.

"I'd want to put myself back together." I frowned. "But I'm not a god, and I very much doubt my own mortal desires are comparable to a god's, not in any meaningful way. And would each of my fragments want the same as all the others?"

She shrugged, obviously not caring particularly what conclusion I came to, or whether it was wrong or right. "Is that all you wanted?"

"Unless you know something about the Black Library of Thraxys, then yes, that's all."

"Why would you want to know about that?"

"Because I need to go there and borrow a book."

She sat up straighter. "What book?"

"Lagna's notebook. Maybe his key, as well."

The guardian smiled, her teeth infant tombstones. "You are amusing, mage. That much I'll grant you."

"Why amusing? I'm perfectly serious."

"Oh, I don't doubt it. So I'll give you this much: Some books aren't books at all, and some books are the reader as much as they are read. You'll need the key to read the book, by the way."

"That's wonderfully vague of you."

She smiled wider. "Some books are also incredibly angry."

"You're really enjoying being cryptic, aren't you?"

"If you make it to the Black Library, you'll see. Ha! See!" and she proceeded to dissolve into gales of laughter that sounded like nothing so much as rusty gate hinges squealing in an autumn wind.

I took my leave. She didn't seem to notice. But at least she didn't bar the gate from opening.

Michael McClung

TWENTY-TWO

I'd gone perhaps fifteen yards down the street when I noticed the first watcher, and I only noticed him because I was using my magesight.

Before I lost my eye, I would only call up my magesight with cause. It could be physically draining if used for long periods, and it could cause visual confusion over time. But for some reason, using my magesight seemed to help me move about the mundane world in three dimensions. It wasn't as good as having two eyes, but it was better than having just the one. I bumped into things less, and had less trouble with my lack of depth perception overall. It had saved me from accident and discomfort more than once aboard ship. And after all the time I'd been forced to use it in Bellarius, I found it much less taxing to use than before I'd become one-eyed.

I did not expect to see any signs of magic on Song Street, so when I saw a fellow sitting on the pavement, grimy begging cap before him and a luminous stripe floating in front of his eyes, I took note.

When I saw the second watcher on the corner of Daudon and Crane, the same strip of light before his eyes, I knew that Kluge had not been making idle noises about keeping me on a short leash.

In other circumstances, it would have amused me. I would have let him hound my every step, set people to watch me while I drank wine or visited the workshop. I might even have waved at the poor sods tasked with surveilling my boring daily routine.

Unfortunately, I was going to be doing something Kluge would, without compunction, kill me to prevent. And while I knew it was almost certainly perfectly safe to reopen the hell gate, I very much doubted he would take my word for it.

So, I needed to part ways with my watchers. And I knew just where and how I could manage it, sadly.

I hailed a hack and told the driver to take me as close to the Rookery as he dared.

~ ~ ~

Lucernis is filled with some of the greatest architectural achievements humanity has been able to create since the Cataclysm. There is a reason it is known as the Jewel of the West. It is filled with the sort of beauty that was almost completely lacking in grim, utilitarian, and frankly ugly Bellarius.

Lucernis is also filled with slums, a veritable patchwork of poverty. Each of these downtrodden neighborhoods comes complete with its own character. Barely-more-than-shacks, breeding sullen desperation and abject poverty, generation after generation. Working class hovels shoved up against each other, proud to sport a second story and badly whitewashed wooden walls. Blocks of once-handsome buildings in long, slow decline, each structure facing inevitable ruin in solitary fashion, home only to the homeless, the hopeless, and the agents of decay. Streets choked with rough commerce, cheap, brightly painted facades projecting false cheer to mask grim interiors.... Lucernis does not want for 'color'.

And then there is the Rookery.

The Rookery has the dubious distinction of being so nightmarish that even Morno's tax collectors refuse to enter it. Which is saying much, as Morno only employs combat veterans to collect the King's fifth.

The Rookery is every bad element of every other slum in the city, only gone feral and festering with it. If I couldn't lose Kluge's watchers there, then I had a serious problem.

The hack dropped me off on the main thoroughfare closest to Lucernis's civic tumor, took my money, and shook his head as he switched the horse. I walked past weed- and detritus-choked vacant lots and burned out shells of buildings in the early evening. It was likely the darkest place in the city; no lamplighters would venture here, even if there had been lamps. There were no lamps, because they would just have been torn up and sold for scrap, and damn the highly flammable natural gas pouring into the neighborhood.

I looked back, once, and standing conspicuous on the corner the hack had let me off at was a figure indistinguishable except for that narrow blue-white glowing strip across the eyes. I waved at him or her and walked deeper into the snake pit.

I had no doubt Kluge was somehow tracking me using the Art. His watchers were not all he was using; he was coordinating them somehow. But whatever magic he was employing wasn't a standard tracking spell. I would have known that the instant he activated it. If he needed eyes on me, then whatever he was doing wasn't something he had much control over, or trust in. Well. First I'd lose my followers, and then I'd see what I could do to defeat Kluge's unknown spell.

The Rookery proper slowly rose up around me, complete with rubbish, vermin, and glassy-eyed toughs lounging in front of doors you never wanted to go in. They wanted to know what was in my pack. And my pockets. And possibly what I'd had for lunch. They'd be happy, most of them, to cut everything open to find out.

Five bravos stood up and started sauntering towards me. Just like that, they had me surrounded on the narrow street. I tapped my well and summoned a brightblade, willing it to lengthen to the size of a cavalry sword.

"Good evening, gentlemen," I said, smiling. "Nice night for a stroll."

Two of them took the hint, as Amra would have said. Three were either too stupid to, or too afraid to look afraid in front of their peers.

"Wotcher got inna pack?" the one directly in front of me asked, fiddling with what was obviously a throwing knife.

"The head of a monster," I replied, truthfully if not exhaustively. Why was I always bringing severed heads into the Rookery?

"Lemme see it." His two friends were positioning themselves to be out of my direct line of sight. I stepped to the side to keep them in view, mentally cursing my reduced vision.

"I'll count to three," I said. "If you're not all back sitting on your stoops before I finish, I'll kill all of you. One."

The one furthest left suddenly broke off and started walking away.

"Two."

The thug in front of me raised his knife to throw at my face, while the second charged in, knife low and ready to go for my gut.

I disincorporated the one in front of me, and swung the brightblade around in a low arc at the same time, sweeping my right flank and lopping off the remaining man's knife hand. The Brightblade made sizzling, crackling sounds as the robber's blood met it, and evaporated.

"Three."

The man fell to the filthy cobbles and started screaming. Rather than let him bleed out, I put the brightblade through his heart.

"Anyone else?" I asked the street in general, silent in the wake of the man's screams.

No one else.

I walked on, brightblade in hand, and was not bothered again. I realized, and not for the first time, that I wasn't a very nice person. I could have disabled my accosters. It hadn't been necessary to kill them. I came to the realization that I could have done what I had done the last time I'd found myself in the Rookery, and simply blown them all off their feet, sent them tumbling down the filthy street like the human debris they were.

I hadn't even considered it this time. It hadn't even occurred to me to use less than lethal force until well after the fact and I wondered, with a vaguely uneasy sort of curiosity, what was different this time around. When the answer came, it was accompanied by a sharp pang.

The difference was Amra. There had been something about her, even then, that had made me not want to be quite such a ruthless bastard.

That was why, after we'd braced my shit-stain of a cousin and the jackals had gathered outside his door to wait for their chance at us, I'd just blown them off their feet and out of our way. I hadn't even killed the one who had attacked me inside the Cock's Spur, though I would have in almost any other circumstance. But Amra was there, watching, and I'd felt the weight of her gaze on me as I crouched over the man. I knew without a doubt she wouldn't be clapping if I dispatched a helpless foe. So he had lived.

When Gavon had asked me why I didn't kill the wretch, he'd been genuinely surprised. He knew me as only family could. Which of course is why he'd made himself scarce afterward. He knew I'd come for him, and I had. I was intent on killing him for what he had done decades earlier. I am not a nice person, but compared to Guache, I am a paragon of virtue.

Michael McClung

He'd disappeared without a trace. Guache Gavon was a dark parody of a human, with a soul as twisted as a corkscrew. But he wasn't in the least stupid.

~ ~ ~

I ruminated my way through the Rookery, walking more or less at random, but generally south and west, as much as the tangle of streets allowed. I gave Kluge sufficient time to set up a cordon of watchers around the loose boundaries of the Rookery. I wanted as many of them as possible waiting for me to re-emerge, or even better, to come in looking for me. If I was lucky, they'd waste the entire night on their fruitless search, and I'd be far, far away.

The River Ose is very big, and very long. One of the reasons it is so big and so long is that it has a damned lot of tributaries that feed it on its long, long journey from somewhere in the Silent Lands to the Bay of Lucernis. One of those tributaries ran right through the Rookery. Or rather it ran *under* it; the River Senna had been bricked and covered over nearly two centuries before, having become a polluted and vile breeding ground for disease. Now it was an all-but-forgotten storm drain.

The things you learn while researching ways not to spend your afterlife in eternal torment.

Case in point: I happened to know that there was a well somewhere in the Rookery whose shaft went down to the Senna, built after the river had had time to become wholesome again, but before the neighborhood had had time to fester. I even knew more or less where the well was, and once I started actively looking for it, it wasn't difficult to find. It was in the middle of a squalid little square, surrounded by tall, narrow half-timbered houses whose eaves rustled with rats or bats or gods-only-knew what vermin, and whose windows were black squares that still somehow managed to give the impression of malevolent eyes.

It turned out I *didn't* know that at some point someone had capped the well with a rough-carved stone that weighed a ton or more. I suppose it had become too convenient a place to dispose of corpses.

I was reluctant to remove the stone using the Art for a few reasons. First, because I wanted to conserve as much of my power as possible. Reopening the hell gate wasn't going to be child's play. Second, once I removed it, it would be impossible to put it back, since I'd have to smash it to gravel. I might as well paint an arrow on the street for Kluge to follow. Finally, I was more than a little worried that Kluge was somehow tracking not *me*, but my use of the Art. It was possible to do so, and there weren't all that many mages running around Lucernis. If I gave Kluge the end of a piece of string, he was perfectly capable of pulling on it.

So I cast around looking for some other way to get at the underground Senna. If it had been re-purposed as a storm drain, then there had to be some way for the runoff to enter.

I have an excellent memory, but not so excellent as to be able to recall with perfect clarity the Senna's course to the Ose. The maze that was the Rookery's streets didn't help. It took me almost an hour to find a grate that I could fit through, and even then, I had a bad time of it. Being stuck in a narrow space that had obviously been used as a piss-hole for decades was incredibly frustrating More than once I was on the verge of using the Art to ease my passage, but I resisted the urge. I was already befouled. Giving my location away to Kluge would mean I'd gotten filthy for no reason. So I wriggled and squirmed, keeping tight hold of my patience and my pack, and after what seemed like centuries I finally squeezed my way past the obstruction that had given me such a hard time, and fell ten feet or more into the lightless, chill waters of the Senna.

The water was deep enough that I sustained no injuries, and wasn't so deep that I had to swim. All in all, not as bad as it might have been. But an underground river doesn't provide much in the way of light, so I pulled out the old, withered glory hand from my pack and hung it around my neck from the chain that pierced the remains of the wrist. The corpselight was enough to keep me oriented, though the stench of whatever had been used to embalm it was enough to make me dizzy. The uneven riverbed threatened to trip me or turn my ankle, and so I felt my way slowly and carefully downstream, shivering and feeling out each step.

It was no scented bath, the Senna, but the Ose was infinitely worse, and people actually ate things that were caught in the Ose. Other people, that is. Not me. The charnel grounds were beside the Ose, after all, and the ground sloped down towards the river. I knew what was going into the Ose every time it rained, and it was considerably more off-putting than sewage.

Soon enough *I* went into the Ose, and swam for the nearest set of moss-slick steps built into the retaining wall. I got out of the water, packed away the hand, and climbed back up into the city, not all that far from Brass Eye Bridge.

There were no watchers that I could see.

My next stop, the last before I went to reopen the hell gate if all went well, was to see Fengal Daruvner.

TWENTY-THREE

Magesight is passive magic; it pulls nothing from the mage's well, simply the mage's vitality. It is just there, and you can choose to see with it or not, just as you can choose to open your eyes or not.

In consequence, I considered the risk of Kluge being able to track my use of magesight to be vanishingly small, whereas the advantage of being able to spot any watchers he set in my path was pronounced. So, dripping and reeking of the Ose, I hailed another hack, then overcame his reluctance to convey me anywhere by paying triple what a reasonable fare might come to.

I had him drop me off two blocks away from Third Wall Road, and then made my way through back alleys that smelled of old grease, urine and fish guts until I came to the back door of Daruvner's establishment.

His nameless eatery was a large affair with high ceilings, though shabby and in a poor state of repair. I doubt he made much profit, considering the pittance he priced his food at and the dauntingly large portions he served out. Third Wall was a working-class neighborhood, and having somewhere to eat that would actually fill you up after a long day's toil without biting too deeply into your pocket had earned him a certain amount of good will. Daruvner's cooks would win no awards, however.

I walked into the kitchen as if it were something I did every day. The three cooks were too busy to give me a second glance. I stepped through quickly into the noisy, crowded dining area, dodging one sweating server, and spotted Daruvner immediately. He was seated at his usual table near the back, bald head gleaming in the lantern light, face flushed with drink. Some things never change, thank the dead gods.

He was having a low conversation with Kettle, his portly runner. Daruvner was speaking and the young man was nodding. None of his nieces seemed to be about, for once. Daruvner glanced up and saw me, and his eyebrows shot up.

"Holgren! I've seen you looking better," he said, taking in my bedraggled clothing and missing eye.

"And hopefully you will again," I replied, taking a seat at his table. Kettle nodded to me and withdrew.

"Wine?"

"I thank you."

He poured, and we both drank. Fengal served bad food and decent wine. It was good to get the Ose off my tongue.

"Not an hour ago," Daruvner said while scratching his ample belly, "I got paid a visit by the recently appointed Commander of the Watch."

"And how was dear old Kluge?"

"Very keen to find out *your* whereabouts, actually. Keen enough to show me a handful of carrots in one hand, and an iron rod in the other."

"I apologize for any inconvenience I might have caused you, Fengal. It was wholly unintentional."

He waved it away. "Part and parcel of the business. Kluge wouldn't be the first to try and get his thumb on me, and he won't be the last. But he did make me curious. Just what have you been up to, to make him so passionate about finding you?"

"I was offered a position he very much wanted. He believes I am utterly unsuitable for it. I happen to agree with him, but not so much so that I'll stick my head in the noose he's braiding for me."

"Do I want to know what this position is?"

"It would embarrass me to tell you."

"Well enough." He swirled the wine in his glass, obviously deciding to broach the subject that had so far not been even hinted at.

"So how is Amra these days? I heard that she went to Bellarius. Then all we've been hearing about Bellarius is how it's been eating its own guts."

I would have liked to tell Fengal everything that had transpired. He had a soft spot for Amra. With me he was cordial; with her he was protective. I decided to tell him the truth, while leaving out the facts that would only beget even more questions.

"Amra was lured to Bellarius. I think she was supposed to die there. She didn't, but she *has* disappeared. I'm trying to find her and bring her back."

"Who—no. You would tell me who would do such a thing if you thought it safe or useful for me to know." He drank down the last of his wine and set the glass on the table. He looked at me and smiled. "Tell me, Holgren, what can I do for you then, this fine evening?"

He said it lightly, but when Fengal Daruvner offered assistance, it meant he was willing to commit his considerable resources to whatever task lay at hand.

"I'll be leaving town tonight. It may be a long time before I return. If I return. I've got people I need to take care of; two retainers and a— protégé, I suppose is the best term. Thanks to Kluge, I can't get them sorted before I depart."

He raised an eyebrow. "That's all?"

I shrugged. "Should there be more?"

"No, no. Don't misunderstand me, please. But please also take no offense if I'm a little surprised."

"It would be rather churlish of me to be offended by what I don't understand."

He laughed and shook his head. "It's not important, magus. But I approve of the effect Amra's had on your character."

"Are you saying I wouldn't have seen to my people before I met Amra?"

"No, I'm saying you wouldn't have had people to see to. Now tell me, how would you like me to sort your people?"

I told him, and he seemed rather disappointed that it would be so easy a thing. Then I told him there was one other thing he could help me with, and what it was, and he didn't like it much at all.

"You might as well slit your wrists now and be done with it," he told me. His frown was impressive.

"I'll only be using it if I have to, believe me," I replied. "But if I need it and don't have it, I'm dead anyway, and Amra along with me."

"I can only take your word. I'll send Kettle to get it. I certainly don't keep any of the stuff."

"I didn't think you did. But I'm not at liberty to go searching for it. Thank you, Fengal."

"For this, I reject your thanks."

~ ~ ~

While waiting for Kettle to return I begged paper and pen from Fengal and write a short note to Keel, Marle and Chalk explaining, what was happening and what I wished them to do in my absence. I hoped that either Marle of Chalk was marginally literate.

A half hour later I stepped out into the street and then directly into the hack that Kettle had anticipated my need for. I twitched closed the dusty, sun-faded curtains on the small windows and settled into the cracked leather upholstery, pack on my knees. For most of the next hour I could relax, as much as possible in the jouncing, swaying carriage.

I was finally on my way to reopen Bosch's hell gate.

THE THIEF WHO WASN'T THERE

TWENTY-FOUR

Once we'd made it a fair distance out on the Jacos Road, man-made light was virtually nonexistent, and the hack's interior became oppressively inky. I opened the curtain. The sky was clear and the stars shone down in beautiful profusion, while the moon rose over the Dragonsea, turning its waters, whenever we hit a rise and I could see them through the scrub, to quicksilver. Yes, I'd missed Lucernis, and I was about to miss it far, far more. Even Bellarius was a paradise compared to where I was going next.

The narrow, sliding window that allowed communication between driver and passenger shot open. "Someone's coming up behind us, sir. Quick-like."

I stuck my head out the side window, and saw another carriage behind us, perhaps a quarter mile away, visible only because of the swaying lanterns it sported.

"Can you outrun them?" I asked the driver.

"No chance."

I dug out a handful of marks and thrust my hand through the gap. "How about now?"

The marks disappeared off my palm as if by magic. "Still doubtful, I have to admit."

"Do your best," I replied, and the coachman applied the whip. We speed up considerably, and I found myself being battered about in the narrow confines of the hack.

I knew it had to be Kluge, and I knew it was unlikely in the extreme that we would outrun him. If he was using the same carriage he had that morning, his team of four were likely fresher and certainly better horse flesh than the rented hack's pair, who had been plying the streets all day.

Which meant that I would have to hurl myself from the hack when we made a turn that took us out of Kluge's line of sight. I communicated this to the driver, with the further instruction that he keep on as fast as he could until overtaken and ordered to stop.

"You're a mad bugger, but your gold's good," the man replied over the thud of horse hooves and the rattling of the hack.

"Can you get the door closed again? I don't want to give the game away."

"I'll manage. Best prepare yourself, best turn you're likely to get's coming up quick-like."

I got firm grip on the pack with one hand and put the other on the handle. I steeled myself for the impact. The fall I wasn't worried about.

The carriage slowed nominally, though it still went into the turn at a rate of speed that was daunting. "Now!" the driver shouted, and I hurled myself into the night, trying to curl myself around the pack. There were things inside that would react very, very badly to being broken.

I landed in a ditch with such force that I lost my breath. Then I kept going, my body getting brutalized along the way by unknowable but decidedly hard and often sharp objects. Nature seems to be full of such things.

I finally fetched up against the trunk of a tree, which did brutal things to my back. Everything hurt. My hair hurt. I lay still and fought for breath. When air finally began to ease back into my lungs, I spat out dirt and debris, opened my eye and saw that I'd bounced down a little leaf-choked ravine. I was definitely out of the line of sight of the road, which was provident. Nothing about my flight felt provident, though.

I lay still until I heard Kluge's coach pass, and saw its lantern light fade as it raced down the road. Then I began to think about getting into a vertical position. With a shaking hand, I pulled myself up the tree that had ended my flight. Nothing seemed broken, though there were definitely rips in both my clothing and the skin beneath.

"Get moving," I muttered to my legs. They didn't seem to want to. I let go of the tree and staggered on anyway. My time was limited. Kluge would discover my ruse soon enough, and be back on my trail. He seemed to be depressingly competent when it came to finding me. I needed to get to the hell gate and get it open before he got to me. If I couldn't, then I was very much afraid I was going to have to kill the commander of the city watch of Lucernis.

That might well give me a sense of satisfaction, considering the trouble Kluge had put me to, but the costs far outweighed the benefits.

I climbed back up to the Jacos and began a stumbling jog towards the cliffs. If Kluge turned around and came back this way, I would be able to hear him in good time and dive back into the brushwood beside the road. I wasn't terribly sure how far I still had to go, but at least I was in no danger of passing my destination by mistake. Beside the fact that there was only one stretch of cliffs along the Jacos, hell gates—even closed hell gates— gave off a stench of magic that was difficult to ignore.

Of course, Kluge was no fool. There was nothing else on the Jacos Road to interest a mage. It wouldn't take much for him to put one and one together and decide my destination.

With a groan, I turned my shuffling jog into a shambling lope.

~ ~ ~

Of course Kluge was waiting at the remains of the villa. Of course he was. He was just that much of a pain. I saw him pacing the ground in the strong moonlight, occasionally stooping to pick up a stone and toss it toward the cliff. His carriage was nowhere to be seen. I stopped at the twisted wreckage of the gate and gave myself time to get my breath back and think of some further plan that didn't involve killing him.

"No need to hide, Holgren," he shouted. "I heard you gasping and wheezing your way up the hill quite some time ago."

"Liar. You can't even hear your own breathing over the surf."

"All right, that was a lie. But you *are* sadly out of shape."

"You try taking a moonlight jog after throwing yourself from a moving carriage," I muttered, and walked towards him.

"I have to admit," I said over the pounding of the waves on the cliffs below, "I am impressed you were able to continue to track me despite my best efforts to throw you off the scent."

"Why? Because I am a mage of lesser abilities? It's simply taught me to use every resource at my disposal. Magic should be a tool, not a crutch."

"I happen to agree with that sentiment," I said, knowing then that he had set some sort of trap for me. He knew I could obliterate him if it came down to a duel using the Art. I wondered what form the trap would take. Bowmen in the brush?

I stopped advancing when we were perhaps ten feet apart. Close enough to speak without having to raise our voices. The hell gate was twenty feet behind him, a patch of seared earth where nothing would ever grow again.

Kluge looked me in the eye, the muscles of his jaw working, working. Finally, he shook his head. "I have never held you in high regard, but I never believed you were a daemonist."

"I'm no demon lover, Kluge."

"Then why are we here, Angrado? For old time's sake?"

"I'll tell you, but you won't believe me."

"Let's hear it, then, before I arrest you."

"Neither of us have time for the full explanation, so I'll abbreviate. I'm going to steal Lagna's notebook from the Black Library. Behind you is my entry point into the eleven hells, since I have no intention of opening a new gate, as I am not a daemonist, or the sort who is amenable to ritual sacrifice."

"You do realize that the crown doesn't recognize insanity as a defense in Lucernia, don't you?"

"Defense against what? What crime have I committed?"

"You just admitted to me that you're going to open a hell gate."

"No. I admitted I'm going to *re*open a hell gate. Not the same thing at all."

"A distinction that all the infernal creatures who crawl out of it will respect, I'm sure."

"Actually, that's the best part. The hells are empty. Or at least Gholdoryth is, and that's where this hell gate leads. So no worries on that score, commander." I gave him a wide smile.

"You're—" Kluge didn't get to finish his thought, because I punched him in the jaw and he went down like a bag of wet sand.

"Yes, Avrom, I am," I muttered, waiting for an arrow in the back. Which never came.

He had really come after me and faced me alone. Very brave, and very stupid.

I tore a page from Gammond's book and scrambled all his senses, in case he regained consciousness before I'd reopened the gate and departed. I made sure it would dissipate as soon as I left the mortal plane. Then I left him a note in floating silver letters:

> *Please close the gate after me. Wouldn't want anybody falling in by accident.*

And then I started picking apart all the threads I'd woven together to seal the damned hell gate almost two years before. It wasn't long before I was cursing myself for being so meticulously thorough. When that was finally done, I started the weary work of breaking to rubble all the dauntingly large stones Kluge had had transported here to fill it in. Though I used the Art rather than muscle power, I was still covered in sweat before I was done.

By the time I'd finished, Kluge was stirring.

"I'll be off now, Avrom. Sorry about the assault and battery. Or is it just battery if you punch someone without warning? I've never been clear on those particular legal concepts."

In response he lashed out with a curse and a brightwhip. His Art-fueled weapon dug an impressive furrow in the earth. Thankfully nowhere near me.

"I'll see you hanged, Holgren Angrado. I swear it."

"All right, then. I suppose asking you to wish me luck would be pointless. Fare well, Avrom. Truly."

And then I secured my pack and turned to face the yard-wide black hole at my feet.

And jumped.

Michael McClung

AMRA: INTERLUDE TWO

Kerf's balls, but eternity was boring. Getting stolidly, ragingly drunk killed some small fraction of time. But I had all of time staring me in the face; or at least all the rest of my life. Stuck in one room. With an inhuman mass murderer for company.

"That's your choice," Kalara said. "Choose again. Choose differently."

"Shut up."

I finally understood what it was that had driven Rui Qi to end it all in Thagoth. Sometimes death really was the best alternative. I had been naive, then. Me, naive. Imagine that. After the life I'd led, I would never have thought it was possible.

"And that's just the hangover talking," Kalara observed. She'd taken up position in a corner, legs crossed tailor-fashion, leaning back on thin arms. Utterly at ease.

"Why are you starting to sound like me?"

"I'm in your head as well as your soul. I'm just taking in the local color, so to speak." She gave a negligent half-shrug.

"Well stop it. It's fucking annoying."

"You and I both know you can't spend the rest of your life in this situation, Amra. You *will* go mad. And when you do, it will be child's play for me to influence you into doing what I want."

"What good would I do to you mad? If a mad bugger was good enough for whatever your plans are, you already had the Telemarch."

She smiled. "You speak as if the mad can never be made sane again."

"Can they? I've never seen anyone come back from being cracked."

"You've seen much. But not nearly so much as I have."

I frowned. The thought was unsettling. *Could* she just wait for me to lose my mind, get me to return to the world, and put a poultice on my sanity?

"I don't think so," I finally said.

"And why is that?"

"Because if me coming unstuck was your best option, you wouldn't talk about it. You'd just let it happen."

"You're absolutely right. It isn't my best option; *that* would be you listening to me and leaving this self-made prison right now. But believe me when I tell you it *is* an option."

"Why should I believe you? About that, or anything?"

She—it—laughed. I waited for that high, child's laughter to fade away.

"Answer my question, Kerf damn you."

"You should believe me, Amra Thetys, because it is impossible for a goddess to lie to her avatar, or her avatar to her. Didn't you know that? This age has lost so much in the way of knowledge."

I felt a sour sickness rise up from my roiling stomach, and it had nothing to do with all the wine.

"I am *not* your avatar. I never agreed to any such thing."

"I am *not* soaked through," she said mockingly, in a voice identical to mine. "I never agreed to let the rain fall on me." She smiled a small, cold smile, and her voice reverted to a child's. "And yet."

"Go to hells."

Her expression sobered. She looked at me levelly. "It may well come to that, Amra Thetys, though I rather doubt the eleven will exist for much longer. Not in any form you would recognize, at least. But keep in mind, if I *did* go there, it would be inside *your* soul."

I stopped talking to her—to it—then, and started drinking again.

Holgren entered my thoughts, naturally enough, and I pushed the thought of him away almost immediately. Firstly, because I wasn't ever going to see him again, and that wasn't something I was going to dwell on if I could help it. Second, because if there was a weak spot in my resolve, its name was Holgren Angrado. And third, because having Chuckles as a voyeur to my private thoughts and emotions made those thoughts and emotions feel slime-coated.

So I drank, and did not think about Holgren.

Eventually I passed out in that big stone chair.

PART III: HELLS

TWENTY-FIVE

I'd opened and stepped through a gate between Lucernis and Thagoth once. Twice, actually; once there and once back. Gating between locations on the face of the world was an experience best described as traumatic, but exceedingly brief.

Going between the mortal realm and Gholdoryth was much, much worse, and lasted for a subjective eternity. I felt as if both my soul and my mind were being flayed a strip at a time. Despair and madness were the most positive reactions I could muster, and whatever else was happening to me, in whatever state of existence or transition the hell gate had transmuted me to for the journey, I could feel a raw pain in my throat, engendered by my endless scream. My eye was open, but I could see nothing but a shade of red that somehow *ate* its way into my eye.

And then I landed. Hard.

The first thing to assault me was the cold. You've heard the phrase 'bone-chilling'. In Gholdoryth, it was not hyperbole. I slowly levered myself to my feet, face already numbing in the brutally chill air. I took a brief look at my surroundings; a gray stone temple-like structure, roughly oval, with stereotypical carvings of the torments damned souls could expect adorning the walls. Walls that went up and up, and never found a ceiling. Wan red light came from somewhere high above. It pulsed erratically.

The second thing to assault me was a daemonette.

One of the disgusting crosses between crab and spider that had infested the villa Bosch had turned into a hell gate, it was roughly the size of a cat. It scuttled towards me sidewise on the gray flagstones. Its two rear legs seemed paralyzed. It wasn't nearly as quick as the others had been. I summoned a brightblade to dispatch it as it approached.

No brightblade appeared, though the light from above flared briefly.

"Oh, hells," I said, and then I dodged the strand of mucus the daemonette shot at my face. The stuff was incredibly sticky, in addition to being both paralytic and acidic when it came in contact with exposed flesh.

I could sense my well, but I couldn't seem to summon any power from it. I had no idea why. Or rather I had several ideas, none of them pleasant, and so refused to believe any of them.

I started backing away from the daemonette as quickly as I could, and it followed, pincers clacking, throwing off blue-white sparks every time. I glanced around, but could find no doors. So. I could run around in circles indefinitely, or I could dispatch the fiend. Without magic. Which meant my only weapon was Amra's knife.

In my favor was the fact that the creature was small, slow, and stupid.

So be it.

I put my pack in front of me, and stopped retreating. It reacted by shooting another strand at my face. I blocked it with the pack, felt it tug, surprisingly forcefully considering the thing's size. Like a fisherman, I kept it on the line, slowly letting the distance between us lessen. And then, when I was one long step away from it, I twisted the pack to the side and stomped on its carapace with all the force I could muster.

Guts shot out in all directions, immediately filling the air with a stench that nearly had me vomiting. Six of the eight legs twitched and scrabbled violently, and then were suddenly still. And then the thing began to be absorbed by the floor.

When they say the eleven hells are always hungry, it isn't a metaphor.

"Well that warmed me up," I muttered, my breath pluming. But I was in serious trouble. If I had no access to my well, I was done before I'd even started, and the trinkets I'd brought along, even if they still worked, wouldn't change that. The cold would kill me much sooner rather than later, making worrying about food and water a moot point. And it appeared I was trapped in any case.

I summoned my magesight. It worked perfectly well. Too well, actually; it recognized everything of my surroundings as magical. The illumination was near-blinding. But I did notice the outline of a huge set of double doors in the wall opposite, and after some exploring with quickly freezing finger tips and my mundane sight, I managed to find the latch to one of the doors, concealed in the frieze that adorned every inch of wall. It was in an unpleasant part of one damned soul's anatomy.

I was hoping that, once I left the chamber, access to my well would return. I thought it at least possible that the hell gate simply absorbed any energy it could in order to maintain itself, knowing what I did about the nature of the eleven hells. I just hoped the same wasn't true everywhere else.

Outside was going to be brutally cold. If I was wrong about being able to access my well, I was going to freeze to death in minutes, rather than the hours it would take me inside the chamber. And if my memories of the afterlife were incorrect, I might well not even get the chance to freeze to death before being torn apart and devoured by demons.

I took a deep breath, sending cold down into my lungs so sharp it cut like knives. I undid the latch, and put all my weight into forcing the giant door open.

It was much, much colder than I had imagined. I felt my lungs seize up. I literally could not draw breath. The cold was such an absolute thing that my mind went into a sort of shock with it, unable to tell my muscles what to do. I fell to the hoarfrosted ground outside the gate house, convulsing in the cold. I was quickly losing even the ability to think. Mortal flesh was never meant for this demesne.

Something. Something I needed to do. Amra's face flitted across my mind's eye. She was frowning, the scar that bisected her eyebrow and continued down her cheek making her look even more fierce.

There was something I needed to do.

My well.

I reached for it, and it was there. With crumbling reason, I constructed a simple, nearly impossible spell, forcing my failing imagination to envision the change I needed.

Not enough. Not clear enough. I did not believe it. I could not feel it. I dredged up a memory from the black ice of my mind. It didn't want to come. I forced it to.

The Hot Wells, on the border between Imria and Lucernia. A setting sun.

More specific, damn you.

The stench of horse sweat. The water bubbling up from the earth there, a little acrid. I remembered lowering myself into the rock-lined pool that unknown hands had constructed, skin at first shrieking in protest at the heat, then slowly coming to an accommodation with it.

And as I remembered the Hot Wells, I pulled magic from my own well to recreate its effect on my body.

The hoarfrost around me evaporated, and I lay on the black, cracked, frozen ground that was now exposed. I took a slow breath. Still bitterly cold, that air, but I could survive it. Slowly, shakily, I levered myself to my feet and slung my pack across my back, sweating in a place far colder than any mortal could survive without assistance. I looked around. Behind me, the bulk of the gate house, a gray tube rising up, up, so far that the eye could never follow. Around me, a featureless expanse of white. And above me, a dark sky from which hundreds, perhaps thousands of stars fell every minute, each in reality a damned soul.

I was back. I refrained from rejoicing.

I pulled the Glory Hand from my pack, hoping it hadn't lost its efficacy by being soaked in the Senna and the Ose. I'd brought it along not for its illuminating property, but for the reason they were coveted by thieves everywhere: It could point the way to that which was to be stolen. If only I'd needed to steal Amra instead of rescuing her, I might have avoided having to capture Halfmoon.

I slipped the chain around my neck and held it by its withered wrist.

"Well, smelly, which way do I need to go to get to the Black Library?"

Ring, middle and little finger curled inward towards the palm, leaving the bony forefinger rigid. Slowly it pointed itself down at the ground.

"Very funny. Not being able to burrow my way through two hells, I'll need an alternate route. Preferably via the Spike."

Slowly the forefinger lifted itself back to a level position, and then began twitching towards the left. I turned slowly in that direction until the twitching stopped and the finger went rigid.

"Excellent. If I survive I'll see about getting you a manicure." I took the unpleasant thing off and dropped it in a coat pocket. Then I started walking in the direction it had indicated.

I noticed, after a few minutes, that all the souls streaking across the sky seemed to be falling in that direction as well.

TWENTY-SIX

Imagine a dozen plates, less one, stacked one atop the other. They vary greatly in size and shape: Some are thin, delicate, small; hardly more than saucers, while others are great lumpy things, serving platters made for giants by a blind, drunk potter. Left this way, the stack would like as not fall.

Now imagine that someone had managed to drive a skewer through the center of the stack, somehow spearing each plate without shattering any.

This, in crude strokes, is the geography of the eleven hells. Each of them is a distinct reality, separate from all the others, and they are held together by the metaphysical force most commonly referred to as the Spike.

The Spike was the only direct means of communication between the various hells that I knew of. I would have to make my way across Gholdoryth to the Spike, then travel down it past Khs to Thraxys.

I wasn't all that clear about just how I was going to do that. While I knew a fair amount about the individual hells, the Spike was something of a mystery. I knew that the demons used it as a highway in their eternal wars against each other. I knew that more than one god had traveled the Spike, for reasons various and generally frustrated. But I did not know much more than that.

I'd died in Thagoth, and my soul had gone to Gholdoryth. I remembered the incredible cold, and I remembered a vast emptiness. Well, not emptiness, exactly. I have the distinct impression that I was one among a countless multitude that was all around me, and at the same time invisible.

I had a very vague memory of endless falling stars, which seemed not to have changed in the intervening months, and the general impression that they were damned souls descending. That impression also had not changed.

And I remember one other thing, if 'remember' is the correct term. I know that I have been somehow blocked from recalling in any meaningful fashion or even trying to speak of it. Who blocked it and why remained a mystery. The most I can say, or even remember clearly, is 'something happened'. A memory of a memory.

Unfortunately, I had no memory whatever of the Spike.

As I walked through one hell on my way to another, I quickly realized being here as a damned soul had not been much of a preparation for being here in living flesh, if for no other reason than when you're already dead and damned, you don't bother much with keeping an eye out for things that can kill you.

Gholdoryth was deceptively featureless. Hoarfrost, that delicate tracery of needle-like ice crystals, coated the ground to a depth of inches, both like and unlike snow, making the ground appear unendingly flat. In truth the ground undulated, sporting little rises and hollows that were invisible until you came upon them. The hoarfrost also concealed fissures in the ground, big enough to turn an ankle in, or even break an ankle in, if your luck was completely out.

A walking stick would have been useful. Not having brought one, I was forced to slow my pace considerably. I cursed the fact and the delay, until I almost died. Would have died, if my pace had been even a little quicker.

I put my foot down on what looked to be just another patch of white, indistinguishable from the rest of the endless world of the stuff. My foot broke through the frost, and met no resistance below it. Instinctively I pulled myself back, stomach lurching as my balance teetered between going forward and going back. The hole I'd made in the frost grew, slowly at first, then faster.

There was nothing below it but black void.

Faster and faster the hoarfrost covering the pit lost cohesion, and uncountable needles of ice fell with the softest whisper, revealing a bottomless pit that had to be a quarter of a mile across.

I did not stare into the void. I was afraid something might stare back. I turned away and called up a brightblade, making it long and thin and good for poking at the ground in front of me.

I hadn't done so before because I wanted to conserve as much power as I could, and just keeping myself from freezing was taxing enough. After seeing the pit, though, I didn't begrudge the extra effort.

~ ~ ~

I walked for hours over the landscape of the damned, stopping occasionally to consult the glory hand. It always agreed with the soulfall in the sky, and I never had to correct my course.

There was no sun, no moon, no stars other than the rain of souls overhead, and so no way to infer time. But soon enough I found myself thirsty, and soon enough after that hunger made its appearance. So I stopped, opened my pack, and took out what I had brought by way of provender.

It wasn't much.

There had been no point in bringing along actual food. One of the things all the eleven hells held in common, a theme as it were, was corruption in all its forms. Moral, spiritual. Physical. As much as I might have liked a bundt cake or a roasted bird, it would have been pointless to pack them. Once-living things were especially susceptible. Within minutes of arriving, any provisions I'd brought along would have been reduced to a rotting, decayed soup. In Gholdoryth, a *frozen*, rotting, decayed soup. If I'd somehow been able to gag something down, it likely would have poisoned me.

So instead I had a little vial filled with a reddish-white powder, procured by Fengal Daruvner over his objections. A drug, of course, from Far Thwyll. Lucernan slang named it 'the Road.' Horribly addictive and ultimately fatal. It made hellweed look positively medicinal. But the user felt no hunger or thirst, had boundless energy, and perhaps most importantly, clear thought. Right up until the moment he or she died of the stuff. And as it was a form of corruption itself, I thought it likely it would be immune to hellish decay.

I considered the vial for a while, and put it back in the pack. I wasn't hungry, thirsty or tired enough yet.

I'd never heard of anyone getting off the Road once they got on it. It was, apparently, a one-way thoroughfare.

With a sigh I slung the pack back over my shoulder, summoned the brightblade again, and began to follow the river of stars once more.

~ ~ ~

At first, I could make no sense of what I was seeing. I was tired, very tired, and my whole existence had become brightblade hissing against hoarfrost, step, and repeat ad nauseum. But slowly something began to intrude on my blurred consciousness; a vague thought that slowly crystallized into a realization.

Something was different.

I stopped and levered my gaze up off my feet, with an effort.

Ahead of me, perhaps a hundred yards, was what looked like a hill. Then my perception changed, and it looked like nothing so much as the carapace of an enormous beetle, blue-black and slightly shiny, and devoid of the frost that covered absolutely everything else.

It was unmoving.

I just stood there for a while, swaying slightly and staring stupidly, letting the novelty of it wash over me.

Then the unmoving beetle-hill moved.

It exploded upward, massive carapace splitting and revealing a beetly set of wings. Wings that battered the air with such force that the back draft knocked me flat.

The monster rose straight into the air, and suddenly stopped, despite the furious beat of its wings. I saw then that a massive chain pinned it to the ground. The lower end was lost to sight, but I could see that the upper end of the chain was fixed to a brutal, barbed spear the size of a ship's mast, and that spear had been driven into the thorax of the beast.

It turned and twisted wildly in the air, and then suddenly it was falling back to earth. I realized, after it was far too late to do anything about it, that its trajectory had me at its terminus. As it came down, the best reaction I could manage was to squint my eyes and throw an arm across my face.

It landed with the force of an earthquake, not a dozen feet from me, and it was all I could do to keep my feet. It opened disturbing catlike eyes in an otherwise nightmarishly insectile face, and each eye was larger than my whole head.

"You missed," I said, and it blinked at me.

Mage.

"Demon."

What do you in Gholdoryth, clothed in flesh?

"I'm taking a stroll. Why haven't you departed along with the rest of your ilk?"

My ilk hold grudges that span eons. I was left to face what comes.

"What comes?"

Ruin. Devastation. Unmaking. Oblivion.

"Are you sure that wouldn't be an improvement?"

Perhaps. Would you choose it?

"Probably not," I conceded. "Well, I would wish you good day if there was any chance of day here. Or good." I started to back away. I had no intention of turning my back on the thing.

Let us strike a bargain, mage.

"Did that once. It didn't work out. I've sworn off bargaining with ruinous powers."

I admit to desperation. You, clothed in flesh and possessing some measure of power, can free me. I am at your mercy. Tell me your desire. I will grant its fulfillment, and then you will break my chain.

"My desire? I have many. Chief among them at the moment is to get around you and continue on my way."

Free me. Or I will eat you.

I was done talking to the thing. There was no way I could break its chain, even if I wanted to. It knew it, and hoped I did not. Making a snack of me might well give it enough power to break the bond on its own, however.

"I'd tell you to go to hells, but..." and I shrugged, and turned away, and circumvented the demon, giving it a wide, wide berth.

It beat the air and the ground with its massive body, raging and thrashing and threatening all the while.

Eventually the sight and sound of it faded behind me, step by careful step.

TWENTY-SEVEN

The eleven hells are for the damned, those who have lived life in such a vile, corrupt fashion as to deserve the punishment that they obviously eluded in life.

That's what virtually everyone says because that is what everyone is taught.

It's a lie.

We put a sober, reasonable face on it, us mortals, but the fact is a certain portion of us go to hells not because it is the afterlife we have earned, exactly, but because of a bargain struck between the gods and demons millennia ago.

Even I don't truly understand the nature of the eleven hells, and I have spent considerable time studying them. Years, literally. But one thing, at least, became clear to me as I'd pieced together thousands of facts and legends and fragmented scraps of knowledge: without a steady stream of that immortal spark that is the mortal soul, all of the eleven hells would eventually wither and die. *We* are what makes their continued existence possible. It isn't just the demons and daemons and daemonettes that feed on souls. It is their entire realm. We are the cord wood that feeds their fires, and without us, all the eleven hells would sputter out and die.

So of course they battled the gods for control of the mortal realm.

Legend has it that the gods and demons only ceased their killing of each other when it was agreed that a portion of souls would be consigned to the hells, a tithe of the damned. The demons were happy enough to get what they needed without conflict, and the gods were happy enough to give the demons a portion of such an infinitely renewable resource in return for peace, especially since it cost them nothing.

Oh, they put a reasonable face on it. Judgment and all that. An incentive to do good while you live. And there are certainly enough evil fuckers dying at any given moment that deserve what they get. But it is a quota system, not a system of justice. If evil ceased to be a force in the world, if every man and woman turned their backs on all sin and truly lived a blameless life, they'd have to scrape the false concept of eternal judgment off the afterlife and label it what it truly is—sacrifice. A tithe to keep the peace between the upper realms and the lower.

To demons, we are food. To the gods, trade goods. Something to barter away when it profits them. Demons are without a doubt malicious, monstrous and evil, but it is worth bearing in mind that they devour souls because they have no choice in the matter. The gods, on the other hand, let them do it because it is, or was, convenient for them to allow it.

I believe in the gods, certainly, living and dead. But I'd be damned if I worshiped any of them.

By the time I arrived at the Spike, however, I was wishing there was some higher power that I could call on. Half a dozen times I'd stopped and taken out the little bottle of slow death that would allow me to keep going without the distress of thirst, hunger or exhaustion. Half a dozen times I put it back in the pack, unopened, and pushed myself forward through the unending hoarfrost.

Then came the point where I stumbled and fell, and wasn't even aware that I'd done so until I let go the spell that kept me from freezing to death. Suddenly, brutally, unignorably, I started to die. Terror and agony slapped me back to consciousness, and I recalled the spell in a panic. Then I levered my face up off the ground, my heart in my throat and my breath coming out in quick, animal pants. Slowly I made it to a sitting position.

If I couldn't stay awake, I was going to die. And I could no longer count on staying awake from one step to the next.

With not a little regret, I reached out and dragged the pack towards me. I shoved a hand in, fingers questing blindly for the vial full of the Road. I was staring off into the distance, my eyes following the flight of all those damned souls, not really thinking anything like a rational thought.

About the same time I found the vial, I noticed something else.

In the distance there was a point where the shooting stars overhead simply vanished. And it wasn't all that far away.

I knew I was simply delaying the inevitable, but I let go the vial and withdrew my hand. With a groan I got myself upright and walking yet again.

~ ~ ~

It was impossible to tell time with any accuracy in that realm, but perhaps an hour passed before I got my first glimpse of the Spike rising from the unending plain. I'd been looking at it for some time before that without realizing it, so near-perfect was its clarity. For it *was* clear, clearer than any glass I'd ever seen, clearer than ice or crystal. It was as transparent a thing as is possible to imagine.

The souls of the fallen entered, and disappeared. That was definitely not the situation that obtained when I last had the misfortune to visit Gholdoryth.

With this new visual anomaly to focus on I found it easier to concentrate. The danger of collapsing, of giving in to my exhaustion retreated. Temporarily, at least. I quickened my pace as much as I dared, and in course of time, I was facing my dim reflection in the glassy structure.

I looked, as Amra might have said, like hammered dog shit.

I reached out one shaky hand to touch the Spike, and was repelled. By repelled I mean thrown back a dozen yards, which had the effect of bringing me fully to my senses, at least. Something like the Telemarch's wards was at play, here. It shouldn't have surprised me that the Spike was defended, otherwise communication between the various hells would have been much more common than my studies on the subject had indicated. I approached again more cautiously, and looked at it anew, this time with magesight.

It was so bright as to make my eyes water. Yes, even the missing one, which was about as unpleasant as it sounds. With difficulty, my sight adjusted. I saw power there, in such quantities as to dwarf the Telemarch's rift, and all of it flowing downward. I also saw wards, the likes of which made my own wards, and even the Telemarch's, look like the crude scribbles of not-especially-bright toddlers.

I tried for a long time to breach those wards, and learned the meaning of abject failure.

"Damn it all anyway," I muttered and, steeling myself as best I could for the inevitable agony, thrust my hand into the pocket that held the magical sink.

As soon as my fingers touched its smooth surface my well disappeared, my warmth fled, and I was dying once again. I tore the thing out of my pocket and slammed it against the impregnable surface of the Spike.

I'm not sure what I expected. Anything from nothing to the utter collapse of the Spike was theoretically possible. What transpired was this: The whole structure began to vibrate in such a way that it rang out one high, pure, deafening, unending note. The falling souls paused in the sky, and then began to meander, as if suddenly unsure of their destination. The surface of the Spike in contact with the amulet blackened and blistered, and that corruption began to spread outward from the point of contact. The amulet itself was not unaffected—the wards ate away at it as surely as it was eating at the wards. An indescribable agony enveloped the hand that held the sink, like nothing I'd ever felt or wish to feel again. I pushed against the wall of the spike with a strength born of desperation; the cold was killing me, surely and not slowly.

And suddenly, as the amulet sizzled away to nothing, the rotten portion of the wall that I'd caused collapsed inward and I fell through it, and I kept falling, endlessly and blind.

TWENTY-EIGHT

"Did you ever see a turtle on its back?"

Something that felt suspiciously like the toe of a boot nudged me in the ribs. An involuntary groan escaped my lips.

"Did you? Pathetic, absurd. Ridiculous, really. Stubby little legs waving in the air in a sort of slow, impotent panic. And yet, you can't just walk away and leave the miserable thing to its fate. Or at least I can't. Get up, you."

I cracked open my eye and saw a man standing over me. Black hair, dusky skin. He was wearing clothes that were centuries out of fashion, and stained with wine. Lots and lots of wine. Here was someone who rarely let the chance at a drink slip past him.

"Who are you?" I croaked.

"What, you don't recognize your god?"

"I worship no god."

"Lucky for you I don't much care for being worshiped, then."

I sat up and took in my surroundings. A huge circular room, pale white, made of some material unknown to me, with a vast hole in its floor, beyond which was only utter dark. A hole I was bare inches from. With a shudder I scrabbled away from the edge until the pack on my back met the wall.

"Right. Now that you're out of the way I can turn this thing back on. You'd be sucked right through otherwise. Might want to avert your eyes. Eye. Sorry."

"I haven't the least clue—" And then he snapped his fingers and all the light in existence, it seemed, was rushing down from above and through the hole below, a torrent, a waterfall, a mighty river whose roar was both felt and heard.

"Something else, isn't it?" I squinted up at him, and he was grinning, looking at the light. "Don't see that every day!"

"What is it?"

"Hells-bound souls, being released back to the Ur!"

"The Ur?"

"The beginning, fool!"

"The beginning of what?"

"The beginning of *everything*!" he shouted, grinning.

"If the beginning is at the bottom," I said a little groggily, "what's at the top?"

He turned back to me, his grin replaced by a frown.

"A beginning of another kind," he replied. He stuck a hand out. I took it, and he pulled me to my feet without the least strain. By the time I was fully upright, my fatigue, hunger, thirst and injuries had all disappeared.

"Who the hells *are* you?" I asked again.

"I told you already, your god. The god of fools and drunkards."

Vosto. He looked more or less how I might have expected him to. Perhaps a bit short for a god.

"Which one am I then? Fool or drunkard?"

"You snuck into Gholdoryth and broke into the Spike. Also, you came without so much as a drop of the good stuff. Which one do you *think* you are?"

I had no answer to that, beyond the obvious.

He pointed to my left. I followed his finger and saw the bottom steps of a very narrow set of stairs that circled up and up the interior of the Spike, the furthest reaches of which were lost to sight.

"Now piss off and don't do any more damage to the Spike. And remember you owe me now. Fool." Then he disappeared.

And that is how Vosto, god of fools and drunkards, saved my life and put me in his debt.

Sometimes I wish he'd let me go back to the Ur instead.

~ ~ ~

It was a long climb. It gave me time to think. I had been given much to think about.

If all the damned souls were being diverted from the eleven hells, then the demons really were gone. They had to be. Without souls, they and their realms would surely die. A point in my favor, certainly; It seemed even more likely that Thraxys would be uninhabited, and somewhat less likely to be the death of me. Thraxys would be far harder to survive than Gholdoryth, demons or no.

It also appeared that the gods, or at least Vosto, were taking an interest. Whether it was to give those damned souls another chance, or just to see the infernal regions destroyed, or both—I couldn't say.

Such thoughts occupied my mind, until the endless climb began to wear me out, and most of my focus was on the pain in my thighs. Luckily, I'd had some practice with endlessly winding stairs beneath the Citadel, else my legs might have fallen off before I reached a simple wooden door with a little placard tacked to it that read:

THRAXYS, FOOL.

Gods know things, no denying it.

With a sigh I sat down carefully on the stairs and took a rest. When I felt vaguely less unready, I stood up, took a breath, put my hand on the knob, summoned my well. And opened the door.

It was night, and sultry with it. It was always a sultry night, in Thraxys.

The door opened onto a small courtyard, its flagstones buckled and broken. A low, vine-choked wall enclosed the courtyard, save for a small, battered, wrought-iron gate directly ahead. Beyond, darkness and the vague suggestion of an orchard of some sort. There was a smell in the air, something sweet. Too sweet. Like overripe fruit.

I stepped into the courtyard and the door closed of its own accord. I looked back. The door had disappeared. Vosto preferred I didn't reenter the Spike, obviously.

The Spike itself had the external appearance of a weathered tower in Thraxys. I imagined it appeared in a different guise in each of the hells. I extended my gaze further upward, to the sky. There a huge moon hung, ten times the size I was accustomed to seeing. A portion of a moon, rather. Someone or something had ripped a chunk out of it. The rest showed some disturbingly deep cracks.

There were no stars other than the falling souls, and not nearly so many of them as had shot across Gholdoryth. Thraxys was one of the smallest hells, but home to some of the most powerful and subtle of all the demon lords.

It was far, far more dangerous than inert Gholdoryth, because unlike Gholdoryth, the realm itself was, in some fashion, self-aware. Or at least portions of it were. I knew I would have to deal with at least one of those regions, and likely two. I hoped no more than that.

Thraxys was where all the old folk-tales your grandmother told you turned gangrenous. Where Gholdoryth was desolation, Thraxys was perversion. Where Gholdoryth was brute elemental force, Thraxys was subtlety. A god had been tricked into coming to Thraxys, after all, and had lost his head as a result. I hoped I would fare better.

I took out the withered glory hand once more.

"Which way, then?" I asked it, and it pointed out through the gate.

"I hope you're not trying to be funny," I muttered, and stuffed it back into my pocket. But I knew the geography of Thraxys tolerably well. If I could find higher ground, I was certain I could orient myself towards the Black Library. I might well be able to see the Black Library, depending on where I had come out of the Spike. Thraxys really was quite small.

I set off, ready to pull power from my well at any moment, but reluctant to call up my magesight after nearly being blinded in Gholdoryth.

~ ~ ~

Beyond the courtyard was indeed an orchard. Its trees were twisted, spiky things; their fruit corrupt and fleshy, reddish-gray in the bright moonlight, vaguely fetal, wholly disturbing. I walked down the aisle between two long rows of the things, and the sickly-sweet odor was enough to bring on gagging. I buried my mouth and nose in the crook of my elbow and increased my pace.

Ahead of me, one of the heavy, melon-sized fruits fell from a low branch, hit the ground with an unpleasant squelching sound, and rolled out into the grassy aisle directly in front of me. I drew up abruptly, misliking the coincidence.

The fruit began to swell, slowly at first, and then rapidly.

"I think not," I muttered, and disincorporated it. The force of the spell flung the fruit's innards away from me, the pulp and juice sparkling faintly in the moonlight. It splattered against the ground, and on the boles of the twisted trees, and on their waxy leaves. Everywhere the stuff touched began to smoke and be eaten away as if by the strongest acid.

"Inedible then," I said to myself. "Not that I was tempted."

Behind me I heard another disturbing thump and squelch. And then, an instant later, several more fruit fell around me, all at once.

I started running, and didn't stop until I'd cleared the orchard and ended up in a field of suspiciously normal-looking, waist-high barley. Heart pounding and lungs working like bellows, I leaned forward and put my hands on my knees, and slowly regained my breath. Upon closer inspection, the barley heads looked more like some unpleasant vegetative variety of centipede than anything else. But they didn't appear to be ripe, and only twitched slightly. Small favors.

In the still air, I heard a sound, a rustling, coming from behind me. And a... mewling sound. Piteous and terrifying all at once. It came from the orchard.

I'd expected the fruit to explode, spraying their acid at me. I realized that none of them had.

I looked back and saw many infant-sized shapes crawling towards me through the rank grass under the trees. Thankfully they were slow, and even more thankfully, the leaves and branches of the orchard put them into deep shadow.

I did not want any more than the vague knowledge of their forms that I already had. I did not want to know what fruit cultivated by demons looked like in its ripeness. I could not afford the pity.

I looked away and saw not far off, just on the other side of the barley field, a small hill. An ancient, weathered standing stone squatted at its top, chalky white in the moonlight.

I set off for the hill.

Michael McClung

TWENTY-NINE

Gholdoryth was home to demons more insectile in appearance and in manners than any of the other hells. They'd lived below the surface of their realm, in great hives, and their thoughts and emotions were generally so alien as to be impenetrable.

In Thraxys, the demons were—had been—much more human in their thoughts, desires, emotions and culture. They were that much more terrifying because of it. As deadly as Gholdoryth had been, there was no subtlety in the peril it presented.

Thraxys, even devoid of demons, was subtle enough in its dangers and terrors to defeat me before I even realized it had happened, because nothing announced its perversion or its danger. There were no warning signs, and everything appeared normal—at first glance.

The base of the hill was ringed in brushwood, spindly trees hardly taller than I was. In these trees roosted what appeared to be, at first glance, large, silent crows with white heads and black beaks.

Then one launched itself from its perch and drove straight towards me, and I realized its head was white because it was nothing more than a bleached skull.

The black wings beat powerfully, scoring the air. The cruel beak was aimed at my eye. I jerked my head away at the last moment and it raked my temple. The scratch burned, and bled profusely.

The bird came around to try again.

I disincorporated it. No blood or guts; only a burst of black feathers. But its end signaled the others. They rose up in a thunderous pounding of wings, and I was forced to call up a wind just to keep them from mobbing me. It kept them at bay, but they were fixed on me. I decided to climb the hill and put my back against the standing stone, then pick them out of the sky with a brightblade, one by one if I had to. So I climbed, and the crows kept after me, a malicious undead flock intent on trying to peck me to death, occasionally scoring a hit when the climb required my attention and my Art-called wind faltered.

I reached the summit, shrugged off my pack, dropped the wind and summoned a brightblade, long and thin, spitting white and indigo light. I put my back against the ancient stone.

As soon as I did, the murder of crows seemed to lose all interest in me. They wheeled away, silent as their living counterparts never were, and in a ragged cloud began to fly off over the barley field.

And then came the sorrowind.

It first announced itself by the bow wave of dread that preceded it. Then, from my elevated position, I saw the barley field suddenly blown flat and reduced to chaff as the sorrowind rushed toward me. The crows were caught by it, and folded their ragged wings, to be flung hither and yon or slammed against the ground as the sorrowind desired. No struggle, no animalistic fight for survival or escape. The sorrowind did with them what it wished. I doubted many would survive its attentions.

There was nothing I could do to avoid it either, or ameliorate its effects, other than put the standing stone between me and it. I simply had to endure.

I got into the lee of the stone, crouched down, put my face against the stone's rough surface and covered my ears.

The sorrowind roamed the eleven hells as it wished, ravaging what it wished. Even demons feared it, or at least thought it prudent to take precautions against being caught out in the open by it. Nothing I'd read had made any suggestion as to what it really was, or what caused it. It simply *was*, and had always been.

The sorrowind blew across the physical landscape, but it blew even more fiercely in a mind, and a soul. And it was no gentle breeze.

Despair, it commanded me, and I did.

Know your utter worthlessness, it suggested, and so I knew it.

See all the sins you have kindled and kept, thorns you have grasped, pressed to your breast and thought so much of, it instructed me, and I did, and felt again all the pains of a life not well lived.

Understand that they are pathetic, paltry things. That you have not even the conviction to be wholly evil. That your moral half-measures damn you to insignificance.

I saw, and understood, and had not even the comfort of my pain.

Now take your own miserable life, it whispered.

And then it blew past, and I returned to myself, and discovered that I was holding Amra's knife to my own throat. I lowered my trembling hand. It was not an easy act.

For the first time since its decapitation, Halfmoon spoke.

That was worse than you.

"Much."

I want you to die. But not here. I do not want to feel that ever again.

"I'll bear it in mind."

I came back to myself but slowly. The sorrowind's effect did not simply abate when it had blown past. My mind, and indeed my soul, was soiled and bruised. I told myself these feelings of worthlessness, of insignificance, of self-loathing were externally applied, phantoms, unreal. I knew it to be true, but the objective knowledge was no comfort in the face of that subjective, brutal emotional violation.

It is still there in some measure, the voice of the sorrowind, lodged in my spirit, the tiniest shard of desolation. Its edges are bitterly sharp, and they never wear down. I have learned to live with it. They say what does not kill you makes you stronger. If only that were true. What does not kill you will likely leave you crippled if you are unlucky, and scarred if you are. Survival is the only reward you can hope for, and the only triumph that matters.

I learned that long before the sorrowind tried to destroy me. Its voice is just another note in the grim symphony.

Eventually I levered myself up off the ground, sheathed the knife and pulled out the glory hand.

"No tricks, now," I muttered. "I'm in no mood. Show me the way to the Black Library."

The forefinger extended itself, in a direct line away from the Spike and the standing stone at my back. I followed its line with my eye and saw, perhaps a mile distant, a glowering dark structure, massive and possessed of many towers and flying buttresses.

And between me and it, a forest, a river and a wall.

I knew now where I was. The forest was the Tanglewood. Bitter was the name of the river. The wall—oh, the wall. It was, and was not, the same Wall that Havak Silversword spent half his life imprisoned behind. Xom Dei, low duke of Thraxys, had thought it such a good joke he'd recreated the Wall in his own demesne, it was said.

Silversword had finally broken out, after thirty years, and in doing so became legend. Thirty years of a life stolen, for a joke.

I did not have thirty years to break in. But I did have something that might make a breach.

I shouldered the pack and resumed my journey.

THIRTY

I descended the hill, brightblade in hand, crossed a dismal little sward, and soon enough found myself facing the edge of the very dark, very tangled wood.

"At least you live up to your name," I said.

I could think of many, many things I would rather do than enter those woods. But going around it would take a long time; the woods paced the river for as far as I had been able to see from the little hill's vantage point. Perhaps even from the river's beginning to its end. The maps I'd studied, or at least my memory of them, were unclear. And I did not want to spend extra hours in Thraxys if I could possibly avoid it. Thraxys was far worse than Gholdoryth, far subtler in its brutality and its danger.

And the misgivings I had about entering the wood irritated me. I couldn't tell whether the disquiet I felt was natural caution or some lingering, cowardly self-doubt engendered by the sorrowind. That inability to judge my own motivation was what decided me. I would rather default to recklessness than a failure of nerve, even if it meant unnecessary danger. Or death.

I summoned magelight and brightblade and stepped into the Tanglewood.

These were not great, towering trees. They were twisted, gnarled things packed close together, their branches and roots so intertwined it was mostly impossible to tell where one left off and the next began. I started by picking my way carefully, ducking, stepping over and pushing stray branches aside; but soon enough I had no choice but to force my way through, and make use of the brightblade more and more. The wood was growing denser and more impassable with every step I took, snagging on my pack, my clothes, and my hair.

I stopped and considered my position. I glanced back the way I had come—and saw that the path I had cut had disappeared.

"Why am I not surprised?" I muttered.

I pulled out the glory hand once more. "Show me another way to the Black Library," I told it.

The fingers didn't so much as twitch. This, apparently, was the only way. With a muttered curse, I shoved it back into its pocket.

Fire magic isn't something I'm particularly good at. It's simple enough magic; almost every mage I'd ever met had some skill with it. My own skill was not great; the amount of power I had to expend when I worked with fire was positively ruinous. Some mages have an affinity for the stuff, and can wield it deftly, artfully, all day long. I wasn't one of them. My fire magic had all the subtlety of a sledge hammer against a ribcage. And just as swinging a sledge would wear me out after a few swings, so too would wielding fire.

So instead of risking a conflagration while I was still in the woods, I laboriously cut my way back out, giving up all the ground I'd just struggled my way across. I emerged from the woods more or less where I had entered them, a little scratched up, and no closer to the Black Library.

I dismissed brightblade and magelight and, raising one arm and gesturing toward the wood, called forth fire. Flames boiled up around my hand and shot forward, turning the swathe of woods directly before me into a bonfire. The heat was intense. I was forced to take several steps back. The trees burned, protesting with a hissing, crackling groan, but the low roar of the flames drowned out almost all.

The fire burned intensely, but did not spread as I had hoped. I began to worry that it would act as a beacon for whatever nastiness was still mobile in Thraxys. Dead, belligerent crows surely weren't the worst, or the end of whatever remained. It was taking too long, this burning, so I helped it along with a gust of wind.

The results were much more satisfactory.

"Stop," came a voice from the woods, melodic and inhuman. "Stop, and I will let you pass."

"Why should I stop?" I replied. "I'm making my own path tolerably well."

"Why take a hard road when an easy one presents itself?" And a path opened up off to the right, a little way from the conflagration.

"I know something about easy paths offered by demons," I said.

"Then you know that we are bound by our agreements, and cannot breach them."

It was true. Demons would honor any agreement made to the very letter—which was why it was vital to understand exactly what they were agreeing *to*.

"Very well," I said. "Offer me a formal compact then, Tanglewood. State your terms."

"Cease your burning. In return, receive safe passage through the wood to the near bank of the Bitter River beyond it."

"Give me safe passage to the Black Library."

"Alas, my demesne does not extend so far."

I hesitated. No good ever came of any compact with a demon. But it was difficult to see the harm in this one. I wasn't trading my soul, certainly. Still, I was reluctant.

"I would not deliberate overlong," the demon said. "You summon wind in the realm of the sorrowind. You usurp its prerogative, and the sorrowind will not abide that. It will surely return to castigate you, if you continue."

I shuddered at the thought. If there was even the possibility that the demon of the woods was telling the truth, I wanted to be moving on as quickly as I could.

"Very well. I'll stop. But what's already been set alight will have to burn itself out."

"So be it."

With deep misgiving I took the demon-wrought path.

~ ~ ~

The path began to curve almost immediately. I stopped as soon as I realized it.

"The agreement was safe passage to the river."

"Indeed," replied Tanglewood.

"Why then is the path leading away from the river?"

"Did our agreement stipulate safe passage by the quickest route? I think not."

"Fire is not the only weapon in my arsenal, demon."

"Calm yourself, mage. I intend a short detour only."

"To what purpose?"

"I wish to meet with you face-to-face."

"To what *purpose*?" I repeated.

"Follow the path and satisfy your curiosity. Or break from the path and make moot our agreement."

Damned demons. I followed the path.

Soon enough I came to a smallish clearing, the ground littered with leaves and bathed in moonlight, as bright as I had seen in Thraxys. The wounded moon stood directly overhead.

In the center of the clearing stood a lone tree, much larger than the others that made up the wood, thicker-boled and marginally less twisted. A figure lounged in the deep shadow of its leaves. Human-like, it appeared to be leaning casually against the trunk. More I could not tell from where I stood.

"The great mage hesitates to come nearer," it observed, melodic voice tinged with sarcasm.

"Why should I?"

"You will have to, if you wish to proceed. The path continues behind me." The figure was still, unnaturally so. No shifting of feet or hand gestures. Nothing.

"You wanted to meet me face to face," I said. "Will you now tell me why?"

"I wanted to see if you were worth another proposition."

"I am uninterested in another deal with a demon."

"Perhaps so, perhaps no. You haven't even heard it yet."

"I don't need to."

"What if I told you there was no way to force a crossing of the Bitter River? That it will surely destroy you if you try? That your drowned corpse will be its plaything until such time as your flesh disintegrates and your bones come to rest on its sandy bed?"

"An unpleasant thing to contemplate," I acknowledged.

"And what, then, if I told you I know the secret of its crossing? Would you remain as disinterested in another bargain?"

Damned demons.

"What are your terms, then?"

"Simple. Take from me a single seed. If you manage to escape the infernal planes, toss it to the ground somewhere, and kick a little dirt over it. And walk away."

"You want me to propagate Thraxys in the mortal realm."

"Not all of Thraxys. Just me."

"You'll forgive me if I point out that would be exceedingly bad for mortals, even so."

"It needn't be. Here, I and indeed all of the eleven hells require souls for sustenance. On the mortal plain, this would not be the case. And time grows short, mortal. I look for the continuance of myself, in the form of my offspring, just as you might."

"A demon? You are immortal."

"Immortal, yes. Eternal, no. I am tied to Thraxys, and Thraxys, soon enough, will be no more." With a faint creak the shadowed figure raised an arm and pointed upward. I followed its direction with my eyes, up past the leaves of the tree, to the dark sky, to the brilliant moon—and saw another piece of it break away and begin to spin off with a stately sort of slowness.

"As above, so below. The Black Library may cease to exist before you reach it."

"That would be bad," I acknowledged. I was all for seeing the hells destroyed. Just not with me still in them.

"Take my acorn, mortal, and swear to plant it in mortal soil. In return I will give you what you need to cross the Bitter."

"So be it. Toss the seed to me, then."

"Oh no. That will not serve. You must come and take it from my hand."

"What for?"

"So that I may know if you intend to deceive me, of course."

"Of course." Of course I *had* intended to toss the thing as soon as I'd got across the river. Now I'd have to make good on my promise. I wondered if it would be safer to plant the demon seed in the Broken Lands, or in the desert between Nine Cities and Far Thwyll, the one called the Anvil.

I walked towards the demon. It wasn't until I came under the shade of the tree it leaned against that I could see more than a silhouette.

It was beautiful, in an androgynous way. At least the face was. The torso and arms were as slender as a child's. Everything below where the navel would normally be was merged with the tree. It had appeared to be leaning against the tree because the trunk bent sharply away from the ground at about waist-height, which was where the demon's body emerged from. Then the trunk bent back sinuously, to merge with the back of the demon's head.

"The nut, then," I said, putting my hand out, palm upward.

It was quick for a tree, I'll give it that. Faster than I imagined possible, it had my hand and wrist clamped in both of its own bark-covered hands.

"Ah," it said, and released me as quickly as it had grabbed me. I stumbled back, ready to send a gout of fire into its beatific face. I raised my hand, and felt a slight itching there.

"You'll have to cut it out, but it won't go deep. No worse than a splinter, and less irritating."

"That was an assault. You've just voided our original compact."

"Oh, come now, it was the smallest of transgressions, and the intent was not to cause harm. Indeed, I wish you nothing but health, so that you may carry my seed away with you. It would not survive long exposed."

I rubbed at my palm, and felt the smallest of lumps under the skin, in the center. There was no wound, or even blood.

"Tell me how to cross the Bitter, damn you, and let us be done with each other."

"Attend: You must tell the river that you love her. She will not believe you, of course, so you must offer yourself to her."

"In what fashion?"

"You must let her drown you, of course."

"Madness."

"Indeed. The Bitter is mad, but not without an interior logic, of sorts. She will drown you, proving to her own satisfaction that you didn't in fact lie to her. She will regret her rash act. She will cast you up on the bank and withdraw."

"I'll still be dead."

"Momentarily. Then my lovely little acorn will do what I have told it to do. It will recall you to life."

"This pip?" I asked, rubbing again at the seed.

"Yes. It contains most of my life force. I'll not need it much longer, and I suspect it will. You will not plant it in a hospitable climate, I think."

"How can you be sure the Bitter will cast me up on the far bank?" I asked, ignoring Tanglewood's entirely accurate assessment of my plans for its seed.

"Because she hates me. I will rail against her for taking my plaything, and demand your return. She will cast you up on the far bank to spite me. That is what sisters do."

"In hells, perhaps."

"In Thraxys, of a certainty. Trust me, mage. All my hopes are attached to your success. Literally. If you fail, my seven thousand years of existence ends, without even the coda you shelter in the palm of your hand."

"Well," I said after a time. "It's good to be needed, I suppose. But why don't I just jump in and let her drown me? Why do I have to pretend to love her?"

"Her bed is littered with the bones of those who merely tried to make a crossing. She does not give those bodies up. Try to be convincing in your professed ardor. Bitter is insane and predictable, but not wholly stupid.

"Now go," it said, but I was already walking.

THIRTY-ONE

The Bitter River. I did not know much about it, other than the fact of its existence, and its location relative to the Tanglewood and the Wall. But it was a river in Thraxys; I was not expecting waters pure and cool.

It turned out that the Bitter was a literal river of blood.

A scant yard separated the river from the wood. I sat down with a sigh on the grassy bank and contemplated the bloody, turgid flow.

"Is there anything more beautiful than a river bathed in moonlight?" I wondered aloud, feeling like a fool.

Nothing happened. I was at a loss as to how I should proceed. Wooing wasn't an art I'd had much practice at.

A branch smacked me in the back of the head. I turned and glared at the Tanglewood, then set my attention back on the river.

"What graceful lines, what secrets, now hidden, now revealed in the serene flow. What murmurings, sweeter than a mother's lullaby! A river—this river—must surely be what mortal women only aspire to. Lover, mother—bah. I wish I were a poet. I would set it to rhyme worthy of the reality. Perhaps not," I argued with myself, shaking my head. "Poets lie far too often. They flatter for effect."

"They do that," the river whispered to me, voice faint as silk on sand.

I sat up straighter. "Whose voice is that?"

"The object of your admiration," Bitter replied.

"Beauty," I breathed.

"Do you think so?"

"I have said so, when I thought my words went unheard."

"What do you want, cunning man, silver tongue?"

"Why should I want anything? I have you to behold, what more might I expect? Unless...."

"Unless what?"

"No. My thoughts are too forward to share. I would not have you think less of me."

"Thraxys falters. Soon I will have run my course. Be forward, before the end, and let me think what I will."

"Very well, since you insist—and because, in your insistence, I am shielded from you finding fault. Beyond admiring you from this dry bank, I would hope to brave your waters, to swim, to dive, to plumb your depths. To lay my hands on your bed, and discover your hidden secrets."

Bitter was silent for a time. Then, an even fainter whisper: "Blandishments. Honeyed words. Encomium. You seek to cross me. You would not be the first."

"You doubt my sincerity," I replied. "Ironic, that the wood behind me declares an affection for me that I do not return, then I in turn declare a love for you, Bitter, and am not believed." I sighed again, woefully. At least I hoped it was a sufficiently woeful sigh.

"Tanglewood fancies you?" the river asked, sharply.

"How else would I have made it through the wood's entanglements?" I shrugged. "It matters little."

The silence stretched.

"I want to believe you," Bitter said in a small voice, barely audible. "But there have been so many liars...."

"Very well. I put myself at your mercy." I stood up. "Drown me if you like, dear Bitter, only let me swim in you while my breath holds out."

I took a deep breath, and dove.

Bitter was as warm as blood usually is. I did not open my eye—to what point? But I swam down, until my hands met soft sand and what I might have mistaken for half-buried driftwood, were it a mortal river. As it was, I guessed it to be a thigh bone.

Bitter caressed me with her current. Even fully clothed, it was intimate to the point of unpleasantness. I repressed a shudder. I resolved not to struggle. I held loosely to the bone, keeping the current from washing me downstream, and submitted for a short span.

And then of course I began to feel the need for air.

"Will you drown me, Bitter?" I asked, spent air escaping my lungs and blood entering my mouth.

"Yes," she whispered against my eardrums.

"I'll try not to struggle, but drowning is hard," I replied. And then I had no more breath, only a burning in my lungs, and then Bitter's flow rushed in.

I began to convulse. The panic that all drowners must feel set in, and I struggled to break for the surface. Bitter held me down with a grip as soft as velvet, as hard as iron.

The last thing I remember is the demon river saying "Shhhhhh."

"Shhhhh."

"Sh—

~ ~ ~

Being resuscitated after being drowned is painful. Having a demon seed do the resuscitation by sending roots through the arteries and veins in your arm, across your chest and finally to your heart, and then *squeezing*, over and over, is like nothing I can possibly relate, and also painful. I only felt the squeezing bit, of course, and only at the end, but as I vomited up the blood Bitter had filled my lungs with, I had the joy of experiencing those roots and tendrils withdraw themselves from my heart, my chest, and back down my arm to my palm. It healed the damage it did to my insides as it went, but it still hurt like all hells.

Luckily, if that is the word, Bitter had cast me onto the bank face down, which made draining my lungs somewhat easier. If 'easier' can truly apply to the situation. My reason says it can, but my memory vehemently disagrees.

Once I was done with the retching and had moved on to gasping, I made it to my hands and knees, and glanced back at the river. I saw the woods on the other side. So it appeared Tanglewood's ruse had worked.

I was in no mood to cheer.

Slowly, dripping blood, I clambered to my feet.

"You live," whispered bitter.

"Barely," I croaked.

"Come back to me."

I spat out another mouthful of blood and bile. "I was mistaken in my affection," I replied. "But believe me when I say I will never forget our time together."

I walked away, ignoring Bitter's hissing, frothing rage.

I enjoyed your death, Halfmoon told me.

"Shut up."

THIRTY-TWO

Perhaps half a mile lay between river and wall, and the Wall was visible the entire way. It was a very tall wall.

By the time I reached the Wall, the blood I was covered in had begun to coagulate in some places, crust and flake in others, and stink all over. You don't want to know what I was reduced to, to clear it from my empty eye socket.

The Wall. It gleamed a bone white in the moonlight. I touched its surface. Glassy. I took in its height—a hundred yards? More? It was the closest thing to impregnable that I had ever seen. That glassy surface was, according to some versions of the legend, impervious to magic.

I did not have the silversword, or thirty years to breach the Wall. But I had two things Havak hadn't had. Magic, and gunpowder. Not enough gunpowder to take down the Wall, certainly, or even breach it. But enough, I hoped, to chip it. And a chip was hopefully all I would require, if the surface really was proof against magic. If the entire wall was impervious to the Art, or if I couldn't get beyond the surface using mundane means, I'd wasted a lot of time and effort on the voyage between Bellarius and Lucernis.

I sat down in the long grass that grew before the wall, and rummaged through my blood-soaked pack, and pulled out what I was looking for.

Gunpowder is ruined by wet, of course—oh, you could dry it out again, but the process was involved and the result unsatisfactory. And that was with water, not blood. I'd kept this small wooden casque of it protected from the elements on general principles. Even the damp in the air could render the stuff useless over time, after all.

So I'd sealed it with wax, wrapped it in oilcloth, and sealed it with wax again. I don't remember my original reasons for doing so. I tend to hold on to things just in case. Amra had laughed and called me a pack rat more than once. If my plan worked, I would get her to acknowledge the usefulness of never throwing anything away. And of keeping gunpowder handy.

If we managed to return to Lucernis.

If I didn't already have a death decree inked out for me there.

"'If' is a foul, foul word," I muttered. "Strange I never noticed before."

I wiped the casque on the grass, clearing off the majority of blood. Then I cut away the outer wax and the oilskin. I left the inner seal as whole as I could. There was no real reason to remove it.

I positioned the casque flat against the wall and took a dozen steps back. Then a dozen more, to be safe. Then I lay flat on the ground, to be doubly safe.

I had no fuse, and was not going to try and make a trail of powder through the grass to act as one. I didn't need to. I did, however, need to hurl fire at it as precisely as I could.

Keeping my head as low as possible while keeping the casque in sight, I pointed at it, and called up my magesight. Thraxys blinded me. But in the wash of illumination was one black dot of mundanity. I focused on it, putting everything else from my mind. I visualized a lance of fire being flung from my finger, narrower than I had ever managed, hotter than the Telemarch's trap. I breathed in, out. And then let fly.

The explosion was something of a disappointment, to be honest. Not as loud as I'd imagined, and not as large as I'd hoped. Bits of the wooden casque and clods of dirt rained down for a few seconds, and the air was thick with smoke and the stench of burnt powder, but the Wall certainly hadn't tumbled down. No great fissures marred its glassy face.

I approached the Wall. I could see no cracks. I tore up a clump of grass and wiped the Wall as clean as I could.

Nothing.

I sighed. I was at a loss as to what I should try next. I did not need a gaping hole for the second part of my assault, but I did need something. Some fissure, some little chip. A foothold, as it were.

"Make sure then, Holgren," I told myself. "The light isn't the best, and your eyesight has been better." I followed my own advice and ran my fingers slowly and carefully along every inch of the surface of the Wall that might conceivably have been affected by the blast.

And I found what I was looking for. The smallest chip, just to one side of where the casque had rested against the Wall. Probably one of the little nails that held the casque together had caused it, blown out through the wood with sufficient force to leave a tiny indentation. Infinitesimal, really. I must have run my finger over it three or four times before it registered. Once it did register, I ran a fingertip over it half a dozen times more, just to convince myself I wasn't imagining it.

I smiled rather grimly and dug out the diamond Moc Mien had grossly overcharged me for; the one I'd spend the entire voyage from Bellarius to Lucernis investing with power and a simple but subtle pair of commands—*unmake* and *spread*.

I took great care to place the diamond against the indentation, working mostly by feel. When I was certain as could be, I set loose the magic.

The diamond began to spin against the wall's surface, heedless of gravity. Slowly at first, then faster. It began to glow with a warm light, then cast out brilliant beams, a prism refracting light that came from no external source. A humming filled the air; ten, a hundred, then ten thousand bees on the wing.

The diamond sank into the surface of the Wall. Light and sound receded. I grabbed up the pack and took several precautionary steps back, and waited.

And waited.

The Wall did not come tumbling down. No great gap suddenly appeared. I could no longer hear any buzzing, or see any light shining from the hole. I did not know if the diamond had been exhausted; it was technically an artifact, existing outside of my direct control. I had no connection to it at this point. It was an arrow loosed. I did not know if it was still in flight or spent.

I gave it a little more time.

Nothing continued to happen.

Cursing, I started back toward the Wall to see if there was anything to see, but stopped dead in my tracks when an almost deafening *ripping* sound filled the air. At first, I thought my spell had finally succeeded—and then I realized with a blossoming dread that the sound was coming from *behind* me.

I looked back over my shoulder and saw that the earth was opening; a huge fissure had appeared and the Tanglewood was now split. As I watched, the crack severed the Bitter; creating a sudden double waterfall, or rather bloodfall, as the river poured away down both sides of the rift—its course fatally disrupted.

As above, so below, Tanglewood had told me. It hadn't lied.

The crack was spreading wider. It was also lengthening, running towards me in a jerking zig-zag path. The rending of Thraxys grew louder as it approached.

"Dead gods. I'm too late." I watched, fascinated, as the rent raced towards me. I didn't even think of trying to run. It isn't every day you see the end of an entire plane of reality, after all, and besides, where was there to run? My only hope of escape lay behind the Wall, in the Black Library.

The rent passed not a yard from me and slammed into the Wall.

For one heartbeat, two, three, nothing happened, no change was apparent—and then there was a tremendous *boom* and the Wall was split from bottom to top, nearly faster than my eye could follow. Cracks began to radiate outward from both sides of the split, and the Wall started to crumble.

"Ha! Damn you, then!" I shouted at the Wall. Exulting in the destruction of an inanimate object was no doubt foolish. I didn't care. "Damn you anyway!"

Chunks of the Wall began to fall. Many of them were very large chunks, and many of those were falling towards *me*. I stopped being foolish and started to run.

It was a deadly rain. The ground trembled with every impact, throwing up great clods of dirt. I ran back towards the Bitter, looking behind me and above, trying to judge where to run to dodge the massive debris. It was difficult, one-eyed and fleeing at speed. I stumbled, I fell, I scrabbled back to my feet. A section of the Wall roughly as big as a door slammed into the ground beside me and threw me off my feet once more. A smaller one grazed my shoulder as I rolled away.

I ended up on my side, looking up. Saw death.

Falling toward me, a ragged portion of the Wall bigger than a barge, blotting out the sky as it rushed toward me.

"Hells!" I threw my arm out and hurled power at it, pure force barely formed.

It split the bastard in two with enough force that the two sections folded into a giant, inverted V just before they slammed into the ground, essentially forming a big stone tent around me.

I blinked and lowered my arm. "That worked out better than I expected," I said.

Then one side of my 'tent' began to slip downwards with an ominous grinding noise, its purchase against the other slipping, failing, the balance between the two slabs shifting as inertia sang its irresistible song.

I scrambled out, and one side fell flat to the ground, and the other side fell atop the first.

"Still alive, you bastard," I muttered, and slowly got to my feet. I surveyed the destruction. It was impressive. Perhaps fifty yards or so of the Wall had collapsed on either side of the rent. It would be easy enough to clamber over the debris to get to the other side. That was the good news.

The bad news was that I was on one side of the fissure, and what remained of the Black Library was on the other. It looked as if some giant cleaver had descended from the sky and sheared off the front of the building. Some of the rubble had fallen on my side of the divide, glossy black stone scattered about the rough grass like giant child's blocks. Not enough to account for what was missing. Much more of it must have fallen into the rent, which at that point was more than a yard across.

I approached the divide and stared into its depths. It did not have a bottom that I could see. Whatever fell into it would keep falling, perhaps all the way to the Ur that Vosto had mentioned. The cosmology of the eleven hells was an imperfect science, and I had only become a pupil of it out of desperation.

I looked back up at the Library. Directly across from me was one huge room. Every surface that I could see was polished black stone. There were no books, but there was a door on the far side, barely visible in the gloom. There really wasn't any other way to enter, and the rent wasn't getting narrower.

Not really having much choice in the matter, I backed up several yards, got a running start, and jumped.

THIRTY-THREE

Half of me made it.

I landed hard, arms spread wide, chest and face taking the blow. Everything below my belt was left dangling down the ragged gap. I scrambled up, away from oblivion, panting through gritted teeth.

A low groan had been building, from everywhere and nowhere, the harmony of destruction. I looked back towards failing Thraxys, and saw it coming undone. Tanglewood had disintegrated. Bitter, it seemed, had forgot what gravity might be, and painted the air as a ribbon of bloody mist. Individual pieces of the moon still cast light, but that light was sputtering and going out, piece by piece.

The Library began to slowly list, like a ship taking on water.

I summoned magelight and pulled out the glory hand one last time.

"Lead me to Lagna's notebook," I told it, "and believe me, this is no time for being funny."

It pointed into the dark interior, and I staggered into the darkness as quickly as I could, fighting to keep my balance on the polished floor.

The Library was more like a palace, heavily ornamented walls, ceilings, and columns—all the same unrelieved black. I got only the barest impression of my surroundings, though. I wasn't there for sightseeing. A black door big enough for any barn appeared out of the gloom that my magelight pierced only in a sullen fashion. I twisted the handle and it swung open silently. Beyond, a room filled with books—thousands of them, scattered across the floor, slowly sliding leftward, every single one of them black bound, with dead black pages. Demon humor.

At the far end of the long room, stairs up and corridors left and right. The glory hand indicated I should take the stairs. I went up them as quickly as I could. The Library was nearly on its side. I finished the ascent using the black balustrade as a ramp of sorts.

"Which way?"

Left. Which meant down now, more or less. A corridor that was now essentially a dark shaft.

"I'm beginning to dislike you immensely," I told it, and slung myself over the edge, holding on to the balustrade. And then let go.

There was enough of a tilt that I half-slid, half fell. Which meant that when I hit the bottom, I did not break my legs. That's about the best that could be said of the experience. I hit hard enough that I wondered for a few moments whether I *had* broken them, though. The pain was exquisite, and raced up from my heels to my knees. It left me breathless. Otherwise I would have screamed.

Above me came a terrible groaning, ripping sound. The rest of the Black Library was coming apart.

There was a door at the bottom. I reached down and turned the handle. The door opened in towards the room, and so gravity took hold and ripped the handle from my hand as the door dropped, and the smell of rain wafted up, clearing from my nose and lungs the noxious odor of Thraxys that I'd become used to.

Beyond was not a room. Beyond was something my eye could make no sense of whatever. Floating stars, cosmic whirlwinds, emotions unknown to me, to any mortal, perhaps—my eye delivered to me this synesthetic chaos, and I could make nothing of it. So I closed my eye and opened my magesight, expecting to be blinded.

Instead I saw only the outlines of a nearly empty room. There was one table standing on what was now the wall. The table did not seem to recognize the change in direction, nor did the black metal box that sat in the middle of the table.

I entered, and the definition of 'down' changed. I didn't stumble too badly. It was a strange sensation, but compared to the previous hours, it barely rated notice. Much stranger was the reluctance to open the box that stole over me as I hobbled towards it. Did it come from the box, or did it originate within me?

I still don't know. But reluctant or not, I certainly wasn't going to *not* open the damned thing. I'd gone through hells to get there, to that moment, and besides, Lagna's notebook was the only way I was going to survive the destruction that had engulfed Thraxys.

When I'd devised my plan to bring Amra back, I'd thought I'd have more time to study the notebook once I'd secured it. Days, perhaps. Hours at least. I hadn't factored in the destruction of the eleven hells. Short-sighted of me. It looked as though I'd be lucky to have a few minutes.

I put a hand on the box. Opened the heavy lid.

It wasn't a notebook. It wasn't a book at all. It was a ball, an orb, roughly the diameter of your circled thumb and forefinger. To my magesight it was crystalline, and glowed brilliantly, giving off a golden-white light. I looked more closely at the thing, and realized it was finely etched.

It was an eye; complete with pupil, iris, delicate traceries of arteries and veins,

The Guardian's words came back to me. 'You'll see,' she'd said. Ha, ha. Her sense of humor wasn't actually very amusing. I suppose that shouldn't have come as a surprise.

I picked it up. Other than a faint tingle, likely more imagined than felt, there was no reaction.

"What now, then?" I wondered, but a creeping sort of dread was washing up my spine. Had the Guardian meant her words *literally*? No doubt it had been an excellent joke to her, if so; a one-eyed mage gone looking for the secret of Lagna's notebook.

It could have been worse. I could have been whole-sighted, and forced to remove my own eye just to test the theory. As it was, I'd already lost an eye, and so had only to lose a little dignity.

"Hurvus would not approve," I muttered, and took off the eye patch and shoved it in a pocket. Then, with not a little distaste, I spread the lids apart with my left hand, while with my right I maneuvered the crystal sphere into my eye socket.

The feeling was unpleasant, undignified, and rather cold. But it fit, that orb, and after a few blinks it seemed to come to some sort of equilibrium or accommodation with the socket.

I blinked a few more times. It was a strange feeling, an odd, unfamiliar weight in a terribly intimate place, and a strange, half-familiar sensation whenever my eyelid slid over the smooth curve of the orb after so long with nothing at all to move against.

And then the crystal eye shifted into the perfect position, and a connection was made between it and whatever a natural eye connects to in the back of the socket, and I saw *everything*.

And was seen.

Lagna's notebook was the god of knowledge's actual eye, plucked from his severed head and put away as a trophy by the demon lord of Thraxys after the execution.

What happens when you put a portion of a god's body into your own, you ask?

You are thrown into convulsions. And then you lose consciousness. Then you die.

And then the really awful part begins.

AMRA: INTERLUDE THREE

The sky was gray.

A banal enough observation. For most people, most of the time. They look at the sky, the dome of light and air that looms above their every moment, seen and unseen, awake or asleep, living or dead, and if they notice it at all, they see it is gray, or blue, or the black of a moonless night, or a-bustle with scudding clouds pregnant with cold, penetrating rain, or pricked with icy stars. No one ever stops to consider whether there *is* a sky; only what sort of sky it might be at that moment, and whether it might change soon, making their lives more miserable or less.

This sky was gray.

When I went to sleep, there was no sky at all; but now there was a sky outside the door, and it was the color of well-used mop water. No sun or moon or star. Below, the rift still burned, golden yellow. Beyond, the absence of anything at all that I chose to think of as blackness.

I did not know what having a sky might mean.

I did not know why there was now a sky, or whether it would vanish as easily as it had arrived. I did not know whether having a sky was a good thing, or a bad sign, or neither.

I *did* know that I had grown very, very tired of *not* having a sky, so on the whole I was satisfied.

"Would you like to know why there is now a sky?" asked the little monster behind me.

"What I'd like to know is how to get my hands around your throat," I replied.

"Contagion," it said. "Contagion of thought and desire. The longer you stay here, the more your desires, and eventually even your idle thoughts, will paint themselves into reality around you. You have no experience controlling the power you now command. And so now there is a sky where once there was nothing. The desire for one bled through while you slept, and the rift reacted."

"Well good. Maybe my desire to see you punished for all the vile things you've done will bleed through as well." I turned away from my new sky and faced her—it.

"Sorry to disabuse you of the notion," it said. "Divine magic trumps what you've got hold of out there." She was sitting in a corner, winding her long, curly hair around a finger, over and over. She hadn't moved from the corner in a long time. Not that she—it—was really there at all.

"Pity," I said, and turned back to my new sky. It was better than nothing. But not much. An unrelieved expanse of gray. Kind of depressing, actually. The horizon was just a hazy line where gray turned to black.

"So, Chuckles, you can't lie to me, correct?"

"Correct."

"You said you made me, more or less. You started wars and had homeless children murdered, just so someone like me would come along. Right?"

"In broad strokes, yes."

"What the hells *for*?"

Suddenly she was standing next to me. My flesh crawled, being so close to the image of the monster that had lodged itself in my soul. That she was a sickeningly-sweet little girl made it much worse. Long practice kept me from flinching. Never let the bastards see you flinch.

"You had a conversation with a bloodwitch in Loathewater, do you remember?" she asked.

"Yes."

"You told her that fate is a slaver, and that you refuse his chains.

That piece of bravado sounded good, I grant you, but the truth is the chains of fate cannot be refused."

"Fuck your truth."

"They *can't* be refused. Trust me on this. I cannot lie to you. They *can*, however, be broken. Or so I believe, and all my sisters with me." She frowned. "We agree on little else, but we do agree on that."

"Answer my damned question."

"You are the pointy end of our argument with fate, Amra Thetys. I can't say more. It isn't my place."

"Then whose place is it?"

"She Who Casts Eight Shadows."

Pretty much all my life I've worked hard to avoid trouble. Not danger—that's part and parcel of being a thief. When you set out to steal rare and valuable things, you're sure to be stealing them from powerful, important people. That's dangerous, and there's no avoiding the fact. You do your best to minimize the risk.

Trouble is something different. There's generally no profit in it, for one. And while danger's something you usually need to go and seek out, trouble will come knocking on your door at any hour of the day or night, uninvited and usually unexpected. At least it did mine, far too often.

So I'd learned to make like I wasn't home.

And still sometimes trouble just went ahead and bashed the door in.

"I truly and deeply hate you," I said.

"I'm aware of that."

"Get away from me, why don't you."

Her image vanished, giving me the illusion of solitude. I stared out at my new sky, but my eyes kept sliding off it down to the horizon. Maybe having a sky wasn't such a....

There was something out there, at the very limits of perception. I'd seen it. A brief flash, then gone. I stared for a long time, but did not see anything else. Then, just as I decided I'd imagined it, it came again, the barest spark of golden light.

"What the hells is that?" I said. It was meant to be a rhetorical question.

"That," said Kalara, smugness practically coating her words, "is an end to our impasse."

Michael McClung

PART IV: NOWHERE

THE THIEF WHO WASN'T THERE

THIRTY-FOUR

Imagine, if you will, that you were able to know every detail of every piece of existence, from the smallest mote of dust settling on a blade of grass to the dance of stars, all ten billion trillion of them—and absolutely everything in between. Now imagine, if you can, knowing all of it, all at once, moment by moment, change by infinitesimal change.

That was what omniscience was.

It was vastly overrated, because it was utterly useless. Worse than useless. A human, mortal mind was wholly inadequate, entirely too fragile, simply too limited in every conceivable way to deal with the unending volume of knowledge that was omniscience.

It killed me.

Lagna's eye killed me, and that's all that saved me. If I'd somehow been able to survive it, I would have been driven permanently mad. Perhaps my head would have exploded, and I'd have lived on like that, somehow. I don't know. It isn't something I like to contemplate.

I don't know how long I was dead. It's not as if time really had much meaning in my situation. At first there was nothing, as you might expect when you die. Then I became aware of the fact that there was still an *I*, and that it was aware. It doesn't sound like much, but without that, you've literally got nothing.

That's what happens when you die, I discovered, if you happen to be already physically present in an afterlife—even one in as miserable a condition as Thraxys happened to be. You don't go anywhere. Your life is gone and your soul loses its connection to its anchor, your flesh—but your spirit does not part from your flesh.

There's nowhere for it to go because, according to the rules it plays by, it's already *arrived*. And so your spirit, in a panic, claws its way back into the very atoms of its earthly container. Or at least mine did. It is not a process I can endorse. In some sense, I feel as if I am *still* dead, and haunting my own flesh, forcing it to maintain all the various bodily functions. It's an unpleasant, distracting feeling, and it does nothing to bolster my sanity.

I came back to life screaming, that much I remember. Instinctively my hands went up to my eye—Lagna's eye. I clapped a palm over it, blocking out all light—and just like that, the torrent of knowledge cut off.

I squeezed my eyelid tight. Took my hands away and scrabbled in my pocket for the patch, and put it back on. My violent trembling made it a challenge, but I succeeded in time. I made damned sure the patch was on properly.

Then I took a rest. I call it a rest because admitting to curling up into a ball and moaning is rather embarrassing.

Gradually, I became aware of my surroundings once more. I was lying on the floor, next to the table. The rest of the room was gone, which was less fine, and the floor was just spinning slowly in a dim emptiness, a sky without end. That wasn't fine at all. Bits of the shattered moon gave off a wan, uneven light, and the wreckage of Thraxys was everywhere. The only thing that I caught a glimpse of that seemed unaffected by the destruction was the Spike, which looked more like an endless wire from my remove. It stretched out of sight in both directions. I could not see any of the other hells. I don't know if that meant they were also destroyed, or if it simply wasn't possible to see one from another one.

I enjoyed watching you die again, Halfmoon informed me.

"Not tired of that trick yet, then?" I wouldn't say I enjoyed my exchanges with the creature, but I did find its blatant, bloodthirsty honesty amusing. And they served to reinforce my decision to never, ever reunite its head with its body.

No, not tired. I think I will not get tired of it soon. Do it more and we can both find out.

"You just tell me when you sense the rift."

The rift is not here.

"I didn't think it was. Now be quiet. I have to master this thing, somehow."

I collected my thoughts, and my courage. Recalled Amra, and put her memory squarely at the forefront of my mind. Lifted the patch by the barest measure and opened my eyelids the most minute fraction.

Was overwhelmed once more.

I came back to consciousness after a time, feeling as if my mind had had blazing hot pokers rammed through it. The patch acted as a dead man's switch, at least, covering the eye when my hand fell away and cutting off the torrent.

You did not die that time, so it does not count. But I liked you being in pain.

"Keep it up and I'll gouge your eye out and put this thing in *you*."

Silence.

"This isn't going to work," I muttered. I needed a filter of some sort. Some way to pick through all that knowledge, and exclude the irrelevant. And I didn't know how to do it. I didn't even know if it was possible. In short, I needed a key. Just as the Queen of Souls had mentioned.

I considered and set aside the idea of using magic to try and tame the thing. Mortal magic was nothing, really, when set against demonic magic, and even less when matched against divine power. I would try if I could think of nothing else, but I didn't hold much hope for success.

The real issue was that I knew less than I'd thought about Lagna's notebook. Legends, I had learned from bitter experience and now more than once, masked as much of the truth as they revealed.

Thagoth had indeed held the secret to immortality, or at least a secret. Lagna's notebook did indeed contain all the knowledge in existence. And yet, having attained both now in my lifetime, I was neither immortal nor all-knowing.

What *did* I know? About Lagna's notebook, that is, beyond the obvious? What—

I smiled a grim sort of smile. The Guardian wasn't a pleasant creature, but she'd given me a clue, hadn't she? Mockingly, laughing at me in unkind fashion, but she'd given me the truth. She'd told me I'd see. What else had she said?

That some books were the reader as well as the read. And that some books were very angry.

Both of those implied there was some sort of intelligence lingering in Lagna's eye. Some sense of self. I would never have suspected a body part could contain, or retain, anything like a personality, but then I was not a god.

If an eye could be a book, then the remaining portion of the god's personality might be a key.

So. So and so. Perhaps I could come to an accommodation with the remains of the god of knowledge. Win its cooperation. Win, or purchase. Or failing that, somehow compel.

I attempted to make contact.

THE THIEF WHO WASN'T THERE

THIRTY-FIVE

I did what I had not done since I'd put the damned thing in. While keeping my eyes firmly shut and the orb covered with my patch, I opened up my magesight. And there he was. Or as much of him as was left, I suppose.

He sat on a rock. The rock sat on a featureless, dust-colored plane, and a sky that looked virtually the same stood above. The light was sourceless and everywhere.

His skin was a dark, dark brown. The hair on his head was close cropped, tightly curled, and graying. The hair on his chin was braided. He was more muscled than I'd imagined him to be. He wore a faded old robe, similar to those Elamners wear, and his feet were sandaled, callused, and dusty. His face... his face was bleak, and his shallow-set, starry-pupiled eyes, when he turned to face me, were hot.

"Lagna, I presume." I sketched a brief bow.

"Where is my body?" he asked, and his voice was leashed thunder. "Where is the rest of me?"

"I do not know," I replied. "The legends do not say what Xom Dei did with your corpse. Does the god of knowledge not know?"

"I have knowledge of nothing, from the time this eye was placed inside the cursed box until the moment you opened it."

I took a few steps toward him. "Lagna, I have come a long and perilous way to recover this portion of you. I ask for your assistance—"

"I care nothing for your needs or your toils, mortal. I find *myself* in need of a body. Yours will have to do. Give it to me."

I raised an eyebrow. "Are you serious?"

"Do you mistake me for the god of humor?"

"I am not giving you my body. It's the only one I happen to have. Sorry."

The sky darkened and the dust at our feet turned rust red. His face suffused with anger. In an instant he was off his rock and his nose was mashed against mine as he screamed in my face.

"GIVE ME YOUR BODY!"

For an answer, I brought my hands up from my sides and shoved him away from me. He stumbled backwards and fell on his posterior. His shock was plain.

"You're not a god," I told him. "You're a piece of petrified meat from a god that once was. He died a thousand years and more ago. Accustom yourself to the reality of your situation."

He came up from the ground swinging, so I assumed he wasn't willing to accustom himself.

I suppose you could say that, in some sense, our fight wasn't real. He had no body, and I never moved a muscle of mine. You might be forgiven for believing it was all symbolic. And maybe that's all it was. But I've been in life or death struggles before. This was as real as any, and the stakes just as high. It was two wills intent on annihilating each other, and it was brutal and vicious.

Lagna's punch connected with my stomach and drove the breath from me and doubled me over. I stumbled back and he followed, bringing down two clasped hands like a double hammer on the base of my neck. I fell to the dust at his feet, gasping it in. I wondered, through the pain, if he'd broken my neck. But the pain told me he had not.

He brought his foot back to kick my teeth down my throat. I took advantage of his imbalance. I grabbed his ankle and yanked with all the strength I could muster. He fell on his back. I suffered a couple of kicks climbing on top of him. I managed a punch to the side of his head, and then we were trading grapples and blows, knees and bites and grunts. We were both sweating and desperate, and murder was on both our minds.

Somehow he got hold of the middle finger of my right hand, and bent it back until it snapped.

I screamed, and he let out a sort of feral growl and shifted, getting most of his weight atop me, our legs tangled. He got one hand on my throat and began to squeeze. His own face was swollen with rage.

It was a special sort of agony, forcing the hand with the broken finger into a fist, but he had the uninjured hand pinned. So make a fist I did, as the need for air and the lack of it began to dim my vision. And then I punched with that fist straight into his throat, putting behind it every ounce of frustration and pain and rage I'd experienced over the last weeks.

His larynx snapped and folded inwards.

I screamed again, my hand in agony.

He did not scream; his voice box being crushed. He just gagged and choked until he died.

And that's how I killed the last remaining shred of the god of knowledge.

~ ~ ~

I staggered to my feet, grinding my teeth to choke back the scream that wanted to escape my mouth. I cradled my mangled hand against my chest. I almost left that place within the eye, to escape the pain, but stopped myself before I made that mistake. Somewhere here was the key to everything, to controlling what I had taken at such a great cost, and getting back what I desperately missed.

Amra.

I went inward, blocking out the agony of my hand. Blocking out all the various injuries I'd sustained in reaching this place, this moment. Blocking out everything, so that I could *think*. And then I opened all my senses to my surroundings, looking for the slightest clue to gaining control of the eye.

Nothing.

So I changed tack, and pretended I was the arrogant bastard I'd just killed.

"Show me the planes, one by one. All of them."

And it did, too fast for me to take in anything. Then suddenly I was back in Lagna's desolate realm.

"Halfmoon, can you hear me?"

Sadly, yes.

"If you have contact with me, then you have contact with the eye through me. Attend, and tell me when you sense the rift."

It grunted. I turned my attention back to the eye.

"Again, but slower," I told it. "Every plane of existence, old and new, so long as it still remains."

It obliged, showing me perhaps two realities for every one of my heartbeats. I saw things, places both wondrous and hideous, and every variation and combination of the two. I caught glimpses of things I am still struggling to forget. Some because they were horrible. Others, because their beauty was haunting.

It went on for a long time. I began to lose hope that I would ever find where Amra had disappeared to. Until Halfmoon spoke.

There.

"Stop!" I commanded the eye. "Which one, Halfmoon?"

Back three. It smells right.

"Back three," I told the eye. It obliged.

I stood on nothing. Lagna's corpse lay on nothing. The rock floated on nothing. Above us, a leaden sky stretched endlessly. And far, far in the distance, a fire, golden-orange.

Mother, purred Halfmoon.

"Get closer to that fire," I told the eye. The perspective jumped. Now I was looking at a rough cube, hovering over an enormous, roiling cloud of gold and orange. The cube was featureless, except for a lighter, oblong patch on one side of it. I was still too far away to make out any detail.

"Closer to the cube," I told the eye. The perspective jumped once more.

The rectangle was a doorway. In it stood Amra, looking out. Behind her a little brown-bronze girl with starlight eyes.

Exactly as the Telemarch's painting had depicted it.

"Amra!"

There was no indication she could hear me.

"Make a doorway that connects us to that realm," I told the eye. Somewhat to my surprise, it did. At least a door appeared in front of me. I released my magesight, and came back to ruined Thraxys. My badly damaged hand was suddenly whole once more, and the relief that is the end of pain practically made me giddy.

Even better, the door had come with me; a plain, featureless white thing with a plain, featureless white knob.

"Finally, something goes my way," I said. Of course as soon as I said it, I became deeply, irrationally suspicious of the door. I was convinced opening it would spring some fresh new horror on me. But there was nothing for it but to open it.

I turned the knob. Instantly it was ripped out of my hand. The door itself was ripped off its hinges, and I was sucked through into the realm I'd glimpsed.

A realm that had no gravity, and no air, but did have the rift, and its poisonous effect on me.

AMRA: INTERLUDE FOUR

After those two flashes, there was nothing for a time. Finally, I turned to Chuckles.

"I'll ask again. What did I just see?"

"Someone has reclaimed Lagna's eye from Thraxys. What you saw was it opening, for the first time in a millennium."

"I don't know how that has anything to do with our current situation."

"I do. Or I strongly suspect. We'll discover soon enough if I am right."

"Right about what, damn you?"

"Keep watch, Amra. What I believe happens next, will happen quickly. When it does, you will have to *move* quickly. If you want to save him."

"Save who?"

"Your lover."

A cold sort of dread crept up my spine at her words. "No."

"Did you think he would just mourn your disappearance? From your memories of him, he doesn't strike me as that sort of man at all. Rather, he seems the sort of man who would climb over a mountain of corpses to find you."

"Damn you," I whispered.

"Me? I had nothing to do with it. If you have a complaint about your love or your lover, you should address it to Isin, if anyone."

"Was this part of your plan as well? Luring Holgren here somehow, to convince me to return to the world?"

"Not me. Fate, if anything. Though I will admit to making sure the rift would poison any mage other than Aither. Which is why you'll have to act quickly when your lover arrives. If the lack of air out there does not kill him, the rift surely will."

"Kerf's balls, I hope you're wrong, you awful bitch."

Her eyes got bigger, and her smile wider. "Oh, look," she said, jutting her chin toward the doorway. "A visitor."

I turned back to face the void. A white door had appeared, maybe fifty feet away.

"Damn it, Holg—"

The door was flung open with such force that it ripped itself off its hinges and flew towards me at speed. It disappeared in flight though—it just vanished.

Holgren followed it. He didn't vanish. He flew toward me, spinning. It looked like he was choking.

"He has no air," Kalara informed me, "and free of its containment, the rift is already killing him."

Holgren slammed into the door frame. I grabbed him before he could bounce away and hauled him into the room. Kerf, he looked bad. Practically emaciated and one-eyed—and that one horribly bloodied. There was no white to the eye at all, only crimson. The other was covered by a patch.

He took a huge gasp of air. Said my name. Then went into convulsions.

"You'd best hurry, Amra. What the rift will do to him will make his death in Thagoth seem like slipping into a warm bath, by comparison."

I could just send him away— I thought, and Kalara laughed.

"You don't have enough control over the rift to be certain where he'd go. He might end up under a mountain. Or under the Dragonsea. Or a mile above it, and sadly lacking wings. And besides, this one is likely to just come right back, if he survives. Stop hiding, Amra Thetys. You can't avoid what will be. You can only delay it, to no good purpose. Delay much longer, and you'll be responsible for his death."

Damn. Damn and damn.

Not wanting to kill us both by trying to go somewhere I'd no experience of, I drew from the rift, concentrated, and put the Telemarch's throne room back where it went. Holgren and I went with it. The rift stayed.

Kalara smiled and smiled.

PART V: BELLARIUS

THIRTY-SIX

I woke in a bed. Blankets were piled high on me, but my face was cold. I cracked open my eye, and realized after a moment that I was back in the Citadel. First floor. Keel's bed, from the smell. I felt... awful.

"Awake, lover?"

I turned my head toward her voice. She was sitting at the table. She'd been reading by lantern light, if the book in her hand was any indication. She was beautiful. Never pretty, but always beautiful.

"I hope so. But if not, it's a pleasant dream."

She smiled, put down the book and came to the bed.

"How are you feeling, then?" She put a hand on my forehead.

I thought about it. "Alive?"

"You mages, you just open your mouths and deep thoughts pour right out." She pulled off her boots and got into the bed. It was then that I realized just how weak I was. I could barely put my arm around her. She had no trouble holding me tight, though, so that was all right.

"I walked through hells to get you back," I told her after a time.

"I know. And I love you for it. But it probably would have been better if you hadn't."

"Better? Better for *who*?"

"Better for every living thing."

"I don't understand."

"I'll tell you about it when you're less chewed up. You'll tell me all about your mishaps, too. Right now, just take it easy. Let me hold you. Rest. Heal. Get your strength back." She paused, and hugged me tighter. "I'll need you strong for what's coming, lover."

"What *is* coming?"

"I don't know, exactly. But it will be a Kerf-damned lot of trouble when it arrives."

"Whatever it is, I'm here," I said. But sleep was dragging me down again.

"*That* I never doubted," she replied, "and never will."

Michael McClung

FROM THE AUTHOR

Thank you for reading this far into the Amra Thetys series. The next book, *The Thief Who Went to War*, is due in the Autumn of 2018. You can sign up for the newsletter If you'd like writing updates.

Meanwhile, there is one other book available set in Amra's World. It's called *The Last God*, and it features the grumpiest old man in Lucernis. You can take a look here.

Again, thanks for tagging along with Amra and Holgren this far, and I hope you're interested in continuing the journey.

mm

THE THIEF WHO WASN'T THERE

CPSIA information can be obtained
at www.ICGtesting.com
Printed in the USA
LVHW09s1547101018
593119LV00001B/215/P